BITTER
WINTER

BITTER WINTER

ILYON CHRONICLES – BOOK FIVE

JAYE L. KNIGHT

Living Sword Publishing
www.livingswordpublishing.com

Bitter Winter
Ilyon Chronicles – Book 5
Copyright © 2018 by Jaye L. Knight
www.ilyonchronicles.com

Published by Living Sword Publishing

Ilyon Map © 2014 by Jaye L. Knight

All Scriptures are taken from the New American Standard Bible, Copyright © 1960, 1962, 1963, 1968, 1971, 1972, 1973, 1975, 1977, 1995 by The Lockman Foundation. Used by permission. www.Lockman.org

ISBN 13: 978-0983774082
ISBN 10: 0983774080

To the One who faithfully leads us
through our bitter winters.

To my new twin nephews, Wyatt and Bradley.
Twins are such a big part of *Ilyon Chronicles*, so you
two were a wonderful surprise.

ILYON

SAMARA

AMBERIN

STONEHELM

SINNAI MTS.

ARCACIA

SIDIAN
OCEAN

GRAYLIN VALLEY

DUNLOW

KINNIM

VALCRE

LANDALE

ARDALUIN BAY

MERNIN
FORT RIVOR

KEATON

FALSPAR

TROAS

ARDA

GRAER MTS.

ARVAEL•

TRAYSE RIVER

•BEL-GARD

ANDROS FORD

DORLAND

WILDMOR

KRELL MTS.

The Lord is near to the brokenhearted
And saves those who are crushed in spirit.
- Psalm 34:18

ANOTHER EMPTY SNARE.

Jace sighed and tugged off his gloves. He loosed the snare wire from the snow and tucked it in a pouch before blowing on his already numb fingers. This bitter cold sucked the warmth from any exposed skin. He looked around the forest. Nothing but white snow and stark gray tree trunks surrounded him. Their brittle boughs creaked and groaned, but no other sound broke the frigid stillness. No bird calls. No signs of life. Not even tracks in the snow.

A chill shivered deep into his core and ached in his bones, especially in his left arm that he had broken over the summer. He shoved his fingers back into his fur-lined gloves and turned to Tyra, who stood in the trail he'd made. Not even his wolf could find signs of game.

"Let's get back."

After over two weeks of empty snares, he didn't bother to set a new snare line today—not with the temperature dropping like it was. He glanced up at the heavy sky. Snow threatened, and the last thing he wanted was to be caught in a deadly blizzard. He pulled his cloak tight around his shoulders and set off the way he had come, praying the snow would hold until he reached shelter. Precipitation threatened constantly, and they seemed to face a new blizzard every week. At this rate, their cabins would be nearly buried by spring.

Despite wearing snowshoes, the deep snow fought his progress. He and Tyra trudged through the drifts until their trail converged with another. They stopped at the split, waiting. Tyra sat down at Jace's side and leaned against his leg as if trying to share warmth. Even her thick winter coat was barely a match for the extreme elements.

A few quiet minutes passed before snow crunched faintly, and Holden approached from the south.

"Anything?" Jace asked.

Holden shook his head, his gray eyes matching the foreboding bank of clouds above them. "Nothing. Not even a squirrel." He brushed away the snow clinging to his pants. "Most of the snares were drifted over, the bait untouched."

His taut, stormy expression reminded Jace of the days when Holden used to glare at him over the fire during meals. He'd never imagined Holden becoming one of his closest friends, but they'd been through some dark times together. This was yet another challenge they had to face.

"Same here." Jace looked back in the direction he had come from. It seemed the hard winter had either driven away or killed the wildlife in the area.

They hiked the remaining distance to camp in silence. Along the way, Jace contemplated their rapidly depleting supplies. Between all three camps, they had a village to feed. Though they'd preserved meat before the winter set in, they hadn't anticipated being unable to supplement it with fresh game. The failure of crops in the region had made it difficult to set aside much else.

Jace prayed every day for success in their hunting and trapping attempts. Though the prayers so far remained unfulfilled, he clung to faith. Elôm had brought them through war and many worse situations. Surely they hadn't come this far only to die of starvation. Whenever doubt crept in, he reminded himself of standing beside Elon in Valcré. Elon loved them so much he had given His life for them. That love didn't change just because their circumstances did.

Smoking chimneys and the warm glow of cabin windows soon welcomed them into camp with the promise of shelter from the harsh climate. The Altair cabin drew Jace's eyes as well as his heart, tugging him in that direction. Warm company was just as desirable as warm shelter. However, he had things to see to first.

"I'll let Trask know about the snares," he told Holden. "You go on."

His friend nodded in thanks.

They split up, and Jace walked deeper into camp, to Trask and Anne's cabin. He hated to bring bad news and didn't envy the camp leaders who would have to decide what to do about their food crisis. So many relied on them. Jace didn't think he would stand up well under such a heavy responsibility. He didn't have the people skills to keep everyone calm and content.

When he reached the cabin, he removed his snowshoes and knocked on the door. A moment later, Trask opened it and invited him in. Warmth from the fireplace engulfed him as he stepped through the door with Tyra. Inside, he found his sister setting the table with Anne. Elanor's happy smile boosted his spirits. She looked so much like their mother with her dark hair and deep indigo eyes. He missed his mother lately, but his sister's bubbly personality made up for her absence. He greeted her warmly, though his attention shifted to a fourth person in the cabin—Prince Daniel. He nodded in greeting to the prince and sent Elanor a curious look. She ducked her head before meeting his gaze again.

"Anne invited us for supper."

While not odd, her use of "us" held hints of more than passing familiarity between her and Daniel. At least it did so to Jace. The two of them did seem to be spending a suspicious amount of time together these days. More so than they would as mere friends. Jace wasn't sure how he felt about this. Part of him bristled just a little at the idea, yet he could find nothing to actually base his feelings on.

Setting aside his musings for now, he focused on Trask. "I just wanted to let you know Holden and I didn't find anything in our snares. There weren't even tracks."

Trask let out a long sigh. "I was afraid of that." He glanced at the door. "I think it's time we called a meeting. When you see the others, let them know I'd like to see everyone in the meeting hall tomorrow after breakfast."

"I will."

He turned to go, but Trask stopped him. "If you're not in a hurry, I have something to show you."

Jace nodded. His heart might be in a hurry, but he did have time.

Trask walked to the table, where his coat lay over the back of a chair. He paused behind Anne and put his arm around her, kissing her hair near her ear. "I'll be right back."

Jace looked away from the intimate exchange, but smiled to himself. It was good to see the two of them finally married and how much they loved each other after everything they had been through with Captain Goler last summer.

Slipping on his coat, Trask joined him at the door.

"If you don't have plans for tonight, feel free to join us for supper when you're done," Anne invited, gesturing to an empty spot at the table.

Though Jace would have liked to accept and observe his sister's apparent connection with Daniel a bit closer, he couldn't give up his previously made plans. "Thank you, but I'm having supper with Kyrin tonight."

Besides, she would surely have some insight as far as Elanor and Daniel were concerned.

He followed Trask outside, where a few light flakes had begun to fall from the sky. They walked through camp along one of the packed paths with Tyra trotting ahead of them. At the far corner, they stopped at a small cabin with darkened windows. Jace zoned in on it, his heart rate accelerating with his thoughts. Could it be?

Trask opened the door, and they stepped inside. The cabin was dim and unoccupied, but Trask lit a candle that sat on one of the window ledges.

"I did some relocating and the cabin is now vacant. It's all yours, at least until spring. We may get more refugees once the snow clears and have to share again, but until then, feel free to make it your own." Trask's eyes gleamed. "I wouldn't waste any time if I were you. I know you didn't ask for this just to have a place to stay by yourself."

Jace bent his head, but a huge smile broke across his face. He'd hesitated to make such a request. A private cabin was a luxury for anyone these days. It must have seemed odd when he'd been perfectly content sharing a cabin with Rayad, Holden, and some of the other men, but Trask had him figured out.

"Thank you. I can't tell you how much I appreciate this."

Trask clapped him on the back, the twinkle in his eyes growing. "I'm sure Kyrin will too."

He then left Jace and Tyra alone. Once the door closed, Jace scanned the cabin. A bed sat in the corner and a table near the cold fireplace. Aside from a couple of shelves, there wasn't much else, but it would do. It just needed a little cleaning and a few finishing touches.

He knelt down and rubbed Tyra's neck. "What do you think? Do you think she'll like it?"

The wolf nosed his chin and wagged her tail. He smiled. "Yeah, I think she will too."

Anticipation thrummed inside of him as plans for the next few days fell into place. He would certainly heed Trask's advice not to waste time. His growing eagerness and impatience would see to that. Finally, it was time. He drew a deep breath to keep his nerves at bay. There would be no backing out or allowing uncertainty to distract him. He was ready for this despite the doubts that threatened to creep in.

With a firm nod, he pushed back to his feet, and the comfortable warmth of contentment filled him. Though it had been a long time coming, this was right.

He motioned to Tyra. "Come on. We don't want to be late."

They braved the weather outside once more, but Jace couldn't keep from looking back at the cabin as they walked away along the icy path. He'd never owned a home of his own before—had never even imagined it. Even if it was temporary, the weight of it exhilarated him. The sight of the Altairs' cabin only fueled these emotions. Now he just had to keep the news to himself if he wanted to maintain the surprise. Such a goal would be a challenge with Kyrin, but he would have to try.

When he knocked on the door, he only had to wait a moment before it opened. Kyrin stood on the other side to greet him with a warm smile that never failed to inspire him.

"Come in." She motioned him inside.

He crossed the threshold and had to battle the urge to pull her into his arms and kiss her with all the enthusiasm stored inside over the excitement for their future. A future where he could kiss her whenever the inclination arose and hold her for far longer than would be appropriate for an unmarried couple. Before his thoughts wandered further, upraised male voices around the table distracted him. He glanced at Kyrin's brothers, who were in the middle of a friendly argument with Talas. The crete came to supper almost as much as Jace did.

Chuckling at the rowdy exchange, he unbuttoned his coat, but his gaze focused again on Kyrin. In the two and a half years since he'd met her, she'd never been more lovely. Her soft eyes squinted slightly. Staring at her surely didn't help his attempt at secrecy, so he slipped his coat off and turned to hang it up.

"All right, boys, that's enough," Kyrin's mother scolded gently. She smiled at Jace as he faced the gathering again. "Come have a seat."

He followed Kyrin, and they both took seats next to each other at the table. Tyra found her usual spot on a small rug near the fireplace. While the others traded a few more passive-aggressive comments, Kyrin leaned in close to Jace.

"Something has you in a very good mood and me very curious."

He looked at her, unable to hold back the smile that only confirmed her observations. He would have made a terrible spy. "It's a surprise."

"Oh?"

"I hope I can tell you soon."

Her lips turned up in a little smile of her own. "Well, I won't ask any more questions then."

Elôm help him, Jace had never loved anything or anyone so much in his life. Some girls might have tried to pry the secret out of him—Kyrin probably could have easily figured it out—but she was content to wait for the moment he wanted to share it with her. It tortured him not to be able to kiss her right now, but he didn't want to send her brothers back into an uproar.

The talk around the table quieted when Lydia joined them, and they all bowed their heads while Kyrin's oldest brother Marcus thanked Elôm for the food and the opportunity to enjoy it together. Jace silently thanked Elôm for the cabin. This set things in motion that he had prayed about for a long time.

When they passed around the food, Marcus looked at Jace. "Was there anything in your snares?"

Jace shook his head, and concern eclipsed some of his joy. Threat of starvation could seriously affect his plans. "Nothing."

Usually the calm and stoic one, Marcus grimaced, betraying his own concern. "We need to start finding other ways to get food. There's no way we can sustain this for much longer."

"Trask wants to have a meeting in the morning after breakfast." Jace served himself from the pot of soup on the table. It was a bit lean on meat and vegetables, making Marcus's statement all the more true.

Though the problem might have lingered in their minds, it did not linger in their conversation. Instead, talk quickly turned to Ronny's thirteenth birthday next month.

"Can I have a sword?" He held his spoon in the air as if wielding the weapon right now. His hair, which was getting a bit long, flopped into his eyes in his enthusiasm. "A real one? Not just a practice one?"

Lydia passed a plate of rolls around to Jace. "I think maybe we'll wait with the sword."

"But Michael has one!"

His mother sent him a pointed look. "Michael is fifteen."

Ronny heaved an exaggerated sigh, dunking his spoon back into his soup bowl. "I hate being the youngest. I'm always last to get anything fun."

"Swords aren't fun," Lydia said seriously. "They're weapons and must be handled appropriately."

"Yes, Mother." Ronny's tone suggested he'd heard this lecture before.

Jace could understand his disappointment. It probably wasn't so much the sword he really wanted but to be one of the men.

Yet, Lydia was right too. To carry a sword came with a huge responsibility—something Ronny would learn over the next couple of years of practicing with his brothers. He may not think a practice sword was much fun at the moment, but that would no doubt change once he saw the one Jace was making for him as a gift along with a matching wooden dagger. He'd be the envy of the other boys in camp when they practiced sparring.

Despite the disappointment of being denied a real sword, Ronny's excitement for his birthday rushed back, and they enjoyed their meal in good spirits.

Once they'd finished sometime later, Jace helped carry dishes to the washtub. When he turned back to the table, movement outside caught his eye. He pushed aside the curtain on the window. Across camp, two people meandered toward one of the cabins, where they paused to speak for a couple of moments before one of them entered.

"What are you looking at?"

Jace let the curtain fall into place and looked down at Kyrin, who joined him at the window. "Elanor had supper tonight with Trask and Anne . . . and Daniel. I just saw him walk her to her cabin."

Kyrin's expression lifted a little. "They seem to be getting serious."

"They do."

"Does that bother you?"

Jace shrugged. Could he really say it didn't? The emotions that wove in and around his sister's possible relationship were very new and not simple to navigate. "Of course I want her to marry and have someone to take care of her . . . I just want her to choose wisely."

Kyrin's gaze turned to the snow drifting into camp. "Are you afraid Daniel isn't a wise choice?"

Jace chewed on this question as he considered how he'd gotten to know Daniel over the last few months. Daniel had allayed all of Jace's suspicions or uncertainty concerning his royal upbringing. "No. He's a good man." Jace breathed out a slow sigh. "It's just strange to think of Elanor with a prince."

"It is," Kyrin reached for his hand and squeezed it, "but as long as they're aware of the challenges, I think they can work it out. After all, look what you and I have worked through."

The loving way her eyes sought his coaxed a smile from his lips.

"Does she ever talk to you about him?" he asked.

Kyrin tipped her head with a cute little grin. "Sometimes. She thinks he's quite handsome, but I'll spare you the dreamy girl talk."

Jace's smile deepened as he ran his gaze over her soft face, pausing at her lips before rising again to her eyes. It was definitely time they were married. "I should probably go before the snow gets any heavier."

She nodded in agreement, but a twinkle lit her eyes. No doubt she read every thought in his expression.

Jace retrieved his coat and slipped it on as he thanked Kyrin's mother for the meal and said goodnight to everyone. At the door, he looked down at Kyrin and spoke quietly. "Good-night. I love you."

Her sparkling grin almost stripped away his restraint not to give her a good long kiss, even in front of her family.

With her face firmly centered in his thoughts, Jace let himself out with Tyra. He pulled his collar close to his neck to shield it from the snow, but even the freezing temperatures couldn't pierce the warmth inside of him. Just a few more days of preparation, and then he would ask her. If she was half as anxious to start their life together as he was, they would likely be married soon.

He glanced up at the large flakes falling around him and pulled in a chill breath. *Thank You, Lord, for working things out with the cabin. But even more than that, thank You for helping me put aside my fears. They still rise up sometimes, but with Your help, I know they can be defeated.*

For the last several yards, he prayed about the life he dreamed of for himself and Kyrin. When he reached the cabin he shared with the others, the comfortable warmth of crackling flames in the fireplace greeted him. Holden, Trev, Mick, and Elian sat around the table with cups of coffee, chatting companionably, while Rayad sat closer to the fire. Jace hung up his coat and pulled off his boots before sliding a chair next him.

"How was supper?" Rayad asked.

Jace nodded. "Good." Another smile took hold.

Rayad's eyes narrowed, and Jace couldn't blame him. He wasn't exactly known for smiling so much. He glanced at the others, who were too deep into their conversation to notice, and lowered his voice.

"Trask cleared out one of the cabins. It's mine until we might have to share again." His heart thumped. "As soon as I clean it up, I'm going to ask Kyrin to marry me."

A broad grin stretched across Rayad's face and, just maybe, his eyes grew a little watery. "That's wonderful, Jace. You two have always made such a good team. Not that I have any experience in this area, but I imagine that will only grow stronger in marriage."

Jace agreed. No one inspired him the way Kyrin did, not only in his life but also in his faith.

THE FROST-COVERED cabin windows blocked the view of camp, but when Jace stepped outside, he found a good four inches of fresh snowfall. He shivered as the frigid air sucked away any lingering warmth from the indoors. It was even colder than yesterday, yet sunshine streamed through the trees as if to signify the excitement of the day. He had lain awake for hours during the night, contemplating all he planned to do in the cabin. The sooner he made it a comfortable home, the sooner he could propose to Kyrin . . . not that he'd wait if the perfect opportunity presented itself before then.

As anxious as he was to begin, he first had to attend Trask's meeting. Hard decisions would have to be made. Between everyone here and the other two camps, they had close to four hundred mouths to feed, plus the dragons and livestock.

Jace followed the others from his cabin toward the meeting hall. Rayad and Holden were already discussing possible solutions, but Jace wasn't sure any were viable. He prayed someone would come up with a sustainable food source.

As they drew near the hall, someone called his name. Elanor hurried to catch up to him, kicking up the fresh snow. He let the other men go ahead and waited for her.

She puffed white clouds into the air when she reached him and paused to catch her breath. "Do you have a minute?"

He glanced toward the meeting hall. It was still early. Trask would allow plenty of time for his core group to show up.

"Sure."

"Good, because I wanted to talk to you after last night."

Jace lifted one brow. Elanor glanced down at her snow-dusted shoes before meeting his gaze. Though she hesitated, a sparkle danced in her eyes.

"I know everyone has noticed that Daniel and I spend a lot of time together. We've both enjoyed talking and getting to know each other and . . . he has expressed his interest in courting me." She paused but then rushed ahead before Jace could even form an opinion on the matter. "He intends to talk to you, but I wanted to tell you myself and see what you think."

Jace offered a slow nod and considered last night's conversation with Kyrin. He should have been more prepared for this.

His sister watched him closely and then prompted him when he didn't speak for a long moment. "Well?"

"I figured as much."

"But is it all right with you?"

Jace let another moment of silence elapse as he gave the situation careful consideration. He wanted to do right by his sister. He was her only true family here in camp. Elian might have been a better choice for her to go to since he was like a second father to both of them. He had come here as her protector, after all. Still, she had chosen to come to Jace, and while he didn't consider himself entirely worthy of such a position, it was up to him to advise her in making wise life choices. If only their mother could be here with them. She could have offered much more wisdom and experience in such matters.

"I just want to make sure any man in your life will take care of you. I believe Daniel is a good man and can do that.

But don't forget, Elôm willing, he'll someday be our king. Are you prepared for what that means if you two pursue a serious relationship?"

"If you're asking if I'm prepared to be queen someday, that's a lot to take in, but I am prepared to face the prospect, yes."

Apparently, she had given it thorough consideration before this conversation based on her straightforward answer. Still, the word "queen" added sobering realism to the possibility. She was right. It was a lot to take in, even for him. A couple of years ago, he hadn't even known he had a sister. A couple years from now and she could be queen of Arcacia. His gut pinched in reaction to the thought, but he wasn't the one who would have to live that life.

"And you've prayed about this?"

She nodded firmly. "Yes."

Well, if she was sure, then he had no real objections. She was strong and capable—just like their mother—and if it ever did come to that, he could see her at Daniel's side when he rose to the throne. For now, though, he would focus on the present and not look too far into the very changeable future.

He let out a long breath. "All right. I still want to talk to Daniel, but as long as he doesn't change my mind, you have my blessing."

A dazzling grin lit up her face, and she reached her arms up around his neck to hug him. He embraced her tightly in return, and a slight twinge pinched his chest. While overjoyed for his sister to have this relationship, reluctance ran with it. Though he had known her for less than two years, he was fiercely protective of her. To have to give some of that up to another man was harder than he expected. Had Kyrin's brothers felt the same way the day he'd expressed his love for Kyrin in Stonehelm's mess hall? What would it feel like if he went through this with a daughter someday? Fear of the prospect of being a father welled up inside of him, though not as strongly as it would have a couple of months ago. Today he pushed it aside to rest in Elôm's hands.

Elanor stepped out of his arms and shone a warm smile up at him. "Thank you. And you're right. Daniel is a good man."

Jace didn't doubt it. He had seen the prince's face when they'd both stood on the execution platform the day Elon died. That moment had changed both of their lives.

"I'd better let you go to the meeting," Elanor said.

They parted, and Jace walked the remaining distance to the hall, where Elian waited just inside the door.

"What was that about?"

Jace glanced back over his shoulder as the door closed to catch another glimpse of his sister. "Daniel."

"I suspected that was coming."

"So did I." Jace turned to face Elian and kept his voice low. "What are your thoughts?"

Elian only took a moment to respond. "I think they're a good match."

"Even if it means Elanor will be queen one day?"

"If she's anything like your mother, which we know she is, she would handle the challenge with strength and dignity." Elian's eyes deepened a bit as they did whenever he spoke of Jace's mother. He had not lost any love for her since coming here to Landale.

This helped settle any doubts or misgivings Jace might have held. Elian was a good judge of character and as protective of Elanor as Jace was. If Elian approved of Daniel, then it boosted Jace's confidence in his decision to give his blessing to their courtship.

Now he turned his attention to the gathering and scanned the large room, his eyes lingering on Daniel, who stood with Trask and King Balen. It was right here in this meeting hall that the spark had first ignited between Elanor and Daniel. She'd caught his eye immediately. Jace should have known what would come.

His thoughts of Elanor and Daniel departed when Kyrin walked in with her twin and older brothers and came to his side. They shared a smile just before Trask called for everyone's attention, and the hall grew quiet.

"Our food situation is no secret to any of you. We still have a long winter ahead, and we already see our food stores dwindling. It's the same in all three camps. Unfortunately, we can't rely on fresh game as we'd hoped. At least not in this area. Even sending hunters south with the dragons won't sustain us long. By the time they return, their dragons are hungry and so are the ones still here. The difficult fact is, we need more meat and other provisions than we are currently able to bring in. We'll need to implement stricter rationing, but even that won't solve our problem in the long run."

After a moment of silence in which everyone mulled this over, Captain Darq stepped forward. "Glynn and I both agree that, aside from those that form our air defense, if we took the remainder of the dragons to Dorland it would lighten the burden of providing food for them. It's a long journey, especially if there's a storm, but we'll bring back as much for supplies as we can when we return. "

Heads nodded. Though Jace would hate to see Gem go, it would be better for everyone. The cretes could provide the food she needed.

"Sounds like a good plan," Trask agreed. "We should see to it as soon as we can. We also need to expand our hunting range even farther south. Perhaps some towns had better luck with crops and have extra to sell. We have to try to bring in more besides meat."

"Too bad we can't get our hands on some of the provisions Dagren has delivered from the queen's stockpile in Valcré,"

Holden said. "He's probably holed up all snug in Landale Castle growing fat on them while he doles out just enough to keep the villagers alive."

Trask nodded slowly. "It's tempting, I admit, but I won't have us turn to thieving. Not if I can help it."

"What if we try getting provisions from Valcré ourselves?" Marcus asked.

Trask winced. "It's risky. The way Davira runs things, one misstep could be deadly. I think we should save that as a last resort. We'll see what we can get from Dorland and farther south first."

Jace released a quiet sigh. Valcré would be the easiest way to gain supplies, but Trask was right. With Davira's nationwide decree that anyone suspected of worshiping Elôm could be killed and sacrificed to Aertus and Vilai, any contact outside of camp was a high risk. Valcré would be the most dangerous of all, being directly under her insidious influence. Anyone had license to murder for any reason; all they had to do was claim the victim was a believer in Elôm. Davira was so bent on destroying believers, she didn't care how many innocent lives it cost in the process.

Jace cast a glance at Leetra. Her pinched lips and clenched jaw gave away her concern. He didn't blame her. After all, Timothy was right in the thick of it. Once Daniel had told them of the gathering of believers in Valcré, Timothy had felt Elôm calling him there. He and Aaron had left just as fall set in. Jace admired their courage, but it didn't relieve the worry they all carried for them and the other believers within the city.

Trask turned his attention to Warin, who oversaw the stables and their livestock. "How are the animals? Will we have enough feed for them?"

Warin nodded, though with some hesitation. "I believe we'll scrape by if we're sparing and the winter doesn't drag out overlong. I will see that we're extra cautious at feeding time."

"Good." Trask looked at Darq again. "You and Glynn see to getting the dragons ready to leave." His gaze switched to each person he addressed in turn. "Kaden, select some of your men to head south. I'll gather funds for them to purchase any provisions they can find. Jace, I'd like you, Holden, and whoever else wants to contribute to continue hunting and trapping around here whenever you can. Even a small yield is better than nothing."

Jace gave a nod. While hunting and trapping was neither easy nor pleasant this winter, he would do whatever he could. Surely, there were still some animals wandering the forest.

"Meanwhile, Balen, Warin, and I will take stock of what we have here and in the other camps and implement a better rationing system. Does anyone have any questions?" Trask looked around at the group.

"What should we tell everyone about the situation?" Daniel asked.

"The truth," Trask answered. "Supplies are low and food is scarce, but we'll do everything we can to make sure everyone is properly fed. It's a serious situation but not dire yet. I don't intend to let it become so. I believe Elôm will provide."

Everyone agreed, and Jace prayed silently over the situation. They just had to hold out until spring. Food wouldn't be so scarce, and they could turn their attention to taking back Samara now that Sam had persuaded the talcrins in Arda to join their already strong alliance with the cretes, giants, and Dorland ryriks. From there, they could figure out how to reclaim Daniel's throne and finally set things right in Arcacia.

Now that they had settled on a plan, Trask dismissed them. Though most of the men lingered to talk, Jace was anxious to get to the cabin. He just had one more thing to see to first. He caught Daniel's eye and the look that said he wanted to talk. Jace turned to Kyrin.

"I need to talk to Daniel, and I have some work to do, but I'll come see you later."

She cast a glance at the prince, her lips lifting in just the hint of a smile. "All right. I'll probably be helping Mother or over at Lenae and Warin's cabin. Now that Mother and I are caught up on new militia uniforms, I promised Meredith I'd help her make some new clothes for her dolls."

They smiled and parted, and Jace made his way through the men toward Daniel.

Daniel drew in a deep breath as Jace approached him. Drat his racing heart. Who knew such a moment could wreak so much havoc on one's nerves? He'd been so confident before this, but what if Jace refused him? He had every right to, as Elanor's older brother and only family member in camp. And to think, Daniel had been less nervous about his coronation.

But this was different and completely new territory. He'd never had any true interest in anyone before. No one had captivated him the way Elanor did. Never mind her beauty; she was everything he'd ever hoped to find in a potential wife— kind, joyful, faithful, strong . . . real. She left all the other women who had practically thrown themselves at him over the years far behind. It didn't matter to her *what* he was, just who he was. The craziest thing was that his father actually would have approved of the match, providing he knew nothing of her faith. She was, after all, from a noble bloodline—not that it meant anything to Daniel.

With another quick breath, he cleared his scratchy throat and focused on Jace, who pinned him with a measuring look— not hostile, but one that said he took the matter seriously. While Jace's mixed blood had never bothered Daniel in any way, it certainly made the man intimidating at times like these. Daniel had no doubt Jace could take on every person in this cabin and come out the victor. He'd certainly have no trouble against Daniel.

"I take it Elanor has already spoken to you," Daniel said when Jace reached him.

Jace nodded. "Just before the meeting."

Daniel wasn't sure if it was a relief that Jace already knew his intentions or not. He paused a moment to see if Jace would deny him outright. When he didn't, Daniel said, "I'd like to talk to you as well."

The two of them stepped to the far end of the meeting hall, away from the others who still mingled, and Daniel raced to gather his thoughts. If this were his old life, his father probably would have taken care of everything—contacting and negotiating with Elanor's father. Well, he'd always wanted to live a normal, unprivileged life. He had that now, for the most part, and facing down a woman's male relatives was part of it.

He faced Jace with what confidence he managed to retain, ready to accept whatever answer he received with dignity. He wasn't about to pull rank if this did not go in his favor. He'd never force Elanor or her family to agree to a courtship or marriage. While his father would have, Daniel never wanted to be that type of man or ruler.

"First, I want to say how much I admire your sister. She is one of the very few truly genuine young women I've met over the years. I've enjoyed getting to know her over the last few months to the point where I look forward to any time we can spend together. I've given it a great deal of prayer and con- sideration, and I very much desire to pursue her seriously through courtship with your permission."

He fought a wince and hoped this rehearsed speech of his didn't sound as stilted to Jace as it did to his own ears.

Jace's cool gaze seemed to pierce right into his soul. He resisted the urge to clear his throat during what seemed to be an eternity-long silence. He'd never wanted anything in his life quite like he wanted to pursue this relationship with Elanor. Neither had he faced the prospect of being denied something like this before.

At long last, Jace spoke. "Once you're crowned king, where does that leave Elanor?"

Daniel lifted his brows slightly. It was not the first question he was anticipating, but he had a ready answer for it. "At my side as my wife and queen."

After all, that was exactly the outcome he hoped for. He wasn't interested in anything other than a serious relationship with marriage as the ultimate goal.

"It's a lot to ask of her."

Daniel opened his mouth but had no prepared answer for this. It *was* a lot to ask. Ruling a kingdom was not easy. It would strain them both. Now he did clear his throat. He took a little longer to answer than he would have liked, but he was confident in his words.

"I would never ask it of her if I didn't believe she was capable of handling its hardships. I think she would make an great queen."

The slightest hint of a potential smile crossed Jace's expression. Or maybe it was just wishful thinking. Daniel wasn't quite sure which.

However, Jace then tipped his chin in a slow nod. "I think she would too."

Daniel's painfully thudding heart picked up a notch.

"You may court her," Jace said. "Just make sure you take care of her."

Daniel let out a great breath of air and put his hand over his heart in a solemn promise. "I will."

Jace appeared to take his measure for another uncomfortably silent moment before he said, "I'll let you go talk to her. I'm sure she's waiting."

Daniel tried not to grin overmuch. This couldn't have been easy for Jace, and he didn't want to rub it in or press his luck. "Thank you."

He made a hasty escape and headed straight to the door. Perhaps he should have checked to see if Trask and Balen had more to discuss, but it wouldn't do to let Elanor wait around out in the cold. They'd find him if they needed him. He had all day to focus on reality and responsibility. Right now, his mind was a little too stuck on someone else.

Jace was right. Elanor waited for him just outside of the meeting hall, her hands tucked into the pockets of her long coat and her cute little nose pink at the tip. Her bright eyes met his and widened a little in expectancy. She stepped forward to meet him.

"How did it go?"

"It went well. I have his permission"

A grin sprang to her lips, and Daniel didn't hold back his own this time.

"So, now that I know I won't mysteriously disappear into the forest or anything for being seen with you," Daniel made an attempt at seriousness but couldn't quite wipe the smile from his face, "I want to officially ask you, Lady Elanor Cantan, if you will permit me to court you?"

"Of course!"

Her enthusiasm warmed his heart. He'd been tempted to kiss her before today, but right at this moment the urge was downright painful. He nearly gave in, but Jace would probably walk out right then and catch him in the act. Better to wait for a more opportune and private moment, difficult as that was. He didn't want to rush anything.

Instead, he offered her his arm. "Let me walk you to your cabin." She must be freezing by now.

With a happy little grin, she took his arm with her gloved hand, and he guided her in the direction of her cabin, though he was in no particular hurry to get there.

After gathering cleaning materials from the supply shack, Jace strode across camp with Tyra and mulled over his conversation with Daniel. He'd seen the two of them walking when he'd left the meeting hall. Elanor certainly looked happy with the way she gazed up at Daniel and laughed at whatever quip he made. Jace had thought he would still hold some hesitation, but speaking to Daniel and witnessing his sincerity had eased his mind. He couldn't help smiling just a little over the memory of the prince's discomfort.

Halfway through camp, Jace took a detour and approached Trask and Anne's cabin. Anne answered the door and invited him inside. Her mother sat near the fire with a cup of tea. Jace greeted her and then turned to Anne.

"Trask probably told you about the cabin."

She grinned. "He did. I'm very excited for you and can hardly wait until you tell Kyrin."

Jace's smile came easily. "Neither can I. Do you or Lenae have extra curtains or anything else that would make a home comfortable for a woman?"

What exactly went in a house beyond the basics? He supposed Kyrin would fill the cabin with her womanly touches once they moved in just like Kalli had done at the farm. Still, he wanted to have it partway furnished and comfortable for her.

Anne's eyes twinkled. "I'm sure we can find some things. If not, we'll make some. You just see about the cleaning up."

"Thank you." Jace didn't know what he'd do without the friends he had made in this camp. "I really appreciate it."

"Consider it an early wedding gift. You both deserve it."

Jace thanked her once more and then went on his way. When he reached the cabin, he paused at the door to savor the weight of the moment. With a smile to himself, he turned the knob and stepped inside. He surveyed the interior now that it was daylight. It wasn't overly in need of cleaning. The floor would need sweeping and scrubbing, the windows washing, and a few cobwebs eradicated. After all, only men had previously occupied the cabin—no women to keep it as neat and tidy as Kyrin and her mother kept theirs.

He lit a fire in the fireplace to warm the cabin and set a bucket of snow by the flames. While waiting for it to melt, he started with the cobwebs and brushed the soot from the wall around the fireplace before cleaning the windows. He looked forward to seeing what Anne would come up with for curtains. Color would really brighten up the place. A nice quilt for the bed and a couple of rugs would also help. He paused to visualize where he and Kyrin would place their things. *Their* things. He was more than ready to share everything about his life with her.

He walked over to the fireplace where a second bucket of snow had melted into fresh water and grabbed a hard brush and a rag to get to work scrubbing the floor. Setting them down in the corner, he dunked the brush into the cold water.

As he pulled it out again, a deep roar echoed like thunder outside. Jace froze. That was no dragon.

FOR TWO HEARTBEATS, Jace could not move, but the answering roars of the dragons jolted him into motion. He jumped to his feet and grabbed his coat as he dashed out the door with Tyra. The chaotic mingling of dragon and firedrake roars blasted the air above him. A wave of fire rolled through the bare branches. He ducked and covered his head as the heatwave struck him. Sparks and flames rained across camp. Thank Elôm for the fresh snow that stopped them from igniting anything.

Jace raced toward the Altair cabin. Men dashed in front of him on their way to their dragons, Kaden leading the way. As Jace rounded one of the cabins, the sight nearly stopped him in his tracks. Black and gold clad men on foot and horseback dotted the tree line.

"Jace!"

His gaze shot to Holden rushing toward him. He tossed Jace his sword. Jace yanked it out and let the scabbard fall, not slowing his pace. Ahead, Marcus and Liam stood outside their cabin. Marcus shouted orders to the militia gathering around him. When Jace reached Liam he skidded to a halt.

"Kyrin?"

"She's inside. Lenae and Meredith too."

The first clanging of swords echoed nearby, and Jace spun to look around camp. Where was Elanor? A moment later, she and Elian appeared and ran toward the cabin. Elanor's wide eyes flashed and darted around camp as battle sounds rang through what had always been a safe haven.

Jace grabbed his sister's arm and hustled her up to the cabin. "Kyrin, open the door!"

It swung open, and Kyrin stood on the other side, her face mirroring Elanor's. In her hand, she clutched the quarterstaff he'd carved for her. Jace guided Elanor inside and grasped the doorknob as he looked down at Kyrin.

"Stay inside and keep the door locked."

She barely nodded, her eyes holding with his, but he had no time to say more. He yanked the door shut with a desperate prayer that no enemy would get past, and then turned to join the rest of the men.

Clanging swords resonated from every direction as a ring of soldiers closed in around the perimeter of camp. Dragons and firedrakes roared overhead and somewhere in the forest the frozen trees cracked and splintered. Jace followed Rayad, Holden, and Elian to the edge of camp not a hundred feet away where Marcus and some of his men were already embroiled in a fierce skirmish.

Warmth burst from Jace's chest, chasing away the cold biting at his bare fingers. One of the soldiers turned to meet him. Their swords crashed together. Jace's left arm ached at the impact, but the surge of heat in his veins masked the pain. He shoved the man's blade away and went on the attack. He would not see this camp fall to Davira's men. He'd lost a home and loved ones already. Not again.

He pressed his advantage against the soldier, who clearly lacked experience, and left the man fallen in the snow. He swiftly scanned the area to see just how many soldiers they had to deal with. The black and gold uniforms appeared to match the number of men from camp. Had any of the dragon riders alerted the militia in the other camps? Would reinforcements come to their aid? Or were the other camps under attack as well?

Jace couldn't dwell on these questions. Whatever happened, he had to focus on the fight before him as he met with a more seasoned warrior, who required his undivided attention. The man aimed a quick thrust of his blade toward Jace's chest and then swung for his legs. Jace jumped back and waited for an opening for his own attack. Out of the corner of his eye, he spotted soldiers making their way deeper into camp.

Kaden latched the straps on Exsis's saddle as quickly as his cold fingers would allow. He shot another glance upward. Captain Darq and the other cretes had already engaged with the firedrakes, taking to the air without saddles. Kaden would have followed, but his men weren't quite that daring. So he stayed behind with his small army of dragon riders to saddle their mounts. Thankfully, they could have done this chore in their sleep and it only took a few minutes, yet it felt like an eternity.

As he worked the last buckle, he eyed the fight taking over camp. A battle waged in his heart as well—to fight the firedrakes or to remain here on the ground to fight alongside his brothers. But he was a captain, and airborne battle was what he and his men were trained for.

With his saddle secure, Kaden scrambled onto his dragon's back and scanned his men. Most were in the process of mounting as well, and the others only seconds behind. The moment everyone was seated, Kaden traded a quick glance and nod with Talas before ordering everyone into the air.

He and Exsis took off first, the dragon's powerful wings shooting them upward, past the treetops. Here the battle played out. Around two dozen firedrakes circled the sky over camp, swirling the smoke rising from the cabin chimneys. Darq and a dozen crete riders darted amongst them, dodging snapping jaws and roiling blasts of fire.

The frozen wind whipped across Kaden's face feeling as though it were taking skin with it. His coat flapped behind him, providing little protection against the cold. He hadn't even had time to button it in his race to get himself and his riders into the air.

But the cold wasn't their biggest threat right now. A firedrake swooped at him from his left. He checked for Talas who was only a dragon-length behind him. Together, they countered with two perfectly-timed attacks, sending the drake toward the trees in a smoking heap. Kaden checked his other men. They worked in pairs as they had all practiced many times. He wasn't worried. He was confident his men would have no problem taking out the drakes along with Darq's riders.

What did worry him was the fight on the ground. Even now as he glanced downward, he spotted flashes of gold rimming camp. He gritted his teeth, but the most he could do was glare at them, at least until the firedrakes were dealt with.

Kaden forced himself to focus on the battle at hand. No amount of confidence would save him if he failed to pay attention to what was going on around him.

The clash of swords, shattering roars, and battle shouts echoed outside the cabin. Sounds that should never have invaded this camp—their refuge. Kyrin clenched her fingers around her staff as her heart thumped with every shriek and cry of the dragons. *Please, Elôm, protect the men!* Locked inside the cabin while the battle raged just outside brought memories of Samara flooding back along with her fear of losing those she loved. What if the men couldn't hold back the soldiers? *Give us victory, Lord. So many innocent lives depend on it.*

She looked around the cabin, her gaze touching each person—her mother, Elanor, Lenae. Their tense faces and frightened eyes were fixed on the door, the only thing shielding them from the danger outside. Meredith huddled in the back corner with Ronny, who held her hand and pretended to be brave. Michael paced in front of Kyrin, his sword in hand.

"I should be out there," he muttered. "I should be helping."

"Marcus wanted you here to make sure we all were safe." Kyrin tried to calm him, but he didn't seem to hear her.

Glass shattered, spraying across the floor from the window to Kyrin's left. She jumped back, and Meredith screamed. A soldier stood at the window, his sword drawn. He used his gloved hand to swipe away jagged pieces of glass to climb through. Cold seized Kyrin, but she pushed herself into action. She rushed to the window and rammed the end of her staff as hard as she could into the soldier's chest. He grunted and disappeared from sight. Kyrin didn't dare get closer to see where he went.

Frigid air rolled through the broken window with the sounds of the battle. Michael stood at Kyrin's side, prepared to intercept if the soldier tried to get in again. Kyrin's heart thudded in her ears. Were soldiers breaking into the other cabins? Would the women and children inside be able to stop them like she and her brother could?

Something solid smashed against the door. Kyrin flinched and spun to face it. Another impact and the area around the lock cracked. Michael rushed toward it but looked back at Kyrin, his face set in steely determination. "As soon as I'm out, lock the door behind me."

"Michael, you can't go out there," their mother gasped.

The soldiers struck the door again, and it threatened to give.

"If I don't, they will get in." Michael swung his gaze back to Kyrin.

She stood frozen in indecision. He was right, but just like her mother, she feared for his safety. Yet, if the soldiers broke down the door, how many might get in? It would be up to her and Michael to hold them off. Could they do it, just the two of them?

Staring at her brother's hard-set face, he suddenly looked much more like a man than a boy. A man who desired to protect his family. Though her heart faltered in uncertainty, she nodded and hurried to the door. She traded a look with Michael as he gripped his sword in preparation, and then he reached for the lock. Unbolting it, he flung the door open and rushed out, taking the soldier on the other side by surprise. Swords clanged, but Kyrin didn't see anything that happened next as she slammed the door shut again and relocked it. She gripped the knob and closed her eyes.

"Elôm, please protect him."

Marcus sidestepped to dodge a blow and then launched an attack of his own. He didn't recognize the soldier he faced, but he did recognize the familiar fighting style typical of all Arcacian soldiers. It was the same one he had trained in and spent countless hours practicing. It was practical, precise, disciplined . . . predictable. Marcus knew it and could execute it as easily as breathing, but thanks to Jace, he had expanded his knowledge and ability. Through the sparring sessions they'd had in the last few months, he'd learned maneuvers to take down an opponent that weren't part of his strict military training.

With one of these newly learned techniques, he twisted his sword around and slashed open the top of the soldier's thigh. The man grabbed for it, and Marcus used that moment to take the soldier down. He scanned the area. A glimpse of Liam brought a quick flush of relief. While his brother didn't like to fight, he could when called upon, and Jace's tips would serve him just as well.

Movement in his periphery yanked his attention to his right. He spun around, his sword ready but froze. A daunting figure in black and gold armor had just entered camp—the General. They locked eyes. His grandfather's narrowed. He took a step closer, his presence as commanding as ever.

"Stand down, Marcus." His deep voice held the same force and intensity it always had while giving orders to his soldiers. "You don't all have to die here. Order your men to surrender."

"Only so they can die on an execution platform elsewhere?" Marcus shook his head and raised his sword. He'd always expected this day would come—when he and his grandfather would face off, not just with words but with blades. "We won't surrender."

The General glowered at him. "Don't test me, Marcus. It won't end well."

But Marcus wasn't a boy anymore, nor was he under his grandfather's command. He was the leader of the militia, and it was his responsibility to protect those within this camp. He gripped his sword firmly and resumed a defensive stance. The General's expression darkened. He raised his own sword and took a deliberate step forward. Marcus drew one quick breath before their blades crashed together. The force jolted up his arms and into his shoulders.

The General attacked again—precise, swift, shattering. Despite his age, the man was the most skilled opponent Marcus had ever faced besides Jace. Though he'd sparred with his grandfather in the past, this was altogether different. The General had more combat experience and expertise than any man Marcus knew. For a moment, Marcus's confidence wavered. Could he even hope to stand up to his grandfather? However, everything he fought for quickly overcame his uncertainty. He had people behind him—people he loved and needed to protect.

Bolstered by this purpose, he pushed forward with an attack of his own. His blade glanced harmlessly off his grandfather's gold-trimmed black pauldron. The armor would make him harder to defeat, yet it would also encumber him. Marcus's only defense was his blade, but he had youth and ease of motion on his side.

He blocked the General's next series of attacks. An opponent like this would require patience and caution to defeat. One slight mistake would give a seasoned warrior the perfect opportunity to strike. At first, Marcus only defended, giving ground strategically under the General's powerful attacks. They couldn't continue indefinitely. The General was not invincible and, strong as he might seem, he was not young either. He *would* tire. Any soldier would. And so, Marcus waited, conserving his own strength for when it would serve him best.

Though brutal, Marcus came to realize that none of the General's attacks were aimed at any vital part of his body. Could it be that his grandfather didn't want to kill him?

Minutes into the fight, sweat soaked through the under layer of Marcus's clothes, despite the cold air. His hands buzzed with the repeated shock of blocking, but finally, he sensed the General growing fatigued. Though his expression remained fierce, his attacks lost power and his heavy breaths left clouds of white in the air.

After one ill-timed attack, the General stumbled over a rut in the snow. This was Marcus's chance. He pressed forward, crashing his blade against the General's. In the beginning, his attacks had been like hitting a wall. This time, his grandfather gave way, taking a step back under the blow.

Now that he'd gained ground, Marcus didn't let up. Though the General stubbornly met each attack with his own, Marcus no longer felt as though he battled a superior opponent. His patience had worn his grandfather down. After an uncharacteristically weak attempt by the General to take out one of his legs, Marcus jabbed his sword toward his grandfather's arm. The blade sliced into the unprotected area just under the pauldron. The General growled in pain. He came at Marcus in a fury now, though his attacks still lacked strength. Marcus blocked each with relative ease and got in a few attacks of his own, including a ringing blow to his grandfather's breastplate. Though it did no noticeable damage, experience told Marcus the impact still hurt.

Blood slicked the side of the General's breastplate and left spatters of it in the snow whenever he raised his sword. His breaths came even harder now. He stumbled again under one of Marcus's attacks. It was over. Marcus knew it was. The General surely did too, though he continued to fight. More blood dripped from the General's wound, and he struggled to raise that arm.

Marcus shook his head. "Give it up. You know you can't keep fighting."

His grandfather just glared at him. Marcus knew him better than just about anyone. He would never surrender. Marcus would have to take him down. Grim regret settled inside him. He raised his sword and pressed forward. It was time to end this.

The General met his attack, surely going on sheer stubborn willpower alone. He held against Marcus for a minute or two, but then one of his hands slipped from his sword as Marcus batted it off to the side. Before he could regain control, Marcus slashed at the General's leg just above his greaves. The General's knee buckled. He fought to push back up, but Marcus slammed his fist into the man's jaw. The sword dropped from his hand as he reached out to stop himself from falling completely. Marcus grabbed it and took a step back, gasping in the frozen air.

For a moment, nothing happened. Then his grandfather spit red into the snow and glanced up at him. Blood oozed from his lip. Marcus stared down at him. Once he'd idolized his grandfather. Growing up, and even just a couple of short years ago, he'd seemed invincible. Now he knelt in the snow—wounded, *defeated*—and Marcus had brought that defeat. Instead of satisfaction, it left him sick inside to have had to fight and conquer his own grandfather, one of Arcacia's most renowned soldiers.

Jace ducked under a high blow and almost slipped on a patch of ice but scrambled to regain his footing. His opponent didn't pursue him immediately. In this moment, Jace glanced around camp. Relief swept through him, boosting his energy. They had pushed the soldiers back. The militia was holding. As long as they didn't let up now and Kaden's riders defeated the firedrakes, they could win this fight. He set his gaze back on the soldier, who prepared for another attack.

Jace sidestepped, avoiding the ice this time, and swung his sword out. The blade caught the soldier in the side, and the man buckled. With a quick glance around, Jace's gaze caught on a brutal one-on-one battle. His heart missed a beat as Rayad barely dodged a heavy-handed blow by a dark-haired soldier in black armor. Deep crimson stained the side of Rayad's coat, and spots of blood dotted the snow around his feet. Jace's breath grew shallow as the soldier pursued Rayad with murderous intent. There was something about him, something malicious in the way he fought.

Jace dashed toward them. In the same moment, the soldier slashed at Rayad's chest. Though Rayad blocked the blade, he must have slipped. Jace sucked in his breath as Rayad fell at the soldier's feet. Heat surged through Jace's limbs, and he charged forward. The soldier raised his sword to finish Rayad off. *No!* Jace wasn't close enough. He pushed his legs hard and shouted as the sword descended, swinging his own blade with frantic effort.

The soldier turned just as Jace's blade glanced off his armored shoulder. Jace's desperate attempt left him open. He twisted as the soldier jabbed his sword toward his chest. Pain like a hot skewer pierced his upper arm but faded in a moment. Jerking back, he held his sword defensively and faced the soldier head on. They locked gazes. He was a tall man with a thin, sharp-angled face and black hair streaked with gray. Though Jace had never met him before, instinct told him immediately who this man was—Captain Dagren. That explained his determination to see Rayad dead.

Jace looked into his cold eyes, his mind flashing back two and a half years ago to two bodies lying in the farmyard and the first home he'd ever known being devoured by flames. This man was responsible for Kalli and Aldor's deaths—for destroying the life Jace had so come to love.

A fresh wave of fury and heat roared through him, the strength of which he hadn't experienced in a long time. This fury demanded vengeance for Kalli and Aldor . . . and for himself. It frightened him, and he fought to rein it in before it led to an action he would regret. In that brief moment he struggled within himself, Dagren launched his attack.

Instinct and reflex took over, fueled by the burning inside of Jace. He smashed his sword into Dagren's, driving it to the side. The captain swiftly raised his blade in defense as Jace brought his own down in a hacking blow. Dagren took a step back under the force of it, and Jace pushed forward, any weariness from his previous fights forgotten. Like the days he'd fought in the arenas, the surroundings faded away. It was only him and Dagren. The memory of Kalli and Aldor's lifeless faces still pulsed at the very center of his mind, though he struggled not to let it consume him.

Attack after attack, Jace forced Dagren back until, at last, the man staggered. Before he could regain his balance, Jace kicked one of his legs out from under him. The man crashed to his side. He scrambled to his hands and knees, about to raise his sword, but Jace stepped on the blade and placed the point of his own sword under Dagren's chin. The sharp tip pierced skin, and a thin rivulet of blood rolled down the captain's neck. The man looked up at him, directly in the eyes. Jace breathed hard, ragged breaths, fighting not to let his sword tremble. With a quick slash, he could end Dagren's life and repay him for what had happened. He had wanted it on that horrible day and at other times since. The man had caused so much pain, and not only to Jace but to others he cared about as well. They deserved justice.

"What are you waiting for, boy?" Dagren growled. "Get it over with."

The overwhelming clamor of past hurts and cries for justice quieted. Jace shook his head and lowered his sword, releasing a long breath. No, he wouldn't do it. It wasn't his place to exact vengeance.

The fire died inside him and heaviness took over his body. Footsteps crunched in the snow. He looked up as Holden hurried toward him. The fighting had ceased. All the soldiers had either retreated into the forest or been apprehended by the militia. However, scattered around the perimeter of camp and even among the cabins, bodies and blood littered the snowy ground—both camp members and soldiers. The sight was like a blow to the chest. Their home had become a war zone.

Jace shook himself. Now was not the time to deal with that reality.

"Watch him," he told Holden tersely, gesturing to Dagren as he turned around.

Rayed knelt in the snow nearby, holding his side, but at least he wasn't lying there dead. Jace rushed over to him. "Are you all right?"

Rayad nodded, wincing just slightly. "I'll be fine. It's not too deep."

Jace blew out another gusting breath. He offered Rayad his hand and helped him to his feet. They needed to get him looked at by their physician Josef or Leetra. He opened his mouth to speak, but a shout cut him off. Kyrin's voice echoed through camp, turning his blood to ice.

"MICHAEL!"

Jace spun around. Several yards from the Altairs' cabin, Kyrin threw herself to her knees in the snow with her mother and Lenae. Elanor stood with Ronny and Meredith, staring down at the body lying in the midst of them. *No.* Jace's legs moved before the thought had fully formed. He ran toward them, disjointed but desperate prayers rushing to his mind.

First, he saw the blood—glaring red and searing into his mind. Too much blood. In the snow. On Michael's clothes. His gaze found Michael's face. The boy struggled for breath, his skin nearly as pale as the snow. Blood stained his lips in vivid contrast. All the air left Jace's lungs, and he couldn't draw it back in.

"I'm sorry," Michael choked, staring up at his mother, who clutched his hand. Lenae knelt on the other side of him, both hands pressed to his chest, but it did little to staunch the blood from the wound beneath them. "I had . . . I had to . . . protect you."

Tears flowed down Lydia's face, and she nodded her head. "I know." She brushed her free hand across his forehead, her lips trembling. "I know."

Michael gasped for another breath that wouldn't seem to come and, for a moment, fear registered in his expression, but then he stilled. His eyes closed, and the hand his mother held went limp. A sob broke from her chest.

"Michael?" Kyrin murmured, timid at first, but then her voice grew more frantic. "Michael! No, please! Please!"

Her brother's eyes remained closed.

Numbness overtook Jace. This couldn't be happening. This family couldn't suffer such loss again. He stepped toward Kyrin, his knees shaking, and dropped down beside her. Putting his arm around her, he pulled her close. Her body shook with sobs that mingled with her mother's and Ronny's. Jace looked around at them, taking in the sight of their grief. How had this happened? Why was Michael even out here?

His attention shifted to the sword that lay at Michael's side, blood glistening along the edges. Why had he been fighting? Guilt sprang up inside Jace. He should have stayed nearby. He should never have let the cabin out of his sight!

Footsteps rushed toward them. Kaden and Liam reached the group first, with Talas right behind. They stopped short, staring wide-eyed.

"What . . . happened?" Kaden rasped.

Jace just shook his head. Did any of them really know?

They stood stunned for a moment before Liam, tears about to overflow his eyes, stepped forward and knelt next to his mother, pulling her into his arms. Kaden crossed to Ronny and Meredith, putting an arm around each of them, though his eyes remained on Michael. Tear tracks wet his cheeks. Jace's own face felt warm, though he was still too numb to even realize tears had formed. How could such a thing happen?

The sounds of grief surrounded him, not only from the Altairs, but all around camp as women and children cried around other fallen men. They were supposed to be safe here!

Others approached, but Jace didn't look up to see who it was. He couldn't take his eyes from Michael's face. He'd been like a little brother to Jace. He *would* have been Jace's brother. Maybe, if Jace had spent more time sparring with him . . . done more to train him . . . maybe he would have stood a better chance. Jace squeezed his eyes shut against a fresh flooding of tears, and he gritted his teeth. *Don't do this!* He couldn't let himself sink into blaming himself. It was a far too slippery path. Guilt didn't bring people back.

Someone gasped Michael's name. Jace raised his head. Marcus stood there now, the horror sinking in for him as it had for everyone else. And just behind him, guarded by two of the militia, stood the General. His face, usually so hard and grim, slackened, his lips parting as he looked down at his slain grandson. No words came. He just stood, like a frozen statue. Were those tears in his eyes?

Kyrin went rigid in Jace's arms and pulled away from him, shoving to her feet. She stepped toward her grandfather, her voice strangled. "You did this!"

Jace jumped up and grabbed her around the waist. She tugged against him, still crying.

"You brought them here! You killed him!"

She almost collapsed then, but Jace held her up, and she turned in his arms, burying her face in his chest as she sobbed. Jace held her tightly and looked over at Kaden. With Kyrin's outburst, would he stand down? His tear-filled eyes smoldered as he glared at their grandfather. However, he held himself back, remaining with Ronny and Meredith, the greatest act of restraint Jace had ever witnessed.

The next few minutes went by in a daze. The militiamen led the General away, while other members of camp helped Kyrin's family wrap Michael in a blanket and carry him into the cabin. Jace led Kyrin along with him. Neither she nor the others wore coats. At the cabin, Jace immediately noticed the broken window and cracks in the door. Things fell into place. Soldiers had tried to break in. That's why Michael was out fighting. He was protecting them . . . just as he'd said. The throbbing inside Jace's chest ached more deeply. Michael had died defending his family.

Daniel still gripped the sword someone had handed him in the chaos. He didn't even remember who. Aric, probably. He only remembered heading toward Trask and Anne's cabin to have lunch with Elanor when he'd heard the roar. He'd never heard anything like it before—a thundering explosion of heart-stopping terror that seemed nearly capable of shattering the frozen landscape around them.

He looked around camp, his eyes drawn from one still body to another. He'd seen death and carnage in the arena, but here was different. This was an attack on a place so many considered home. Unexpected and devastating.

Now his gaze dropped to his blade, stained red. Today marked the first day he had ever fought in battle. The first day he'd ever killed someone. His heart still raced with adrenaline, each breath still heavy with exertion. All those hours spent training and sparring at Auréa—they had done nothing to prepare him for the true reality of fighting for his life and those in this camp.

He blinked, snapping himself from a shock-induced haze. The fight was over. They had won. But at what cost? A fresh surge of adrenaline flushed through him, though a kind that fed panic more than fighting. He kept it in check, but questions pounded the inside of his skull. Where was Elanor?

He hurried forward, picking up speed toward the heart of camp. He paused along the way to help with their wounded soldiers. Some were able to move under their own power while others bore grisly wounds and wouldn't likely survive the night. He helped wherever he could but always searched for Elanor's face amongst the crowds gathering outside. Had the soldiers broken into any of the cabins? Had any of the women and children been caught outside?

"Daniel!"

His heart reacted to the feminine voice, and he spun around. Elanor rushed toward him. She threw her arms unashamedly around his neck when she reached him, and he wrapped his free arm around her, still holding his sword in the other. He let out a huge breath.

She released him just as quickly and looked him over. "Are you all right?"

He nodded.

The concern in her expression deepened. "You're bleeding."

What? He looked down at himself. Blood covered his sword hand. He thought at first it was someone else's, but then realized he had a long gash along the back of his hand and wrist. He hadn't even noticed it. With the realization came the pain, but it was the least of his concern. Elanor's eyes were red, her cheeks pink and damp. Was she afraid or was she hurt?

"I'm fine." He put his injured hand on her shoulder. "Are you all right? Are you hurt?"

She shook her head, all at once pain crumpling her face. "Michael is dead."

A boulder slammed his chest. "What?"

Tears poured from her eyes. "Soldiers were trying to break in. He went out to stop them."

Daniel could only stare at her for a moment as the adrenaline finally died and his body grew cold. Another Altair dead. Michael was just a boy. Heat flared in his blood. This was all because of his sister. Because of her unsatiated hatred for all of them. He knew beyond all doubt she had ordered this attack. Right in the dead of winter when they would least expect it. No one fought wars in the winter, but she was just crazy enough to send her men out into the snowy wilderness to do it.

Daniel clenched his fist, fighting his own hatred. But the weak sob Elanor released snapped his attention back to her. He pulled her close again, holding her against his chest as she cried. His nose stung, moisture filling his eyes as he thought about the agony the Altairs faced once again. Two of their family members were gone now because of his family and their bloody quest for power.

Jace sat at the fireplace with Kyrin, holding her close, just as he had the day her father died. And just like that day, he wished desperately for a way to take her pain upon himself. He hated to see her and her family suffer so. Hadn't they borne enough pain and loss? Why Michael too? He couldn't help asking Elôm such questions. He trusted there was a purpose—there had to be—but, in the midst of grief, it felt so . . . pointless.

He rubbed his burning eyes with his free hand. Below him, Tyra shifted, her chin resting on his foot. He'd lost track of her during the attack but was thankful when she had turned up at the cabin with Elian. She'd obviously done her part in the fight. Blood matted her fur in areas—both her own and others'—but his quick inspection of her hadn't revealed anything more than minor cuts she had already licked clean. She peered up at him, a sad look to her crystal blue eyes. She couldn't know what had happened, but she sensed the mood in the cabin.

Jace glanced around them. Kyrin's brothers sat at the table with their mother, their faces dazed, occasional tears falling. Lydia cried more openly. Aric sat beside her, consoling her as best he could. Talas had stayed, his typically bright green eyes dimmed. He surely felt as though he had lost a brother too. Others came and went, offering quiet sympathies. Some of the men had boarded up the broken window and cleaned up the glass.

Jace stared back into the crackling flames in the fireplace and tried to make some sort of sense of what had happened. A moment later, a quiet voice said his name and a hand touched his shoulder. He looked up to find Lenae. Her eyes were full of moisture and shared grief.

"Why don't you let me look at your arm?"

His arm? He looked down at the blood staining his sleeve. That's right; he'd been wounded. He hadn't even noticed the throbbing ache until now. Slowly, he took his other arm from around Kyrin's shoulders. She barely reacted, staring vacantly toward the fire. It always scared him to see her like this, but he reminded himself how strong she was. She would get through this . . . eventually, and he would be there to help her.

Standing, he slipped out of his coat. Red stained his shirt-sleeve down to the wrist. He peeled it away from his skin and pulled his arm out. Dagren's blade had sliced into his flesh just below his shoulder. Blood caked the wound, though it no longer bled. He sat down again and let Lenae take over cleaning it. He barely felt it when she stitched the torn flesh.

When she finished bandaging it, Jace stuck his arm back in his sleeve, but the blood held his attention. He should change. He shouldn't sit here with blood on his clothes. Though he hated to leave, he turned to Kyrin and cleared his throat.

"I'll be back in a few minutes."

She didn't respond at first but then nodded slowly. Firelight flickered on the pooled tears in her eyes. Jace leaned over to press a soft kiss to her temple and then stood, looking down at her. She always appeared so small and frail when grief hit. He passed the table, glancing at her family, and then let himself out of the cabin with Tyra, who followed along.

Outside, he took in the sight of camp—a world of white and gray . . . and red. Blood. It spotted camp in a glaring reminder of just how fragile their life was here. The safety they'd experienced for so long had shattered, proving to be little more than an illusion. Of the only two places Jace had ever considered home, both had now faced attack and left him in mourning. Why couldn't one place remain safe and protected? He glanced up at the sky, longing for Elôm to answer. *Please comfort Kyrin and her family . . . and the others who have suffered loss.*

Heaviness dragging at him, Jace crossed the snow to the other cabin. Amidst the sorrow, concern crowded in. He hadn't seen Rayad since the fight with Dagren. He'd appeared all right, but what if he was more seriously injured than either of them realized? Jace's pace quickened. The possibility of losing Rayad too snatched away his ability to breathe.

At the cabin door, he hesitated. He had no reason to believe Rayad wasn't all right, but his fears escalated faster than he could contain them. With a desperate prayer, he opened the door and walked in.

His breath finally returned, seeping out slowly. Rayad sat in his usual chair and looked back at Jace as he entered. Holden, Elian, and Trev were also present. Each of them bore tight-lipped, grim expressions. Rayad carefully pushed to his feet, holding his side, and met Jace near the door.

"How are they?" he asked quietly.

Jace just stood a moment, the heavy numbness of what had happened returning. He shook his head. What could he even say? Devastated? Crushed?

Rayad gave a slight nod. His gaze dropped to Jace's shoulder. "Have you had that looked at?"

"Yes. I just came to change. I need to get back to Kyrin." He walked over to his clothing chest and pulled out a new shirt. As he changed, a question rose that he hesitated to ask. "How many others did we lose?" He didn't look back, too afraid to see Rayad's face and the possibility of dealing with more loss.

"Five dragon riders—three of Kaden's men and two of Darq's," Rayad answered soberly. "Sixteen men from the militia and another five who weren't. Several more are injured. Two women were killed in one of the cabins the soldiers broke into. I haven't heard yet, but I'm assuming our lookouts were killed as well."

Jace let out a long breath. If not for Michael, that could have been Kyrin and Elanor. "Balen and Daniel?"

"They are fine."

Jace nodded slowly. Over thirty dead. Perhaps more if some of the wounded didn't survive. A large chunk of their community just . . . gone. They hadn't even had any warning. It wasn't that they'd grown complacent, but . . . Jace would never have imagined their enemies finding them here. For nearly three years it had stood as a safe haven. What would happen now that its location was no longer secret?

All at once, the questions and the sorrow overwhelmed Jace, and he found himself sinking down on the edge of his cot and putting his head in his hands. They were all in danger—Kyrin, her family, Elanor, Rayad. Not only that, but they were hurting, and there was nothing he could do about any of it. He blinked hard, his eyes burning, yet try as he might to stop them, the tears soon rolled down his cheeks.

The cot creaked as Rayad sat down beside him with a heavy sigh. He said nothing, but the strength of his presence helped Jace bear the pain. Finally, he wiped the tears from his chin and looked over at Rayad, speaking hoarsely. "Why does this keep happening to her?"

Of all that had happened, the most painful was knowing the agony Kyrin had to endure and that it would forever remain fresh in her memory.

KYRIN STARED AT the ceiling for hours; her eyes burning as if full of sand. She drew in a slow breath past her lips, her nose congested from crying. Her body felt heavy, numb . . . cold, even being under the blankets with her mother. Kyrin tipped her head to look over at her. She seemed to be asleep, finally. The sorrow had exhausted them both. It had been late when they'd given in to the gentle urgings to get some rest. Even then, they had lain awake, soon breaking down into tears. Kyrin had held her mother tightly as they'd both sobbed in loss.

Kyrin closed her eyes as the sting of tears returned. *Elôm?* She was out of words beyond this simple, aching plea to feel His presence in this. She struggled to remind herself of His work behind her father's death and the joy that had grown up amidst the soil of sorrow. Surely, He also had a purpose in her brother dying. She begged for the answer, but reasons eluded her, the pain far too fresh to see beyond it.

Afraid of breaking down again, Kyrin silently slipped out of bed, careful not to disturb her mother, and changed into a dress. A pale light filtering through the windows signaled a cold dawn as she left the cabin loft. She looked to the back of the cabin. The canvas partitions were open enough for her to see each of her brothers—four of them . . . no longer five. Her lungs struggled to expand and draw air as she gazed at them. Ronny shared a bed with Liam. All of them appeared to be asleep except for Kaden. He stared up at the ceiling much as she had been. He glanced at her as she approached the fireplace. Though the cabin was dim, the small flames from the fire glinted in his eyes, which looked overly moist.

Fighting to swallow down her own tears, Kyrin's gaze fell on Jace. He sat on the floor, his back resting against the stones of the fireplace. His eyes were closed, his arm draped over Tyra, who lay beside him with her chin in his lap. Though they had told everyone who had been with them during the long, hard day to return to their cabins for the night, Jace had stayed. Stayed right here, disregarding his own comfort just to be near. A couple of her tears spilled over in an overwhelming combination of love and sorrow.

She brushed her hands across her cheeks and sat down in the chair she'd occupied yesterday. Though it barely creaked, Jace's eyes opened. He blinked, and his gaze locked on her. Concern filled them immediately, and he started to rise, but Kyrin held up her hand to stop him.

"Don't get up on my account," she whispered.

Jace rested back again and rubbed his hands over his face. His usually brilliant and clear eyes were red. He'd been crying too, something he did so seldom. The thought of that robbed her of breath. He and Michael had shared a growing bond, especially since Jace had saved his life last summer, nearly losing his own as a result. After all that, why had Michael had to die now? It felt so meaningless. She closed her eyes again and bit her lip. *Elôm, please give us peace in this. It's too hard.*

The sound of Jace moving around again drew her attention. He had gotten to his knees and quietly put wood on the fire. Once the flames had caught, he got up and claimed the chair next to her. Still weak, she reached for his hand, needing his strength. His worn but gentle fingers closed around hers and squeezed tightly. Resting her head against his shoulder, Kyrin let the tears fall freely. She didn't have enough strength to fight them.

Daniel stared at his bandaged hand and flexed his fingers as he sat on the edge of his bed. The wound beneath the blood-stained strip of linen ached, but pain meant he was alive, unlike so many others. He let a heavy breath seep from his lungs. The last time he had faced death like this had been the night his father died. Many, including Daniel, would say his father had deserved his fate. Those here hadn't—especially not the innocent women and young Michael. What a tragic waste of life.

While Daniel hadn't been in this camp nearly as long as most, like them he'd felt safe here. It had long been a haven that had seemed untouchable, even before he'd arrived. But like the days leading up to Davira usurping his throne, he'd grown far too comfortable and confident in his position. Too caught up in the simple freedoms he'd found here.

He rubbed the sore muscles in his neck. He couldn't help but feel like this was his fault. Maybe because Davira was his sister. If he'd just been wise and stopped her from taking power, then none of this would have happened. Somehow he always failed at doing the one thing he should do.

"Are you all right?"

Daniel looked up and found Aric watching him. Realizing how tightly he held his brows together, he probably looked like he'd swallowed spoiled milk. "I was just wishing I had thrown Davira in a cage where she belonged before she had a chance to do it to me. I could have prevented this."

"I was there too," Aric said. "You can't blame yourself."

Daniel shook his head. "I was the one who was supposed to be king. I should've known better."

From across the cabin where he poured a cup of coffee, Balen joined in. "Just because you're king doesn't mean you can know or see everything. Don't forget it was my stepmother who surrendered Samara into the hands of your father."

He brought Daniel and Aric both a cup of hot coffee. Daniel raised his cup to Balen in a mock toast. "To being betrayed by family."

He then sipped the coffee that was about as dark and bitter as his feelings toward his sister at the moment.

A knock at the door interrupted his uncharitable imaginings of all the horrible things Davira deserved to have happen to her. When Balen answered it, Trask, Warin, and Captain Darq stepped inside. The flames in the fireplace wavered as if shivering at the cold air that followed them in.

If he'd been the suspicious sort and not a believer in Elôm, Daniel might have wondered if his sister had somehow conjured this vicious winter weather herself. It was just the sort of thing she would do given the power. Thank Elôm she was only human like the rest of them.

"Have we lost anyone else?" Balen asked.

Trask shook his head. "No, but some are still in bad condition."

Balen gestured to the table, and the three of them took seats. Once they each had a mug of steaming coffee to help warm them up, Trask spoke again.

"I didn't want to have to call everyone out for a meeting this morning, but we need to discuss the security of camp now that our location is no longer a secret."

"We won't be able to stay here now," Warin said.

Regret hung heavy in his low tone. Daniel couldn't blame him. This camp had been home to a good many people for a long time. He'd only been here a few months, but he would already hate to leave it.

"There isn't much we can do until the snow clears," Balen responded. "We may be able to evacuate to the other camps, but who's to say their location is still a secret?"

Trask rubbed his neck with a sigh. "You're right. We can't evacuate until spring. Even if we had enough dragons for everyone, we don't have the supplies to set up a new camp in this weather." He turned his attention to Darq. "Does it look like we need to prepare for another attack?"

"My men and I patrolled throughout the night. The surviving soldiers and firedrakes retreated to the barracks. It's too soon to tell if they will wait for reinforcements and try again."

Now Trask looked at Daniel. "What do you think?"

Daniel straightened. He still wasn't used to being part of this governing body of men where decisions he helped make could mean life or death. He scolded himself for his uncertainty. One of these days he needed to start acting like the king they all were prepared to fight and die to see him become.

"If Davira was crazy enough to attack us now in the dead of winter, then she's crazy enough to try it again. We won't know for sure unless reinforcements show up."

"We'll keep a close watch on any activity at the barracks," Darq said.

"How did she find us in the first place?" Daniel asked. This was surely the one question on almost everyone's mind. "And why didn't our lookouts have a chance to warn us?"

"Your sister must have had scouts searching the forest from the air," Trask answered. "Most likely at night when we didn't notice. They were probably crete traitors. They could even have used the trees. From what we can tell, they knew the location of our lookouts before the attack and made their way around to cut them off and ambush them before they could warn us."

Daniel gritted his teeth. "So they're dead?"

Trask nodded slowly, his jaw taut.

Daniel had expected as much, though he hadn't heard for sure until now.

"So, what options do we have?" Thank Elôm there were men here who knew this camp and how to defend it much better than he did.

"Since we can't evacuate, our best chance is to have as much advance warning of an attack as possible. We should have dragon riders patrolling at all times." Trask directed his words at Darq again. "Kaden's men can cover daytime shifts while you and your men take the night."

Darq nodded firmly.

"We'll monitor all activity at the barracks and in Landale," Trask continued. "Beyond that, there's nothing we can do until spring."

Daniel swallowed down a sigh of frustration. Even here Davira had them under her thumb now. Waiting around to see if she would attack again would put a strain on all of them and wouldn't help morale, especially when combined with their food shortage.

Jace looked over the top of Kyrin's head at a quiet knock at the cabin door. By this time, Kyrin's mother had gotten up, and her brothers were in various stages of doing the same. Lydia opened the door to Lenae, who stepped in and gave her friend a hug. They talked in subdued tones, and Lenae went to work making breakfast for them.

Giving Kyrin's hand another gentle squeeze, Jace murmured, "I'm going to get some wood." The wood box was nearly empty, and the least he could do was fill it.

Kyrin only nodded.

Jace pushed up from the chair, stretching his muscles. His lower back ached from sitting all night. Trading a sad look with Lenae, he walked to the door and slipped on his coat. Tyra followed him into the frigid air outside. He pulled on his gloves as he stood for a moment and looked around camp. Many of the men were up and about, but their movements seemed weighted by the invisible gloom that hovered.

Jace's gaze strayed in the direction of his cabin. Had only twenty-four hours passed since he'd been full of exciting plans for his future with Kyrin? He hung his head. It would take time now for the sorrow to fade enough for such excitement to return. The future he'd just started to build for himself and Kyrin could be snatched away just as quickly as lives were yesterday.

Trudging through the snow toward their wood supply, Jace struggled with the terror that always rose up whenever he considered losing Kyrin. It was as if the frozen air were seeping right into his chest, freezing up his lungs and making it difficult to breathe. He shook his head to rid himself of the sensation. He would do whatever he could to protect her. Beyond that, he had to trust Elôm to keep her safe.

At the woodpile, he filled his arms with firewood, ignoring the throbbing from his wound. After a moment, footsteps approached, and Holden walked up. Jace glanced at him, catching the sympathy in his friend's eyes. They said nothing at first. Finally, Jace cleared his throat and asked, "How's Rayad?"

"Sore, but Josef was over a bit ago and wasn't concerned."

Jace nodded, relief settling amongst his other emotions. He could still see Dagren standing over Rayad, about to kill him. If only Jace could have saved both Rayad and Michael.

He wrapped his free arm around his bundle of wood and turned back toward the Altair cabin.

"I'll come see him later."

Holden nodded and reached out to grip his shoulder encouragingly before letting him go.

Back at the cabin, Kyrin and her family slowly gathered around the table where Lenae had laid out breakfast. Jace placed the wood in its box and put a couple of pieces in the fire before joining them. He sat down next to Kyrin and all was quiet. No one seemed to know what to do. Jace glanced around the table. Kyrin and her mother looked lost, while her brothers all sat redeyed and grim-faced.

At last, Marcus bowed his head, and everyone else followed his example. He took a deep breath, but his words didn't come for a long moment. When he did speak, his voice lacked the confident strength Jace was used to, and it wavered at times. Marcus thanked Elôm that they'd driven the soldiers back and hadn't been defeated and that most of them were still here to have this meal together. After that, he prayed for strength for everyone. That was all he could manage and ended with a hoarse "amen". Jace added his own internal plea for divine comfort for the Altairs and for all those dealing with loss this morning.

Silence fell again as they all picked at their food. Even Jace found it hard to force any down. A heavy and stifling gloom hung over them. No one said a word for a long time. The silence was only broken by another gentle knock at the door. As if coming out of a trance, Marcus straightened, and then rose to answer it. Aric and Talas entered the cabin when he opened the door. To see Talas was almost startling. Jace was so used to his grin and air of mischief, but his red-rimmed eyes lacked any sort of sparkle. Even the times Talas had been injured, his good humor had remained. Today, however, there wasn't even a hint of it.

Aric approached the table, hesitating, and focused on Lydia. His voice was rough but compassionate. "We came to let you know Trask and Darq are gathering the dragons to help clear a burial site. It will take some time to get through the ground, but it should be ready by tomorrow."

At first, Lydia barely reacted, but then she blinked at the tears building in her eyes and shook her head. "No, he should be buried at home . . . with his father."

Everyone looked at her, but Marcus responded first. "I agree."

Kyrin and the rest of her brothers nodded. Jace could understand their desire to keep their family graves together.

With a slow nod, Aric asked, "When do you want to do it?"

Lydia bit her lip, and when she spoke, Jace could tell she fought mightily not to cry. "We should get it done . . . as soon as we can."

"We could leave tomorrow," Marcus suggested.

Silent agreement passed through the family. Jace prayed no snowstorm would blow in and delay their plans. A funeral would help provide closure.

"I'll let Trask know," Aric said. He stood for a moment before heading back to the door.

"Thank you," Lydia said after him.

He glanced back and nodded.

Once he was gone, Marcus took his coat from a peg on the wall. He faced his family as he pulled it on. "I should go check on my men."

Kaden rose from the table. "Me too."

He, Marcus, and Talas left the cabin, and Lydia got up, quietly clearing the breakfast dishes. Before Kyrin could join her, Jace put his hand on her arm.

"I'll go with you to Mernin, if you want me to." He didn't want to intrude, but he also wanted her to know he was more than willing to be there.

"Yes, please," she murmured, her eyes watery.

He squeezed her arm. "Then I'll go get ready and be back in a little while."

Nighttime darkness engulfed the cabin. Kyrin's brothers had lit some lamps, and Jace added a couple of pieces of wood to the fire. He glanced at Kyrin, who helped her mother finish the supper dishes. Neither of them spoke. No one did. Jace wasn't used to the cabin being so quiet. It had always been so lively with Kyrin's brothers around. Would it ever be the same again? Jace let out a long sigh. Why was joy so easily snatched away?

Glass clinked as Kyrin and her mother placed the dishes in the cupboard. Lydia then turned to her sons at the table.

"Ronny, why don't you get ready for bed?" she said softly, weariness weighing on her voice. "We all need rest."

Ronny said nothing, just got up and walked toward the back of the cabin, his head bowed. Jace didn't think he'd spoken since the attack. He was too young to have had to face so much heartache already. Liam followed Ronny, and Marcus and Kaden both got up, pushing in the chairs around the table. As they prepared to turn in for the night, Kyrin joined Jace at the fireplace. She stood beside him for a moment, staring at the fire before looking up at him.

"You should go so you can sleep in your own bed tonight."

He shook his head. "I don't mind staying." His back might, but it was a small price to pay.

The briefest hint of a sad smile lifted her lips. "I know, but I do want you to rest comfortably." She breathed a deep breath. "I'll be all right."

He watched her for a moment, debating, but he wouldn't insist. Slowly, he nodded and headed for the door. As he slipped into his coat, he turned to Kyrin, who had followed him. Her face seemed especially pale in the dim light. The emotions and grief were taking a heavy toll. He hated seeing her in such a state.

He reached for her, pulling her gently into his arms. She latched onto him, burying her face in the folds of his coat. For a long moment, they just stood there. When Jace gently pulled away, Kyrin's cheeks were wet. He reached up, wiping the moisture with his thumbs, and cupped her face in his hands. His throat clogged up, strangling his voice. "I wish so much that I could bear this for you."

"I know," she barely whispered. She closed her eyes to collect herself. Finally, she opened them again and stared up at him. "Thank you for bearing it with me."

TRASK PULLED ON his boots and then sat back in his chair with a heavy sigh. Today would be one of their first funerals held in camp. The only other one had been for Mr. Hagen, and that was due to an unfortunate accident, not an attack. Thirty freshly-dug graves waited on the edge of camp. Another thirty-eight deeper into the forest for the fallen Arcacian soldiers. So many.

A hand rested on his shoulder, and he looked up. Anne gazed down at him, her deep green eyes dimmed by sorrow and sympathy. One of those graves could have been hers. Had the soldiers broken into the cabin, they could have slaughtered her and her mother. He could hardly bear that thought.

"It's my fault." His voice dragged hoarsely past the knot in his throat.

Anne's forehead wrinkled, and she sat in a chair across from him. "What is?"

"The attack. I got complacent. I never imagined there would be an attack in the dead of winter. With all the snow and the cold, I didn't think . . ." He shook his head, the guilt wearing him down. He'd failed the people he'd set out to protect. "I should have done more. I should have had more security in place."

Anne reached for his hands, squeezing them between her soft fingers. "You're the one who started this camp, but you're not the only one responsible for it. We *all* grew complacent. It isn't only on you. None of us could have predicted an attack now. I still don't know how they managed to reach us through all that snow. And that's probably exactly why they chose to attack now. They knew we would be unprepared."

Trask nodded and sighed again. "We relied too much on the cold and snow. Unfortunately, that's what made us easy to find. They probably had their crete spies flying over the forest at night looking for us now that the trees are bare."

"We can't change what has happened; we can only make sure it doesn't happen again."

She spoke with such attractive strength and determination. She hadn't once broken down in a weepy panic since the attack. He knew men with less fortitude. A slight smile worked its way to his lips. How he loved this woman.

Her eyes narrowed suspiciously. "What?"

He just shook his head and lifted her hands to his lips to kiss them. "I just love you, that's all."

Mernin. The last time Jace had visited this area, he'd just been whipped and beaten by the General's men at Fort Rivor. The pain from that experience crawled along his back like a phantom whip and stabbed through his ribs. He looked ahead to the large, gray-brick Altair house as he dismounted Gem. It reminded him of a couple of the homes where he'd once been a slave, though the Altairs had never kept slaves.

Giving his dragon a light pat on the shoulder, Jace cast a glance over at Kyrin. The memories of pain faded, and real pain squeezed his heart. Kyrin's gaze was fixed on the spot where her father was buried. What a tragedy that her childhood home held such a difficult mix of both fond and painful memories.

Jace scanned the yard for any sign of danger even though Talas had scouted ahead of them with Storm. Everything was quiet and frozen. The only sign of life was the smoke rising from the house chimneys, and the area seemed just as devoid of wildlife as Landale.

With a low creak, the back door to the house opened, and an elderly man stepped out into the snow. He wore a familiar, bright smile, but it faded quickly once he noticed the misery on their faces. Pulling on his coat, the Altair's old groundskeeper, Carl, crossed the yard to meet them, the lines in his face deepening.

"What's happened?" he asked when he stood a few feet away.

Jace looked over at Lydia, who struggled to form even a simple word. Marcus stepped up and put his arm around her shoulders.

"Camp was attacked." He hesitated, clearing his throat. "Michael was killed."

Tears slid down Lydia's cold-reddened cheeks. Kyrin's weren't far behind. Carl stared at them as if frozen for a moment, but his eyes turned watery. He blinked hard and shook his head, murmuring, "I'm sorry."

Marcus cleared his throat again, though his voice came out husky. "We wanted to bury him here, with Father."

Silence engulfed them as Carl let the news sink in. He then said hoarsely, "Let me help you bring your things inside."

Everyone turned to unload the dragons. After taking his things from Gem, Jace turned to help Kyrin. With their packs in tow, they followed Carl up to the house. The warmth inside enveloped them as they stepped into the back entry. Carl's wife, Ethel, waited there, her stern face knitting in concern. Carl set aside the pack he had carried for Lydia and gave his wife the news. Though she was stiff and not particularly friendly, Jace could see the sorrow in her eyes. She even stepped forward to give Lydia a hug. Why did it always have to be death that brought people together?

Once things were settled, Jace followed the rest of the men back outside. It didn't seem that Marcus or his brothers would rest until they had accomplished their task. With the dragons to clear most of the snow and help thaw the ground with their fire, they went to work digging a grave. Since only a couple could work on it at a time, Jace turned his attention to the gravestone just to the left. The top barely peaked out through the snow.

Calling to Gem, he set about clearing the snow here as well. When his dragon had scraped away most of it with her powerful claws, he used a shovel to remove the rest. Before long, he had a large area around the grave cleared. Resting against his shovel, he stared at the gravestone. *William Altair. Traitor.*

Jace let out a long breath, tight bands wrapping around his chest. Kyrin's father had been a good man. If only Jace could have gotten to know him better, especially now with all that he had planned for a future with Kyrin. Would he have approved?

Yes, Jace believed he would have. Kaden had told Jace that his father liked him even though they'd known each other for only a brief time. Jace's eyes stung, and he closed them for a moment. *Lord, please spare Kyrin and her family any further pain.*

The only funeral Daniel had ever attended before today had been his father's. How was that even possible? He felt like such an imposter standing here with all these grieving people. He hadn't been in camp long enough to know any of the deceased that well. Yet, they were his people. He should have been able to prevent this.

The sounds of women weeping added a backdrop to Trask's voice as he spoke over the graves. His words were thick, and he had to clear his throat several times. Really, these were more his people than Daniel's. Trask had been leading men for far longer than Daniel had even thought about it. Trask had grown up learning that responsibility. Daniel had squandered any times his father had tried to teach him how to be a leader. And yet, somehow these people still intended to make him their king. They were prepared to die to accomplish it. He certainly hadn't earned any such loyalty. Trask would have made the better king.

Daniel's vision blurred, his eyes stinging. He blinked hard. Would he ever be able to do right by these people and protect them from future heartbreak? Sometimes he wondered why Elôm hadn't just wiped out his family and started with someone new. He had many good men to choose from who had far more experience and wisdom than a once-pampered prince.

A firm hand gripped his shoulder. He blinked the wetness from his eyes and looked over to find Sam. The talcrin's gold eyes beamed compassion that bolstered Daniel. Sam had been his friend since long before any of this. He'd known Daniel as a child. He had seen Daniel at his worst, and that was strangely comforting. Sam held no grand illusions about.

The funeral ended a short time later with a few final words from Trask and everyone slowly dispersed. Daniel blew out a gusting breath, standing at the graves a moment longer before turning toward the cabins. He didn't realize that Sam had remained behind as well until the talcrin fell into step beside him.

"How are you holding up?"

Daniel shook his head. "I keep thinking that this is my fault. I should have been able to prevent this, but I was too foolish and naïve to secure my place on the throne. If I had suspected Davira and taken precautions, none of these people would even be here. They would be at home with their families, finally living in peace. I'm supposed to be king, but I can't even prevent a massacre of my own people."

"You may be king, but you are not Elôm," Sam said in a tone far more fatherly than Daniel's own father had ever used. "You can't see or know all."

Daniel sighed again. "Yes, but shouldn't a king be wiser than that?"

He glanced at Sam, who wore a faint smile.

"Kings are people, just like the rest of us. They must be wise, yes, but not a single one is perfect."

"I don't know. Balen seems a lot more perfect than I'll ever be."

"Yet, his people are suffering under Davira's rule, and he is here, same as you."

This did give Daniel a bit of pause. After all, if Balen had suspected his stepmother of treachery, things might be very different in Samara. Really, they'd made the same mistake. Still, Balen had far more experience and wisdom as a result.

"At least he took his position seriously. All I did was fight any training my father tried to give me."

"You will learn," Sam assured him. "You're more than willing now. And don't forget that Elôm is working, even in our mistakes. He would not have allowed Davira to succeed if it was not part of His plan."

As hard as it was to accept and understand, Sam was right. Daniel just had to trust Elôm to see it all through.

"Don't sell yourself short." Sam squeezed his shoulder again. "Anyone can see that you love your people and want to do what is right for them. You've come a long way from where you were when you let me walk out of the palace with the Scrolls, but even then, you knew what was right."

The memory of that night brought a small smile to Daniel's

lips. It seemed like a lifetime ago. Thank Elôm he had let Sam leave. He looked into his friend's gold eyes.

"Thanks, Sam."

They held Michael's funeral shortly after preparing the grave. A few snowflakes fell from the overcast sky as they all gathered at the edge of the frozen hole in the ground, where Marcus and Kaden laid Michael. Jace stood next to Kyrin and rested his hand against her back to let her know he was there to support her. At first, no one said a word, but then Marcus spoke, softly and sadly. He spoke of how much Michael loved his family and his great desire to protect them. He shared memories of their time growing up—memories that drew brief, teary smiles. In conclusion, he reminded them all that Michael was with their father and grandfather now, enjoying the blissful life Elôm promised His children.

By this time, Kyrin and her mother cried openly, and her brothers each had tear tracks glistening down their cheeks. A few tears fell from Jace's eyes, and he put his arm around Kyrin's shoulders, drawing her close. She leaned into him, weeping.

After a few minutes to compose themselves, the men grabbed shovels to fill in the grave. Gently parting from Kyrin, Jace joined them. The shovel felt strangely heavy, as if weighed down by the memories. He'd taken part in too many burials—first Kalli and Aldor, then Josan, and now Michael. So many good people gone from this life. They were in a better place now, but many people sorely missed their presence and positive influence.

Once the grave was filled, they stood for a while longer before the cold drove them inside, where they gathered in the dining room. Memories of their previous visit returned to Jace again. His gaze focused on the end of the table where he'd sat bloodied, beaten, and in agony. He then looked at Kyrin. She too stared at that spot before meeting his gaze. As painful as it had been, the memories weren't all bad. In those moments, her gentle care for him had first awakened feelings he'd never had for anyone before her.

Her attention shifted away from him when Carl spoke.

"Will you be staying?"

"If you don't mind," Lydia said. "We won't stay long. We don't want anyone to come by and notice."

He smiled gently. "It's still your house. We are merely its caretakers."

"You're far more than that." Lydia peered around the dining room with a longing expression and ran her hand along the edge of the table. Jace could only imagine the memories playing in her mind.

He glanced at Ethel. Her pinched expression didn't show pleasure at harboring fugitives, but she didn't speak against it. Instead, she murmured, "I'll start dinner."

She left the room, and Lydia turned to Jace and Talas. Her eyes and cheeks were still red from crying, but she appeared more in control of her emotions than she had all day. "We have two guest bedrooms you can use. I'll show you."

They collected their things from the entryway and followed her. Jace had never been upstairs. The long hall at the top of the staircase had three doors on either side. Lydia opened the first one and motioned to Talas.

"I'm afraid you won't find anywhere to hang your hammock."

Talas shook his head and replied graciously, "The bed will be just fine. Thank you."

Lydia opened the next door for Jace. He thanked her and stepped into the room. A thick blue quilt draped the bed in the corner, and a large braided rug covered the middle of the wood floor. He glanced out the window, which faced the front of the house, toward the road. Though he didn't anticipate trouble, he appreciated the vantage point.

He set his pack on the bed and took a seat beside it, breathing out a sigh as he reached up to rub his arm. The wound ached from all the digging. In fact, his entire body felt drained. How could only three days hold enough emotion and exhaustion to fill an entire month? It would take weeks just to recover.

He sat for a few minutes, contemplating the funeral and being here in the Altairs' house, before everyone gathered downstairs again. Kyrin and her mother disappeared into the kitchen to help Ethel while Jace followed the men into the living room, where a fire crackled in a large fireplace. Here they discussed the goings-on at camp until joining the women in the dining room for a warm meal.

They passed the food around quietly. After a minute or two, Lydia broke the silence and asked Carl, "Have you had any trouble while we've been away?"

"Nothing to speak of. We're still getting a monthly sum and supplies from the fort. It seems the General is holding out hope you'll someday return and wants us to look after the place."

"Hopefully that won't cease. My father led the attack against camp and was taken captive."

Carl raised his brows. "Who managed that?"

"I did," Marcus said quietly.

Carl sent him a look that hinted of pride. "Well, whatever happens, I'm sure we'll make do."

This didn't appear to ease Lydia's concern. "I hope so. This winter isn't being kind to anyone."

Carl grunted in agreement. "We've heard of the food shortages. How are you faring?"

"There's concern over how we'll feed everyone," Marcus answered. "It's not dire yet, but we'll have to figure something out. We had planned to send the extra dragons to Dorland for the winter, but after the attack . . ." He shook his head. "It's something we'll have to discuss when we get back."

Jace hadn't considered how the attack would change their plans. Could they afford to send away so many of their dragons? What if Davira launched another attack? Could they risk it? Either choice presented them with the possibility of grim consequences.

"Have you heard much news from Valcré?" Carl asked.

"Not recently. Most of our dragon riders are out looking for food, and now that Aric is at camp, we don't hear much from the palace. Our only other informant isn't included in much of Davira's dealings. Last we heard, though, things were bad. Sounds like people don't even want to leave their homes for fear of being murdered right on the street. I don't know how Davira thinks her proclamation will help her destroy us. It will sooner destroy the country."

"It's bad," Carl agreed, "and it has only grown worse. Did you hear of the Miner's Fever?"

The mention of the dreaded sickness brought memories to Jace's mind from when he was a boy, about ten years old. It had reportedly originated in the mines of the Graylin Valley and spread rapidly through most of western Arcacia. People had died by the thousands. He remembered the fear of his fellow slaves who would never receive the proper treatment if they did contract the illness. There hadn't been any cases of it that he knew of since that winter.

Marcus shook his head. "No, what of it?"

"I'm afraid it's back. We just heard a few days ago that it's sweeping through Valcré and the forts."

"That may be why Davira didn't send a larger army after us."

Jace had to thank Elôm for the timing of the fever. They would not likely have been able to hold back a much larger army.

"There is a remedy for it, isn't there?" Kyrin asked.

Jace had never heard of a remedy, but Kyrin would know. After all, she would have been in Valcré at Tarvin Hall during the first outbreak.

Carl nodded slowly. "Yes, but supplies are limited. Word has it the queen has taken control of that supply and only doles it out to those who can prove their loyalty to her and the gods."

Kaden scowled. "So she's using it as a tool to kill us."

"Yes, and unfortunately she doesn't believe the poor are worth saving either. Many are turned away simply for being too far beneath her. It's the same with food supplies. Not only is crime rampant in the city, but Davira holds them all in a suffocating grip."

The rest of the afternoon passed quietly with a light snow falling outside. It reminded Kyrin of days long ago when she, Kaden, Marcus, and Liam were little—the days they would play on the living room floor in front of the fireplace or listen to their father tell them stories. She had always loved winter because he was home every day instead of at the fort.

A couple of hours after lunch, Kyrin wandered upstairs. Her brothers too had found their way back to their rooms. Stepping into her own, she stood and looked around for a few minutes. Her mother hadn't done much to change it since she was a girl. The bed and lavender colored quilt remained the same, and her toys were still present. It was as if time had stood still in this room. It didn't take much to imagine herself as a little girl, listening to her brothers play and fight in their rooms and hearing their father call them from the staircase. Their bare or stocking-clad feet would pound down the hall in their race to meet him.

Kyrin's breath snagged, and she had to pull it in hard. Blinking away the wateriness in her vision, she crossed the room to a little white shelf and picked up the doll sitting on the edge. Its brown yarn hair was a bit of a mess, and the hem of its cotton dress had frayed. However, the red thread of its mouth still formed a happy smile, and its blue button eyes matched Kyrin's almost perfectly. Though other dolls sat on the shelf, this one had always been Kyrin's favorite. Her father had given it to her on her fifth birthday. She'd so badly wanted to bring it with her to Tarvin Hall.

Cradling the doll in her hands, Kyrin sank down on the rug at the foot of her bed and stared at the doll's face, getting lost in the memories it held.

Jace reached the top of the stairs. Kaden and Talas's voices drifted from just down the hall. Approaching the open door, he glanced into the one to the right—Kyrin's room. He paused. She sat on the floor against the end of her bed and stared down at something in her hands—a doll. The sight mirrored her sitting on the mountain overlooking Valcré, her father's necklace in her hand. She bore the same small, fragile look she'd had then.

He stepped into the room and quietly sat down next to her. She glanced at him. Her cheeks were dry, but her eyes were red with held-back tears. For a few moments, both of them sat silently as Kyrin continued to stare at the doll.

"I wanted to name her Kyrin since I thought she looked like me, but my father suggested Kiah." She ran her fingers over a line of stitches on the doll's arm where it had obviously ripped. "Kaden impaled her with a stick."

A flicker of a smile appeared on Kyrin's face, and Jace had to smile too as he imagined how little Kyrin must have screamed at her brother in horror. But the smile faded at the sadness engulfing Kyrin's expression.

Her voice wavered as she clutched the doll more tightly. "She belonged to a little girl who never imagined her family would be ripped apart in so many painful ways. A little girl who laughed and played with her brothers and thought everything would always be all right."

Now the tears spilled over, sliding one by one down to Kyrin's chin. Sharing her pain, Jace reached his arm around her and held her close, much the same as he had done that day on the mountain.

FOR TWO NIGHTS, they remained at the Altair house. When it came time to leave, Jace sensed Kyrin's desire stay longer, but their presence risked exposing Carl and Ethel. The day and a half long trip back to camp thankfully passed without major snowfall to delay them. Landing in camp put a hard knot in Jace's stomach. It was as if it sank in right then that they'd left Michael in Mernin. Nothing about this felt right. One look at Kyrin told him that she experienced the same emotion, though infinitely stronger. Her eyes glinted with abundant moisture, and she didn't seem to know what to do once she dismounted Ivoris.

Clearing his throat, Jace hurried to her side and helped her unsaddle her dragon. She sent him a grateful look, and he offered a sad smile. He helped carry the family belongings to their cabin. The fireplace was cold when they entered, so he built a fire for them. Once the warmth began to seep into the room, he turned to Kyrin. She appeared to have conquered her emotions for now. Tears no longer threatened to fall, and she managed a small smile of her own.

"Thank you."

He put his hand on her shoulder, rubbing it gently. "I'm going to go check Rayad if you're all right."

She nodded. "Go. I'll be fine."

He hated to leave her, but he hoped she would rest while he was gone. They all needed it. He left the cabin and headed toward the one he shared. Tyra met him along the way, bounding through the snow, her tail wagging. He paused to pet her. Though he hadn't been gone nearly as long as he had in the past, she was just as excited to see him. He was thankful to have people he trusted to look after her whenever he had to be away. Motioning to her to follow, he continued to the cabin.

Josef was there when he walked in and appeared to have just finished examining Rayad's wound. Setting his pack down next to the door, Jace asked the physician, "How is he?"

"He is healing well. I don't see anything to be concerned about."

Jace breathed out, releasing some of the tension he'd been carrying. He shouldn't have worried, but life felt too fragile lately.

As Josef packed up his medical supplies, Jace shrugged off his coat. He eyed the coffee pot hanging at the fireplace. The journey back had been cold. Josef bid them both goodbye, and Jace crossed the cabin to pour himself a mug of coffee. He then joined Rayad, where he'd taken a seat at the table.

"How did it go?" Rayad asked.

Jace stirred a little sugar into his coffee and then met Rayad's gaze. "It was tough . . . Kyrin didn't want to leave."

Rayad nodded slowly. "It's hard when you feel like you're leaving family behind."

Jace agreed. He'd hated leaving Kalli and Aldor's graves at the farm. "Did anything happen while we were gone?"

"Two of the wounded men died. We buried them yesterday."

Jace grimaced, but at the same time, he thanked Elôm. The loss could have been much greater. If Marcus had not trained such a skilled militia, this camp would have fallen. Everyone would have been killed or destined for execution.

"I'm heading over to Trask's cabin after lunch," Rayad said. "It seems there's talk concerning the captured soldiers. Many aren't happy with the idea of feeding them when there's so little food to begin with. Add that to the losses, and no one will feel charitable toward them."

Jace could understand that. He didn't feel very charitable himself, but what could they do? Let the soldiers go? He didn't envy the decisions Trask, Daniel, and Balen would ultimately have to make.

A couple of hours later, Jace followed Rayad outside and toward Trask's cabin. Whatever they chose to do about the soldiers concerned Dagren and the General, and Jace wanted to know what their leaders would decide. Along the way, Marcus joined them.

"Is Kyrin coming?" Jace asked.

Marcus shook his head, his expression set in a determined frown. "I don't think she wants to hear about the General right now."

Jace didn't blame her.

When they reached the cabin, Trask, Daniel, Balen, and several others of the group were waiting for them around the table. Anne poured fresh coffee for everyone before Trask began.

"I'm sure most of you have heard the grumblings going around. Maybe you even feel the same way. Emotions are raw right now, and though I expect them to settle with time, it's an issue we have to deal with. We have eleven soldiers held in the meeting hall. That's eleven more mouths to feed."

"What does everyone think we should do?" Sam asked.

"It's mostly just displeasure at the thought of feeding and sheltering them but . . . there have been a few veiled suggestions of execution."

Jace raised his brows. Execution? It was hard to imagine the people of this camp turning to such extreme measures. Who would even carry out such a sentence? But then, many of them were hurting deeply. If he searched his own heart, wouldn't he find similar feelings when it came to Dagren—the man responsible for the murders of Kalli and Aldor? Still, these men couldn't truly be labeled as murderers—they were soldiers.

He glanced at the others to gauge their reactions. They said nothing, but no one appeared comfortable with the idea.

Trask focused his attention on Daniel. "I would leave such a decision up to you, but I personally wouldn't be willing to pursue such action, at least not right now."

Daniel seemed to squirm a little at the prospect of such a decision. Jace certainly wouldn't want the responsibility. Still, he was to be their king, not to mention, perhaps, Elanor's husband. He had to rise to the challenge.

Whether he caught Jace watching him or not, Daniel straightened in his chair as if to accept the burden. "I understand why some might want this . . ." he cast a look at Marcus, "but I won't start executing captives. Murder is one thing, but most of these men are just soldiers following orders. As for General Veshiron and Captain Dagren, I'm not sure just how highly my sister values them, but they could be worth something should we need bargaining pieces in the future."

The next morning, Jace stared up at the rafters in the cabin from his cot as dawn slowly brightened the world outside. He let his arm hang over the side as he scratched Tyra's head. Sleep had eluded him for the last couple of hours since waking from a dream—not one of the nightmares he still suffered occasionally but one of life on the farm. He ached for that life—ached for Kalli's mothering and Aldor's humor. He tried never to let himself dwell too deeply on the pain of the past, but discussing Dagren at the meeting yesterday opened the old wounds.

Finally, he sat up, swinging his legs over the side of the cot. Tyra pushed herself up with a yawn, and Jace scratched her under the chin. A shiver passed through him at the chill in the cabin. Only embers glowed in the fireplace. He pulled on his clothes and walked over to the hearth to stir the coals and add some wood. Flames soon sprouted from the dry kindling, and he started a pot of coffee. The others would appreciate it being ready when they got up. Rayad and Holden already stirred in their cots.

While the coffee brewed, Jace sat down at the table with a couple of pages of the King's Scrolls that Kyrin had copied for him. He felt especially in need of them this morning, though his mind kept straying. Frustrated, he closed his eyes and prayed—first for Kyrin and her family and the others who had lost someone in the attack. Then he turned to his own struggle, pouring out the troubling issues in his heart.

When he finished, he released a long sigh and rested back in his chair. Rayad was just getting up across the room. He moved slowly, favoring his side, but at least he'd escaped serious injury. Jace again thanked Elôm for this blessing.

Once dressed, Rayad joined him at the table and eyed him perceptively. "Are you all right?"

Jace gave a slow nod. "It's Dagren. I've been struggling . . . with revenge." He didn't have Kyrin's memory, yet the pain of riding up to the farm and finding Kalli and Aldor murdered still stabbed into his mind and heart. The desperation to take down the man responsible had remained buried inside him, reawakened now that he was only a couple of cabins away.

"Understandable," Rayad murmured. He'd been right there beside Jace at the farm, the only one stopping him from seeking revenge that very day, starting with his old nemesis, Morden.

Jace drew in a breath to fortify himself. "I know what I have to do."

The moment he finished breakfast an hour later, Jace pulled on his boots and coat. He reached for the door but then paused to pick up his sword. He hadn't felt the need to carry it in camp for a long time. The attack had changed that. He buckled it on and stepped outside. The cold air bit his face immediately, the heavy clouds threatening yet more snow. Spring couldn't come soon enough.

Setting his mind on his task, Jace strode toward the meeting hall. At the door, he paused for prayer before letting himself inside. Two guards Trask had posted sat at a table near the fireplace playing cards. The captive soldiers were chained together at the far end of the hall. Trask planned on rearranging the occupancy of some of the cabins and converting one into a jail of sorts. Though Jace would have willingly given it up, he was grateful Trask hadn't asked for his. He still clung to his dream of soon beginning a life with Kyrin even though recent grief shadowed it.

The guards looked at him as he approached their table, and he said, "I need to talk to Captain Dagren."

They nodded, seeming unconcerned about his sword or any other weapons he might carry. Jace would have to mention that to Trask. While he didn't want to think anyone in camp might try to murder their captives, he knew how grief could lead to actions one might never take otherwise.

His steps echoed as he crossed the hall toward the captives. Dagren watched him the entire way, his cool eyes narrowed.

Jace stopped a few feet short of them, and the man stared up from a mat on the floor. His captain's uniform was wrinkled and stained with other men's blood, but he sat with a stiff arrogance, as if he were still far superior to Jace, even as a prisoner. Jace forced a hard breath into his lungs that had begun to tighten up. This was even harder than he'd anticipated. Yet it must be done. He cleared his throat.

"Two and a half years ago, you sent a company of men to Kinnim to find Rayad. You gave them orders to kill anyone found with him."

Dagren lifted his chin slightly and didn't deny it.

"Your men killed a man and woman. An innocent elderly couple."

Dagren sneered. "Anyone who associates with criminals and traitors isn't innocent."

Jace squeezed the hilt of his sword, fighting old temptations and to keep his voice calm. His throat clogged, but he pushed on. "I loved them. Dearly. They were my family." He cleared his throat again. "I've wanted to kill you for what happened to them. I wanted to kill you when we fought . . . Instead, I've come to tell you . . ."

He grimaced. It was so hard. His mind would barely form the words, let alone his lips, but he forced them out. "I came to tell you . . . I forgive you."

He breathed out heavily. He might not feel it completely, but he meant every word, and a burden lifted with the declaration.

Dagren released a harsh bark of laughter. "You think I care about your forgiveness, *half-blood*?"

Jace didn't react to the intended insult. Such words held no power over him anymore. He shook his head. "No. But I'm not doing it for you. I'm doing it for myself."

Since he'd accomplished what he had set out to do, he turned to go. His gaze snagged on the General. He didn't look anything like the commanding man who'd had Jace whipped and beaten half to death at Fort Rivor. He looked . . . old . . . worn . . . remorseful. Perhaps that wasn't what he felt but something like it weighed on his expression, deepening the age lines in his lean face. Though still projecting a stubborn pride, his eyes contained a troubled look.

They held each other's gaze for a moment before Jace spoke again. "I forgive you, too."

He didn't wait for a response this time.

Leaving the meeting hall, he walked across camp to his cabin. The weight of the last week dragged on him, but getting back to work seemed to be the best thing right now. Tyra trotted along with him, his always-faithful companion. He hadn't visited his cabin since the attack. The cleaning buckets and brushes still sat in the corner where he had left them when he'd heard the firedrake. The water had turned to ice, and he lit a fire to melt it.

Tyra found a cozy spot near the hearth, and Jace went to work scrubbing the floor once again. He was almost half done when someone knocked on the door. It was more of a light tap, obviously female. He pushed up from his knees and walked to the door. When he opened it, Anne waited on the other side, a bundle of fabric in her arms. Holden stood behind her, carrying an even larger bundle.

Anne smiled. "I found a couple of things for you."

He let them inside, and Anne set her bundle on the table. "I went through our supplies and found these curtains. I know how Kyrin likes blue."

She lifted one of the curtains made of a soft, sky blue fabric. Kyrin would like them indeed.

"I also found a nice rug." She gestured at Holden, who set the roll he carried on the floor. "Trask said he can help you carry over some furniture later."

"Thank you," Jace said, brushing his fingers along the smooth curtain material. "I really appreciate it."

Anne smiled again. "I'll hang the curtains."

As she crossed the cabin to one of the windows, Jace turned to Holden. His friend grinned at him.

"I saw you coming over here. It didn't take much to figure out what you were up to."

Jace's own smile broke out. Something about his friend knowing made his plans feel more real.

Holden surveyed the cabin. "It'll be nice once you get some furniture in here . . ." he looked back at Jace, a twinkle in his eyes, "and permanent female company."

Jace agreed, but his smile faded. "It would've been nicer if the attack hadn't happened."

Holden sighed and nodded but gave Jace an encouraging clap on the back. "It will still be good for both of you to start your life together."

A few minutes later, Anne finished smoothing out the last curtain. "There, much better."

Jace looked around at each of the windows. Just the simple addition of color made a big difference in transforming the empty cabin into the start of a home.

"I'll see about getting a nice quilt and linens for the bed," Anne said, buttoning up her coat.

Jace thanked her again, and she left the cabin. Holden, however, stayed behind and helped Jace scrub the floor. Jace appreciated his company, especially after the emotions he'd had to deal with that morning. By the time they finished cleaning and arranging the rug and table, it was nearly noon. Banking the fire, they headed out to have lunch.

Nearing their cabin, Jace caught sight of a large group of men gathering around the meeting hall. Tension knotted his stomach. Had one of the soldiers tried to escape or cause trouble? He glanced at Holden and they hurried to join the others.

"What's going on?" Jace asked when they reached the edge of the group.

Aric turned to them. "One of the soldiers has fallen ill."

Jace frowned. He'd seen their captives only hours ago. None of them had shown any apparent signs of illness.

Their attention shifted to Trask, who asked Josef, "Do you know what ails him?"

A cold premonition took hold of Jace at the way the old physician's face grew taut.

"I'm afraid it's Miner's Fever."

THE KNOT IN Jace's stomach constricted, and a visible reaction swept through the others. Murmurs rose around them. Jace prayed to Elôm that Josef was wrong. How could they deal with something like Miner's Fever when the attack had already devastated them? The cold that had overtaken him chilled him right to the core with a sudden wave of helplessness. This was not something he could fight against to protect those he loved.

"Are you sure that's what he has?" Trask asked, his voice calm yet hinting at uncertainty.

Josef nodded regretfully. "I wish I weren't, but this fever strikes much more swiftly than less serious condition, and one of the earliest symptoms is a red rash along the neck and chest, and sometimes arms. A rash this soldier, unfortunately, has."

"Have you dealt with Miner's Fever before?"

"I have seen some cases in Samara."

"Can it be treated?"

"There is a remedy; however, we do not have it here, nor can I make any with our limited supplies."

Trask's expression hardened in determination. "Then we must find where we can get some." He traded a glance with Jace and the others. Marcus had told him of the situation with Davira and the remedy yesterday. "Surely we can find some somewhere."

He refocused on Josef. "If we can't get the remedy, what *can* we do?"

"We must quarantine the soldiers and any who have been in close contact with them."

Jace hung his head. That included him.

"How likely is it to spread?"

"That is uncertain. It seems to strike at random, but when it spreads, it spreads rapidly."

"And for those who do get it, what are their chances?"

"Without the remedy?" Josef shook his head. "The prognosis is not good. While some do survive it, many more do not. There is no way to know for certain. Young and old alike have succumbed to it."

After a silent moment of consideration, Trask gave a short nod. If he felt the same deep fear of this new threat as Jace did, he did not show it. "All right. We'll use the meeting hall as a quarantine for the sick. We also need to isolate those who have been exposed."

Jace stepped forward. All his plans were about to be dashed again, but it must be done. "My cabin. Those who have been exposed can stay there."

Trask nodded gratefully at him. "Thank you, Jace." He looked at Josef again. "How long will they have to remain in isolation?"

"If there are no symptoms within a week, they should be safe."

Jace clenched his fingers. A whole week separated from Kyrin. He glanced skyward. Why now when she needed him most? If only this were a physical threat he could just fight and be done with. *Please just protect the people in this camp, Lord.* They had already suffered so much.

Trask turned to Warin, Balen, and Daniel. "Get word around. Everyone who has had close contact with the soldiers in the last couple of days needs to move into the vacant cabin. We must take every precaution to contain this. Until we do, we need to limit contact with the other camps. No close contact with anyone here." He rubbed his forehead. "We also must keep anyone from panicking."

"This will make many even less charitable toward the soldiers," Balen warned.

"I know," Trask sighed. "But there's nothing we can do about it now. We just need to deal with this and pray it doesn't spread."

News traveled swiftly around camp. Jace helped several of the men move into his cabin, one of them being Marcus. Kyrin's brother took this new threat with a steady acceptance of the facts, as he did everything. While Jace wished Marcus didn't have to be here, he was thankful to have his companionship for the next week. He wasn't nearly as well acquainted with the other men.

After getting them situated, Jace left the cabin to get a few of his own things from Holden. Along the way, someone called his name. He turned to find Kyrin hurrying toward him. Her taut expression betrayed her concern, and it hurt deeply to have to hold up his hand to stop her. He didn't know if he could spread the fever already, but he wouldn't risk it.

"You probably shouldn't come any closer," he said gently.

Her face crumpled, and her eyes filled with tears. She appeared too overwhelmed to speak for a moment. Finally, her voice made it past her lips, though it wavered. "I can't believe this is happening."

Jace ached to reach for her but held himself in place. He had to be strong, even now. "These are just precautions. If we can keep it contained to the meeting hall, I'm sure everything will be all right."

Her shoulders drooped. "How long until we know . . ." she cleared her throat, "you won't get sick?"

"A week." Just saying it hurt. A week would feel like eternity, every uncertain moment torture for both of them.

She closed her eyes as if to hold back the tears.

"Kyrin."

She met his gaze again.

"We will get through this."

Sucking in a breath, she straightened and nodded. He had to smile. She was so strong, even after all the heartbreak she had endured. It was one of the uncountable things he loved so much about her.

"Where will you be?"

"We're using a vacant cabin for anyone who was exposed." He gestured toward his cabin—*their* cabin—if he could only get to proposing to her without some calamity postponing his plans. He was tempted to tell her now, but not under these circumstances.

"And Marcus is there too?"

"Yes."

She rubbed her arms, though he doubted her chill came from the weather. "Will you come out and see me every day so I know for sure you're all right?"

"Of course." Jace couldn't imagine anything else, as long as they maintained a safe distance.

His attention shifted when another feminine figure approached. Elanor reached Kyrin's side, her face showing signs of distress as well. She looked longingly at him, her blue eyes, which were just like their mother's, a little watery.

"Elian told me." Her lips thinned. "Do you think you were near enough to them to get sick?"

Jace shook his head. "I don't know. I was only near them for a few minutes." Whether that would make a difference or not, he couldn't say. He attempted a slight smile, wanting so much to cheer them up. "I'll be fine. My ryrik blood usually prevents illnesses."

This did seem to bolster them.

He grew serious again. "Just make sure to stay clear of the meeting hall until this blows over."

They both nodded, and Kyrin promised, "We will."

Kyrin rubbed the dull ache that wouldn't leave the pit of her stomach. Four more of the soldiers and one of their guards had fallen ill since yesterday. She felt as though she had spent every minute praying that the fever would be confined to those in the meeting hall. The fear surrounding the first outbreak in Valcré hovered in her mind. No one had been allowed to leave Tarvin Hall for over a month. Kyrin had been terrified of getting sick, but at least there they'd had access to the remedy. In a community like this, with no cure, it could wipe them out.

Kyrin pulled herself from these depressing thoughts and set her focus determinedly on the work before her. She had started a new shirt for Jace to replace one of his older ones. Making something helped with the pain of losing Michael and the fear of more loss. It comforted her to think of Jace wearing it. And he always seemed to wear the shirts she made more than those she hadn't. This succeeded in bringing the slightest smile to her lips. She really did enjoy doing such things for him. It made her feel . . . like his wife.

She glanced at her mother, who sat across from her, also sewing. With three camps full of people, more men than women, mending was a never-ending job. She then looked over to the corner of the cabin where Ronny sat on his bed fiddling with a toy dragon Jace had carved for him. He didn't even seem aware of what he was doing, his face cast down. Kyrin let out a slow sigh as her chest constricted.

A moment later, the door opened, cold air rolling in ahead of Liam. He closed it quickly and stepped toward the table. Something in the hesitant way he moved and his pensive expression sent a jolt through Kyrin's heart.

"Is someone else sick?" Her thoughts turned immediately to Jace.

"No," he quickly assured them.

Kyrin released a long breath, as did their mother, yet Kyrin's anxiety didn't fade completely. She waited, her heart still thumping an anxious rhythm. Liam rested his gloved hands on the back of a chair and looked at their mother, whose face paled.

He didn't speak immediately, which was agony, but finally he said, "I'm going to help Josef and Leetra with the sick."

Kyrin's heart plummeted, and their mother sat very still for a moment before her mouth opened to speak. However, Liam stopped her, raising his hand.

"I know it's a risk, and I know how hard it is for you, but if any more of the soldiers fall ill, Josef and Leetra will be short-handed. And what if one of them gets sick? They need help. I haven't spent all this time training with Josef to stand aside now when there's a real need."

Again, their mother just sat silently but moisture gushed into her eyes. Though her lips trembled, she nodded. "You're right. You should help them if that's what you want."

"I do."

Kyrin struggled with a combination of pride and fear as her heart both swelled and ached in her chest. So many people had deemed her brother slow or incompetent over the years, completely missing his strengths—his bravery, compassion, and desire to help people. This was his passion. She would have fought anyone who stood in his way.

"I came to gather my things," he said more quietly. "I'll have to stay at the meeting hall until the threat of the fever has passed."

That could take weeks. First Jace and Marcus were separated from them, and now Liam. The cabin was starting to feel depressingly empty.

Doing well at holding back her sorrow, their mother pushed away from the table. "I'll pack food for you and the others. I'm sure it's difficult to prepare meals while caring for the sick."

Kyrin set the incomplete shirt aside and rose to help her. All the while, she prayed for Elôm to protect her brother while he served so selflessly.

After Liam had filled a pack with his belongings, they all gathered near the door. He gave Ronny a hug first. Though their youngest brother fought hard to hold back tears, a couple slipped out that he quickly swiped away. He knew as well as they did that they could lose Liam too.

"Everything will be all right," Liam told him with a comforting air of confidence.

He then gave their mother a long hug, speaking encouragingly to her as well. Finally, he reached Kyrin. She tried to give him a smile that would show how proud she was of him, but she was afraid she didn't quite accomplish it. She stepped into his strong arms, relishing one of his almost-too-tight hugs.

"Help take care of mother," he whispered in her ear. "I think you're the strongest of all of us."

Kyrin raised her brows. She felt anything but strong lately. Parting, she looked up into his eyes. A hand seemed to close around her throat as she asked, "Will you be all right around the General?" Just the thought of their grandfather intensified the sick aching in her stomach. He'd always been so cruel to Liam.

He nodded, though just a hint of uncertainty lurked in his eyes. "I'll be fine."

At least Josef would be there. He understood Liam and would be a strong ally if things got unpleasant. And Leetra was more than a match for the General's harshness. After bonding over the summer, she was confident Leetra would step in to defend one of her brothers in Kyrin's stead if the need arose.

Liam looked between her and their mother. "Kaden knows what I'm doing, but could someone let Marcus know?"

Kyrin nodded. "We will. If not today, I'll see Jace in the morning and can let him know."

"Thanks." Liam turned and let himself out.

As the door closed behind him, Kyrin wrapped her arms around herself, fighting to ward off the chill creeping in at the fear of losing another member of her family.

Leetra rifled through all the herbs and vials that made up their medical supply. She gritted her teeth and forced a sigh out through her nose. If everyone had just caught a cold, they'd have plenty to work with, but Miner's Fever? It didn't help that she had no experience with this particular illness. They'd never had an outbreak in Arval, but there were remedies her people used that may provide some relief. Problem was, they were on the other side of the continent.

Leetra braced herself against the table and listened to the hoarse coughing around her. She should have been more prepared. She should have stocked up on the more potent remedies they used in Arval. Not that they could cure this illness, but at least she would have had more to try.

Pushing away from the table, she turned to face the dilemma that lay before her. While there were only six cots now, the number was bound to rise. She cast a narrow-eyed look at the soldiers in the corner—the cause of this entire mess. Dagren sat glowering at everyone—high and mighty pig. General Veshiron sat stone-faced. She wasn't sure she'd heard him speak a single word since the attack. Maybe they'd be the next to fall to the fever. She scolded herself not to hope they would. She was a healer; she shouldn't wish harm on anyone. In this instance, she would surely need Elôm's help to banish such feelings. Elôm's help and a moment of fresh air.

She strode over to Josef, who tended one of the soldiers. "I'll be back in a few minutes."

The old physician nodded, and Leetra headed to the door. She grabbed her leather coat and let herself outside. The chill air usually didn't bother her much, but today it seemed mockingly harsh, even for a crete. She quickly buttoned the coat and stuck her hands in her pockets. Doing what any true-blood crete would do, she headed straight toward the dragons gathered in a group at the edge of camp. There was almost no snow here in contrast to the rest of their surroundings. The dragons' warm bodies melted it as fast as it fell.

Her dragon greeted her with a chirp as she approached. It *almost* drew a smile from her but not quite. She walked to the dragon's side and rested against her, her cheek pressed to the animal's warm neck. The feel of smooth, warm scales both soothed and strengthened her. She didn't say anything, just let the warmth radiate through her taut muscles.

It was at times like this she missed home—missed her parents and siblings. Whenever the first snow fell, her father would take them to the ground where they would have snowball fights and build snow forts. She hadn't gotten to be there for that this year. She could just imagine her siblings' shrieks and her father's deep laughter. Her heart squeezed inside her chest. She missed it.

But even more than all of that, she missed Timothy. Somehow, he understood her better than anyone else outside of her family. He could see her most vulnerable parts, something that had once terrified her. Now she longed for his understanding and strength. She'd wanted to beg him to stay last fall, but she couldn't stand in the way of his calling.

Moisture pooled in her eyes and burned. She blinked hard and straightened resolutely. Timothy was not here. Her family was not here. She had a job to do—people to save. *Elôm, I don't have the resources I need, but please show me what I can do.*

She turned at the sound of footsteps. Darq, Glynn, and Talas walked toward her. Leetra locked eyes with her cousin. Talas had been spending most of his time with the Altairs, and she saw the toll Michael's death had taken on him. From the start, they had been like a second family to him. She hated seeing her cousin hurt.

"Don't get too close," she warned them when they came within several feet. Just because they'd never experienced the fever in Arvael didn't mean they were immune.

The three of them stopped.

"How are things going?" Darq asked.

Leetra focused on her captain and mentor. "It's too soon to say how the soldiers will fare. There's not much we can do to treat them. Maybe if I had more supplies from Arvael." She shook her head. "There's so little we can try."

"Do you want Glynn and me to go to Arvael for supplies?"

Leetra sighed. "It would take you two weeks to get back here. Only Elôm knows what shape we'll be in then. I don't even know if we have anything that will work. If only we had the ingredients we would need for the remedy."

While they might be able to scrape together some, the important ingredients were rare and only found along the west coast of Arcacia. She knew of nothing in Dorland that could work as a substitute.

"I'll send a couple of riders," Darq said. "Make a list of what you want. If nothing else, they can bring back food. We already have riders heading out to the surrounding towns to see if they have the remedy."

Liam drew a cold breath into his lungs as he stopped at the door of the meeting hall. His grandfather was on the other side of that door. That shouldn't make any difference. He wasn't the coward the General always made him out to be. He'd proved that and had found his calling—his purpose in life. There was nothing his grandfather could say to change that.

Even so, the tight knot in his stomach was the same he'd felt every time he had faced his grandfather as a soldier. Old familiar dread and fear mingling into a nauseous ache. He pulled his shoulders back and stiffened his spine. The General had no authority over him anymore. This time, his grandfather was the prisoner and at their mercy.

Liam opened the door and strode inside. Familiar healing herbs scented the open space. Josef had cots lined up near the fireplace, each one occupied by a prone figure. Those soldiers had brought death to this camp, but as a physician, that was not his concern. Healing was, even if that meant caring for the enemy.

He crossed the hall to the table where Josef worked and had his supplies organized. "I'm here to help."

The old man did not say a word, but the flash of pride in his eyes and firm nod were all Liam needed. Josef had been far more a grandfather and mentor to him than the General ever had.

"I'm mixing a tea for their fevers," Josef told him. "Why don't you finish?"

Liam accepted the task and took Josef's place at the mortar and pestle. He knew exactly what to do here—what herbs he needed to add. It came so much more naturally than training drills and formations ever had. He chanced a glance at the General, who sat chained up with the others not far away. His grandfather was watching him. Did he have any knowledge of the skills Liam had learned since leaving the army?

Liam focused on his work. Right now, it was all that mattered.

JACE PULLED HIS blankets over himself and tried to get comfortable in his bed on the floor near the fireplace. Eight other men shared the cabin, including Marcus, and were in various stages of drifting off. Jace stared at the flames of the fire, struggling to quiet the unease that never completely faded. After only two days, he already missed Kyrin. It was too cold to stand outside and talk for long, so they barely spent any time together. He couldn't wait for the week to pass, yet if anyone in his cabin fell ill, that week would begin all over again.

Jace reached out as Tyra settled down next to him and stroked her back. Breathing out a sigh, he closed his eyes. However, his body fought relaxation, his mind too full. So, he turned to the one and only thing he knew he could do in this situation—prayer. He prayed for everyone who was sick or had been exposed. He even prayed for the soldiers. This camp had already seen enough death.

Eventually, he must have fallen asleep because a sharp knock jolted him right back to consciousness. He lifted his head and listened. The knocking came again at the door, not loud but urgent nonetheless. The flames in the fireplace had died out leaving only glowing embers and darkness still cloaked the cabin.

Heat shot through his blood. No one would be here in the middle of the night unless something terrible had happened.

As the others stirred, Jace jumped to his feet and crossed the cabin to the door. Another knock came as he reached for the knob and pulled it open. Holden stood on the other side—a dark silhouette against the snow. Jace's stomach caved in on itself at the taut, shadowed lines in Holden's face.

"Rayad is sick."

The words cut into Jace like a knife blade. He stood frozen for a moment before he spun around to find a warmer shirt and his boots. The others were awake now, either standing or sitting up in their beds. Jace caught Marcus's remorseful gaze. Even though he repeated Holden's words in his mind, every fiber of him wanted to deny their truth.

Back at the door, he grabbed his coat, but Holden held up his hand.

"He doesn't want you to come and expose yourself to the fever."

"I need to see him." Jace stepped outside and strode toward the other cabin. No danger would keep him away. He struggled to breathe in the frozen air. *Please don't let him die.*

When he entered the cabin, Josef was there, but Jace focused on Rayad as he approached the bed. Even in the dim light of the cabin, the sheen of sweat on Rayad's forehead and the red splotches on his neck were apparent. Jace met Rayad's fever-glazed eyes.

"Jace."

He already sounded weak. Another stab pierced Jace's heart. Rayad was the only father he'd ever had. He knelt down next to Rayad's cot, opposite of Josef.

"You shouldn't be here," Rayad told him.

Jace shook his head. "You'd come if I was sick."

Rayad didn't respond, but Jace knew it was true. He looked up at Josef. "What can we do?"

"I'm brewing a tea." Josef nodded toward the fireplace. "Hopefully it will help bring down the fever. That is the greatest concern."

Jace gritted his teeth and breathed out slowly. Tea. That was all they could do? He tried not to let his fear reach his expression and forced himself to remember that, if nothing else, Rayad was a fighter. They'd been through life and death situations before. But this was not a foe either of them could fight with their hands, and that left him frustratingly helpless.

Rayad reached up and touched his shoulder. He didn't say anything, but his look said he understood Jace's internal struggle. They were both powerless. *Elôm, please don't take him. Not yet.* Elôm willing, Jace would one day soon make Kyrin his wife, and Rayad had to be there. He'd helped shape Jace into the man he was today—a man who could even hope for a life with a woman as wonderful as Kyrin. He owed Rayad everything.

Josef stayed another half an hour before he prepared to leave. He gave Jace the extra herbal mixture to make more tea when it ran out and instructed him to keep cold snow compresses on Rayad's head and neck to try to bring the fever down. Jace joined him at the door as the physician slipped on his coat.

He hesitated a moment, afraid to speak, but needed answers. "What are his chances?"

Sympathy shone in Josef's pained eyes as his head shook slightly. "I'm afraid that's impossible to answer. I know of nothing that clearly distinguishes why some live and others die. All I can say is that it's in the hands of Elôm."

Jace nodded. If only he were more comforted. "Thank you."

"Keeping him cool and prayer are our best weapons against this. Just send for me if he gets worse."

Jace watched dawn break over camp from a chair next to Rayad's cot. Holden and Elian had taken turns sitting up with him. Though Rayad slept, it never seemed very restful. At least the fever hadn't grown worse. But it hadn't lessened either.

After a while, Holden started breakfast. Stretching his sore back, Jace got up and grabbed a basin to gather fresh snow for Rayad's compresses. Once he'd changed them, he accepted a plate of eggs and slice of toast from Holden. He could have eaten twice what was on the plate, but everyone had started cutting back to conserve food. What would they do if the fever continued to spread and they ran out of supplies?

Shortly after they finished, Liam entered the cabin. He cast a glance at Rayad as he pulled off his coat. "How is he?"

Jace rubbed his hand along the back of his neck, fighting discouragement. "The same." It wasn't that he had expected any improvement overnight, but he had prayed for it.

"Josef sent me to check him. Leetra also made up broth for the sick." Liam handed Jace a canteen.

Jace brought it to the table and poured some of the warm liquid into a mug while Liam walked over to Rayad's cot. By now, Rayad had awakened. He greeted Liam quietly and offered Jace a hint of a smile when he joined them.

"Do you feel up to a little broth?" Jace asked. One of the keys would be to keep Rayad's strength up and not let his body weaken from lack of nourishment.

Rayad nodded slowly. "That sounds good."

Liam arranged a blanket under Rayad's pillow so he could sit up, and Jace carefully helped Rayad raise the mug to his lips. Rayad took a couple of sips and sighed, then started coughing. Jace waited for it to subside before offering more broth. He clenched his teeth as the pit of his stomach squeezed. It was so hard to see Rayad in such a weakened state.

Once the mug was empty, Rayad thanked Jace but seemed to be slipping toward unconsciousness again. Jace removed the blanket to let him lie down and replaced the compresses. Straightening, he turned to Holden. "Will you watch him for me for a few minutes? I need to go see Kyrin."

Holden nodded, and Jace grabbed his coat before letting himself outside. The cold air was invigorating, but weariness had taken hold of him that not even fresh air could erase. With Tyra at his side, he waited not too far from the Altair cabin. A couple of minutes later, the door opened and Kyrin stepped out. She approached him with a slight smile on her face, but it disappeared, her expression morphing into fear.

"Is it Marcus?"

Jace shook his head. "Rayad." He hated giving her bad news.

Kyrin's gloved hand went to her chest. "Rayad?" She drew a hard breath, her eyes tearing up.

"Holden came to get me during the night."

"How is he?"

"He has a fever and is weak already." Jace shrugged his shoulders, the powerlessness gripping him like a vise again. "There's really nothing we can do but try to keep the fever down. And pray."

"Jace, I'm so sorry." She blinked hard, but determination overcame her face. "I'll come and help you take care of him."

"No," he said quickly. The thought of her anywhere near the sickness left him cold. "I just need to know you're safe." He'd told her same thing in Dorland last summer.

Her shoulders drooped. "I just wish I could help."

"I know. But the fewer people who are exposed, the better."

"You probably want to get back to him. We'll be praying," Kyrin promised.

"Thank you. I'll come out again after lunch and let you know how he is doing."

Kyrin returned to the cabin and closed the cabin door slowly, the emotions so heavy inside her that she wasn't sure what to do with them. She'd prepared herself for the possibility of Jace having to tell her that Marcus was sick, but she had not expected nor prepared for his news this morning. Her heart ached for him.

She pulled off her coat, her arms feeling weighted, and hung it on a peg before facing her family—her mother, Kaden, and Ronny. Only the four of them in the cabin. She cleared her throat, swollen with held-back tears. They all seemed to notice that something was wrong at the same time.

"Rayad is sick," she told them.

Their faces registered shock.

"With the fever?" Kaden asked.

Kyrin nodded, biting her lip to keep her tears at bay. She might not be with Jace, but if nothing else, she desired to be strong for him. "He fell ill last night. Jace is with him."

Her mother must have seen the struggle in her expression and stepped forward, pulling Kyrin into her arms. Kyrin hugged her tightly and closed her eyes against the intense burning of tears. *Why is this happening, Elôm?* They'd faced so much already.

"Jace won't let me, but I wish I could go over and help him," Kyrin said, her voice cracking.

"I know." Her mother rubbed her back and then released her. "We just need to pray."

Kyrin nodded and joined her brothers at the table. That's when she noticed the fretful storm brewing in Kaden's eyes.

"Rayad wasn't one of the men we thought were exposed," he said, "so that means . . ."

Kyrin drew in a heavy breath and let it out slowly. "Anyone could get sick."

Daniel stepped outside, fighting back a shiver. Right about now, he missed the fur-lined cloak he used to have at the palace. Not that he would have been out and about in this weather were he still there. In his old life, he'd probably still be in bed, sleeping the morning away.

Well, he wasn't that lazy bum anymore. He set out for the wood pile. Usually Aric brought in their firewood, but he was perfectly capable of the chore. It would give him something to do at least. Everyone was adamant he stay clear of anyone who might spread the fever. Such precautions seemed to consist of him staying cooped up in his cabin all day. Surely a trip to the wood pile wouldn't put him in too much danger. Balen hadn't tried to stop him at least. The king was as restless as he was.

When he approached the wood pile, two other men were there—Gavin and Ket, if he remembered correctly. His father had always been good with names. He'd made a point of it since arriving, but still struggled to remember everyone in camp. Gavin nearly matched Balen in bulk and muscle mass, though he was shorter, while Ket was more average. Neither one seemed to notice him approaching, or at least didn't realize it was him. Not that he wanted any special treatment.

"We're wasting resources on an enemy that came in and killed our people," Gavin stated heatedly.

Ket nodded in agreement. "I wonder if they knew they could be bringing in the fever."

"Wouldn't put it past them," Gavin grumbled. "We should have dealt with them right away. Maybe we wouldn't be dealing with this now. I still say they should be eliminated. It might stop the fever from spreading further."

Clearly they didn't know about Rayad yet. Trask had brought the news this morning that now one of their members was ill.

"Someone should just go in and end the problem. We'd all be better off for it."

Daniel sucked in a breath. Would he be a hypocrite to speak against them when he understood their feelings and maybe even harbored them himself? It would solve a lot not to have to worry about the soldiers when their own people were facing the threat of a deadly illness and starvation.

No, it wouldn't be right, and it was up to him as their king to set an example. He cleared his throat. Both men turned and, upon recognizing him, dipped their heads.

"My lord," they murmured. Only Ket looked slightly shame-faced over their conversation.

Normally, Daniel would have protested such reverence, but in this instance, their respect was more important than his discomfort with the mantle of leadership. If he didn't put a stop to this unrest now, then he and the other leaders in camp might have to deal with murder later on. He would avoid that at all cost and peered at the men, attempting to project just the right amount of kingly authority he may have inherited from his father.

"I understand the situation with the soldiers is difficult," he said, "but we don't have much choice."

"They killed my brother," Gavin ground out.

His gaze bordered on a glare, though Daniel could see in his watery, red-rimmed eyes that it came more from sorrow than anger. Good thing, because Daniel wasn't in the mood to get punched in the jaw for defending the soldiers.

"I am sorry." He tried to convey the deepest of sympathies. All it took was imagining if Elanor had been killed to understand the man's pain. "If there was anything I could do to change what happened, believe me, I would. But it is my sister, not these men, who are directly responsible. She ordered them here. I'm sure most had no desire to go trudging through a frozen forest to find us."

The men's faces remained hardened, but neither one spoke against him.

"I know you want justice for your brother and feel like eliminating the soldiers is the way to get that and help everyone still here. But we are followers of Elôm. We must live our lives to a higher standard. We can't allow ourselves to become murderers just because some of them may be. It would do far more harm than good."

Gavin and Ket hung their heads. After a heavy, silent moment, Gavin nodded and met Daniel's gaze.

"You're right, my lord."

With that, they wandered away. Once they were out of earshot, Daniel released a long breath. Trying to be king was exhausting. Would he ever feel ready?

Liam carried a handful of used cups to a basin of hot wash water. There wasn't much else to do besides administer tea, clean up, and monitor the sick. But that was all part of the job. He'd choose it any day over soldiering.

He scrubbed the cups in the steaming water and set them on a rack to dry. He should go check on Rayad again soon. Was anyone else from the cabin getting sick? He'd have to check for any symptoms. The fever set in so quickly—

"How are your mother and the others?"

Liam's attention snapped to the General. It was the first time he'd heard him speak since the attack. His silence, though unusual, had been a welcome blessing. Up until now.

Before he could think of how to answer, Leetra's icy voice cut in from where she worked near Liam. "How do you think they are after your attack and the threat of this fever you brought?"

Her purple eyes smoldered with the glare she sent his grandfather. The General looked away and bowed his head. Liam had never seen him daunted by anyone before. It was probably the first time in his life that he wasn't in control of a situation.

Liam focused on his work again. He didn't want to be part of the exchange. He had hoped to avoid interaction with the General.

A couple of minutes later, Leetra walked away to check on the sick soldiers. Liam held his breath. Just as he anticipated, his grandfather broke the silence left by the crete's absence.

"So, you're a physician now?"

He'd kept his voice low and void of the ring of any of his usual derision. Even so, Liam stood still and silent for a long moment. Technically, he was still under Josef's training. He was more an assistant, but Josef did trust him now with nearly all his work. He swallowed and forced confidence into his voice. He *was* confident in his profession.

"Yes."

He looked over at his grandfather, waiting for a response. Would he call Liam weak? A coward for choosing to heal people instead of kill them?

But the General only nodded slowly. Liam narrowed his eyes. His grandfather was never so quiet, so calm. For some reason, such a response left a coal burning in Liam's chest. Never in his entire life had he ever dared nor wanted to antagonize the man, but with everything they now faced, just enough anger simmered inside him to propel him to speak. He stepped in front of his grandfather, standing straight and tall. He would never cower before this man again.

"And to answer your other question, Mother and the others are grieving and scared. How could they not be after what you've put us through?"

The lines in the General's face deepened. Just a little of his usual sharpness crept out with his words. "I did not know Michael would die in the attack."

"But you knew some would. We are not the only family grieving." Liam shook his head in disgust. "Your men killed helpless women!"

"Had you surrendered, you could have avoided such death. I warned Marcus."

"No," Liam said with enough force that his grandfather blinked in surprise. "You of all people know that surrender is not an option. We would have been thrown into prison camps, bound for the execution block, if we hadn't died of starvation or fever before that. And who knows what harm your men might have done to us in the meantime. Michael and the others, their deaths are on you."

Liam turned away and joined Josef and Leetra before the burning in his eyes could turn into anything more.

The day dragged by. Jace spent almost every moment at Rayad's bedside praying for a miracle or even just a small sign he would recover. Rayad wavered back and forth between consciousness. While his fever didn't get worse, his coughing did.

Liam came to check on him a couple of times and said this was the normal progression of the illness. That didn't make it any less difficult for Jace to witness.

They also learned from Liam that Dagren and a few of the others had fallen ill. Now all the soldiers except the General and two other men were battling the fever. The first man who'd come down with it was not doing well.

Though Holden and Elian insisted he get rest, Jace hardly slept that night. He hated the feeling that every moment he spent near Rayad could be one of the last. It made him want to cling to each moment they had.

When morning arrived again, Jace tore himself away from Rayad's cot to head outside for his daily meeting with Kyrin. Heaviness pressed down on him this morning even greater than it had the day before. He should have slept more, but rest wouldn't come easily for a while. Even if he tried, his mind refused to quit imagining the worst.

When Kyrin left the cabin and walked toward him, she didn't appear to have slept well either. Her reddened eyes stood out in her pale face. She almost looked sick. A painful jolt stabbed his chest.

"Are you all right?"

She nodded slowly. "Just tired." She looked into his eyes. "How is Rayad?"

"The same. Josef says it could be days before we know if he'll recover." The wait would kill Jace. He just prayed Rayad had the strength to fight that long. He rubbed his forehead. "We've been through difficult things before, but seeing him like this . . ." He shook his head.

Kyrin's eyes flooded with moisture and sympathy, and she wrapped her arms around herself as though she wished, as he did, that they could hold each other. Why must they be apart during such a trying time?

"If there's anything I can do, let me know," she said.

"Just keep praying."

"We will."

They talked for a few more minutes before turning back toward their cabins. Jace had only taken a step when he heard a muffled thump in the snow behind him. He looked back, and his heart plowed into his ribs.

Kyrin was on her knees, one arm out to brace herself.

"KYRIN!"

Jace rushed toward her and dropped to his knees. She looked up, both fear and despair flashing in her eyes. He yanked off his glove and put his hand to her face. Her skin radiated heat into his palm. *No!* His stomach lurched, and he pushed aside her coat collar to expose her neck. Red splotches tinged her skin. They met each other's eyes and, for that awful moment, Jace felt everything he loved most dearly crashing down around him. Like losing Kalli and Aldor and the farm, he saw himself losing the foundations of his life again. *Please, Elôm, no.*

He scooped Kyrin up into his arms and carried her to her cabin. Knocking the door with his foot, he looked down into her face. Tears had filled her eyes. He didn't like the shadow of resignation in them.

"You're going to be all right," he said.

The door opened, Kyrin's mother standing on the other side.

"She's sick."

Lydia's face paled. She hurried back to let them in.

"Kyrin?" Kaden stepped toward them, his face going slack. "Is it the fever?"

"Yes," Jace answered grimly.

"Bring her over here." Lydia led the way across the cabin and gestured to the empty bed that used to be Michael's. Jace set Kyrin carefully down on the edge of the mattress, keeping his hand on her shoulder to steady her. Lydia felt her forehead and then helped her get her coat and boots off.

"I'll get Josef." Jace strode to the door and outside. On his way to the meeting hall, his heart pounded a hard, sluggish beat. First Rayad and now Kyrin. He'd never been in danger of losing them both at once. Clenching his fists, he forced such a possibility as far away as he could. He wasn't sure he could survive losing both of them.

When he entered the meeting hall, the sickness permeated the air along with the pungent scent of herbs. Josef, Liam, and Leetra all looked up from their various places along the row of cots containing sick men. Josef straightened and stepped toward him.

"Is Rayad worse?"

"No." Jace glanced at Liam, his throat constricting. "Kyrin is sick."

Liam's eyes widened before his expression went taut. "What are her symptoms?"

"Fever and the rash. She collapsed while we were out talking."

Liam immediately strode across the room for his coat. As he slipped it on, Josef brought him a small pouch.

"Here are the herbs for the tea. Get her to drink as much as she can, and start compresses like the others. Come and get me if there is anything out of the ordinary."

Liam set his face determinedly and nodded. He did a better job at hiding his fear for Kyrin than Jace probably did.

Back at the Altair cabin, Lydia had Kyrin in bed and had already put cold compresses on her head by the time they arrived. Kaden and Ronny stood nearby. Ronny's eyes were wide, while Kaden watched with a deeply furrowed brow. Jace had seen him in many dire situations, but the look on his face lacked all of his usual confidence. Jace understood. It was the same helplessness he had been battling since Rayad had fallen ill. They were too used to taking action when their loved ones were in danger.

Jace stopped at the end of Kyrin's bed as Liam gave her a quick examination. Though alert, she was clearly miserable. She did attempt to give him a brave smile, and he did his level best to return it. If nothing else, he had to be her strength and keep her hopeful, even if his own hope withered.

After a moment, he looked at Lydia. "I'll let Marcus know."

Her worry-strained face softened as she glanced at him. "Thank you."

Though he hated leaving, Jace walked outside again and crossed camp. At the door to his cabin, he knocked and stepped back so he wouldn't be too close to whoever answered it. Marcus did a moment later.

"Jace?" He peered at him questioningly, but a look of grim knowing settled in his eyes.

"Kyrin's sick." Every time he said the words, the cords of fear around his chest wound even tighter.

Marcus processed this for a moment in the calm way he faced every calamity, though his concern wasn't hidden. "Is she in our cabin?"

Jace nodded.

"I'll get my things." Marcus turned back inside.

Jace didn't try to stop him. Marcus was Kyrin's brother. It was up to him whether or not he wanted to expose himself to the fever.

"You go," Jace said when he returned. "I need to check Rayad and let them know."

With a nod, Marcus hurried on to the Altair cabin and Jace toward the other. Inside, he found Elian sitting at Rayad's side while Holden brewed more tea. They both reacted in concern when he gave them the news.

"She's young and strong," Holden attempted to comfort him. "I'm sure she'll be fine."

If only Jace could find any confidence in that. Josef had said both young and old succumbed to the fever.

"You go on and be with her," Rayad's weak but determined voice grabbed Jace's attention. He hadn't realized he was awake. Rayad nodded at Jace. "You don't have to keep sitting with me. It won't help me recover any faster."

Jace sighed heavily. He wanted to be with both of them. "I'll come back later," he said finally.

"Don't wear yourself out trying to be both places at once," Rayad said with a little of his usual stubbornness.

Jace had to smile. It was heartening, if only for a moment. He turned for the door but paused near Holden. "Come and get me if there's any change."

"I will."

Daniel pulled on his coat and headed outside. It didn't feel exactly right to be paying a social visit to Elanor while the camp was on the verge of crisis, but what else was there to do? At this point, it was a waiting game. Either their dragon riders would return with the remedy or they wouldn't. Josef, Liam, and Leetra were doing all they could for the sick. Beyond prayer, there was nothing Daniel could do personally. So, if he couldn't be useful elsewhere, he might as well do something in pursuit of Elanor. If nothing else, it might cheer her up and distract her from worrying about Jace and Elian who were now exposed to the fever.

Along the way to the cabin Elanor shared with Anne's parents, Daniel smoothed his hair. He was so out of his element here. Had he been courting a lady back in Valcré, he would have brought her some token of his affection. Here, he would show up empty-handed. He had nothing to his name beyond a title and a hope for a future. Of course, Elanor didn't care about any of that, but it did add to the insecurities he battled lately.

When he had first arrived last summer, he had been more than happy to adopt life here in camp. It was exactly the sort of life he'd always wanted. However, time and this brutal winter had exposed how little his privileged upbringing had prepared him for the stark realities of life. Once, he might have been able to affect an entire nation with little more than a spoken word. Here, he was next to powerless. Simply another fugitive fighting to stay alive.

"You look very deep in thought."

Daniel nearly tripped in the snow at the sound of a female voice. He turned quickly to find Elanor's pink lips quirked in amusement. So now he was both powerless and clumsy, not to mention completely unaware of his surroundings. Shrugging off any sting to his pride, he smiled back at her. "I was."

She crossed the short distance between them, her skirts sending frozen bits of snow scattering along the path. "Where are you off to?"

"I was actually coming to see you. I thought you would be at the cabin."

Her smile blossomed more fully as she learned of his plans. "I was just out for a walk. It's cold, but the fresh air helps clear my head."

Though her smile lit up her face, her weary eyes betrayed the deeper turmoil inside.

"It's hard being cooped up when there's nothing you can do to help."

Her delicate brow wrinkled, and she nodded in agreement. They started walking slowly, but neither one said a word for a minute or two. Both had so much to think about. Still, this was not the way he intended to court Elanor. Surely he could find something to bring the smile back to her face while learning more about this young woman he hoped would someday be his bride. Lingering in the oppressive mood that permeated camp wouldn't actually help anyone.

"So, tell me, what were winters like for you growing up? Did you have any fun as a child with James?"

Her entire stance perked up at the questions, and he smiled to himself.

"We did have fun. We loved to play Fox and Geese in the snow. Sometimes we built snow dragons, or at least attempted to, and pretended we were on grand adventures. James was kinder then, though still a handful."

"Did you ever go sledding?"

"Oh, yes, we loved sledding. Father wasn't much into joining us, but Mother and Elian took us out to a hill not too far from the estate. We would spend hours there until our toes and fingers were numb with the cold. Then we would come back and huddle by the fireplace with mugs of tea or hot chocolate."

"Those sound like very happy memories."

Elanor looked up at him, a little of the sparkle having returned to her eyes. "What about you? Surely you have happy memories as a child. Did you and Davira ever get along?"

Daniel shook his head. As far back as he could remember, Davira always hated him. "Not so much. But I had friends, so it never really bothered. Whenever we had winter gatherings and my cousins were around, we had grand snowball battles in the courtyard. We built some pretty impressive snow forts back in the day."

Elanor grinned. "I would have loved to see them. I always wanted to make forts, but James would get bored of helping and end up destroying them."

"Little boys do tend to like destroying things."

"I guess they do."

In his mind's eye, Daniel saw a little boy about six tumbling about in the snow with slightly wavy dark hair like his and deep blue eyes like Elanor's. And perhaps a petite little girl with her mother's long, beautiful locks toddling after him. Longing squeezed his heart. If such a future ever took place, he would be sure his children both knew how deeply loved they were by him and each other. He wouldn't let them grow to be enemies like he was with Davira.

Daniel didn't realize his imaginings of the future had caused him to pause until Elanor turned to face him. Her brows scrunched in a questioning way, but all Daniel could do was stare down at her as the scene replayed itself in his mind. He could die a happy man if nothing else became of his life except for his dream of his own family. He could see it far more clearly than any of his other aspirations for the future.

Overwhelmed by such thoughts, he took a step closer to Elanor and stared down into her eyes. He'd resisted kissing her for months. He'd burst if he didn't do it now. He bent his head toward hers, but forced himself to wait for her to accept such an advance. To the delight of his pounding heart, she tipped her head up to meet him.

Daniel had kissed more girls than he ever cared to admit, but this kiss meant the world to him and completely outshone the others. Any chill from the cold vanished. He was going to marry this woman. That was about the only certainty he had right now.

When they broke the kiss, Daniel studied her face. Her eyes danced and her cheeks were rosy red from more than just the cold. Those soft lips of hers gave him a pert little smile, begging for another kiss, but he resisted. Instead, he reached for her gloved hand and tipped his head toward her cabin.

"I suppose we best go inside before we freeze."

Not likely the way his blood still thrummed through him.

Trask trudged back to his cabin after checking in on all those who had fallen ill. Four more in camp had contracted the fever. They had done their best, but it didn't look like they would be able to contain this. Now, if nothing else, he had to make himself available to help wherever he could. He hadn't planned to go back to his cabin after making his rounds, not wanting to expose Anne to the sickness, but she wouldn't hear of it. She had told him they would face whatever happened together.

When he entered, Anne stood at the table, putting together baskets of food for the sick and their caretakers. She would probably take them to the meeting hall as soon as she was finished. If more fell ill, Josef would need all the help he could get.

"How is everyone?"

Trask sighed and shrugged off his coat. "Scared. No one knows who will be next, and they know it's only a matter of time until people start dying."

Suddenly overwhelmed, Trask sank down in a chair by the fireplace and rubbed his fingers against his eyes. He opened them when he sensed Anne's presence. She sat down in his lap, and he wrapped his arms around her, holding her close and inhaling the sweet scent of her hair. Being leader of the encampment, he had a responsibility to be strong for everyone and keep his emotions in check or well hidden. That, however, didn't erase the deeply rooted fear of losing her in all of this.

"I've done everything possible to protect this camp. But now, after the attack and this sickness, I don't know what to do. How can I continue to protect them if everyone is sick? And what if there is a second attack while we're too weak to fight?" He'd put his heart and soul into creating this place. He couldn't bear to see it crumble now and lose the people who had come to rely on it.

Anne rested her soft hand against his cheek, and he looked deep into her eyes.

"We'll pray," she told him softly. "Remember, it isn't the lookouts you've had in place or all the precautions you've taken that have kept this camp safe the last couple of years. Elôm has. I don't know why He now allowed the attack and this fever, but He will show us what to do if we ask Him."

Her gentle reminder brought a smile to his lips. Elôm had blessed him with a wonderfully faithful life partner and helper.

"I love you," he murmured and drew her closer for a kiss.

Jace rested his elbows on his knees and his chin on his clasped hands as he stared at Kyrin. She hadn't started coughing yet, but the rise and fall of her chest seemed labored. Like Rayad, she drifted in and out of consciousness as they sat around her in the quietness of the cabin. Jace could tell they were all restless, especially Kaden. His knee kept bouncing, and he wouldn't stop fiddling with one of his daggers, drawing it in and out of its sheath and flipping it agitatedly in his fingers. No doubt he wished as Jace did to have a physical foe to use it on.

Evening encroached, bringing with it the foreboding promise of torturously long night hours. A knock at the door sent a jolt through Jace. He straightened, his back and shoulders stiff, and then rose to answer it so the others wouldn't have to. When he pulled it open, Holden stood on the other side, and Jace's heart plunged toward his feet.

Holden held up his hand as if to stop Jace's sudden spiral of panic. "It's not Rayad. Glynn just returned from scouting the nearby towns. Sounds like he has news. He's heading to Trask's cabin."

Could the crete possibly have the remedy? Jace glanced back at Kyrin and then at her family, their own burst of fragile hope displayed in their wide eyes. He then grabbed his coat and stepped out with Holden. He had to find out.

The two of them strode toward Trask's cabin, Jace's pace barely below a jog. Did he dare hope that the cure for Kyrin and Rayad was within his grasp? When they reached the cabin, Holden knocked on the door. Jace could hardly remain still in the few seconds before Trask answered it and motioned them inside.

"Anne and I are helping with the sick, so you might as well come in. We've both been exposed."

They stepped in. Anne greeted them quietly, but Jace focused on Glynn. Even being a crete, he looked cold as he stood near the fireplace.

"Did you find the remedy?"

With a tight-lipped expression, Glynn shook his head, and Jace's hope crashed to the ground. However, the crete wasn't finished. "But I did find out where we might be able to attain some."

"Where?" Jace held his breath, waiting to see if his shattered hope might be rebuilt.

Glynn looked between Jace and Trask. "Alex Avery."

Jace drew his brows together in a deep frown. Avery was the one who had poisoned the emperor. No one had seen or heard from him since, despite Davira's months-long manhunt. What did he have to do with the remedy?

"From what I heard, he never fled Valcré like everyone thought. Turns out, he's set up an underground smuggling ring. They say anyone who can't go to Davira can go to him, for supplies as well as the remedy."

Jace looked over at Trask who appeared to mull this information over. But, for Jace, there was nothing to consider.

"I'll go."

"It would be a risk," Glynn warned. "We've all heard the stories out of Valcré, and there's a bigger bounty on Avery's head right now than on any of ours. Just getting close to him would be dangerous."

Jace shook his head. Even if it meant walking right into the heart of Davira's rule, he would do anything to help Kyrin and Rayad. "We don't have a choice. We need the remedy, and I am willing to get it." He looked at Trask again. "That is, if I can borrow some money for the payment."

Trask glanced at Anne but said, "You can have whatever you need."

Jace let out a deep breath. He wasn't sure he'd expected Trask to agree so quickly. It just proved how dire the situation was. Without the cure, their camp would be completely devastated in one fell swoop.

"When will you leave?"

"Right away." Jace wouldn't let Kyrin or Rayad suffer for a minute longer than they had to. Their lives could hinge on a mere moment of lost time.

"Let me see what we have," Trask said, reaching for his coat. "I'm sure Avery won't sell cheaply."

Jace nodded. "I'll gather my things and meet you back here."

He rushed to the other cabin. Now that he had something he could do, he wouldn't be slowed down by anything. Holden followed him. He was disappointed to find Rayad asleep when they arrived. He'd hoped to talk to him before he left, but he didn't want to wake him. Kneeling down next to the cot, Jace watched him for a long moment. How long would it take to get the remedy from Avery? What if it took days? Did Rayad have that long? Jace swallowed hard. *Please let him hang on until I get back.*

He then pushed to his feet and gathered his pack and extra clothing.

"Where are you going?" Elian asked from the table.

Jace glanced back to where he and Trev watched him questioningly.

"Valcré. Alex Avery has the remedy. I'm going to get some."

They were quiet for a moment before Trev asked, "Do you want some of us to go with you?"

Jace shook his head. "It will be dangerous to head into the city, and I don't even know if I'll be able to find or meet with Avery, but I have to try."

They were quiet again until Holden walked over to his cot and pulled out his own pack. Jace looked at him.

"None of us should head out alone, especially not into Valcré," Holden said. "I'll come along to watch your back. Besides, I know the types of places men like Avery tend to hang out. I used to frequent them myself."

Jace gave him a grateful nod. He wouldn't have willingly dragged anyone else into danger, but he would be glad to have Holden's expertise.

Once they finished packing, Jace turned his attention once more to Rayad. He still didn't stir from sleep. What if this was the last time he ever saw him? The possibility knifed deeply into his chest with a violent twist.

A hand gripped his shoulder. Elian stood at his side. "We'll take care of him."

Jace blinked at the burning in his eyes. He cleared his throat. "Thank you."

Focusing on his purpose, Jace took the lead, and Holden followed him back to Trask's cabin. Trask, Balen, Daniel, Aric, and Warin all waited there for them. Jace would have thought Trask would've insisted on keeping Balen and Daniel away from the sickness. Yet, now that it was spreading so quickly, most of them were probably exposed in one way or another anyway.

Trask set a pair of leather saddlebags on the table. "This is what we could gather. It's not a fortune, but hopefully it'll be enough for what we need. And, if there happens to be any left over, perhaps you can also get us supplies."

Jace lifted the flap to look in the saddlebags. They were full of coins, including a few gold ones, and valuable jewelry.

"I'll bring back as much as I can." He closed the flap. "Holden is coming with me."

"Good. I'll feel better knowing there are two of you with how things are in Valcré, especially toting around money like that."

Jace agreed. With Davira's proclamation, there wouldn't be anything stopping someone from murdering for this money. He would have to be careful to keep it concealed, even with Holden there.

"When you speak to Alex," Daniel said, drawing Jace's attention, "you can let him know I'm here if you think it will help. We were always good friends. I would hope it still means something to him."

Jace would keep that in mind. He'd dealt with many different sorts of people in his lifetime, but never smugglers. It was hard to guess how sympathetic Alex Avery would be to their plight.

He turned to Holden. "Ready?"

His friend nodded. After trading goodbyes with the others, they left the cabin. Outside, Jace said, "I just need to see Kyrin once more."

"I'll take your things to Gem," Holden offered.

Jace handed over his pack and hurried to the Altair cabin. Kyrin's family was still gathered around her bed, but Marcus and Kaden rose from their seats to meet Jace.

"What was that about?" Marcus asked.

Jace glanced at Kyrin. Like Rayad, she was asleep. "Glynn found out that Alex Avery is still in Valcré and has the remedy. I'm going to try to get some."

Kaden jumped on this. "I'll go with you."

"Holden is going with me. You might be needed more here." He cast another look at Kyrin. Her family needed to be together after the sorrow they already faced. Kaden's riders would also need their captain if they were attacked again.

Kaden sighed but seemed to understand and didn't press the issue.

Jace sank down in the chair next to the bed and reached for Kyrin's hand. He desperately needed to speak with her before he left. He couldn't walk away without hearing her voice once more, just in case it was the last time. Biting back the emotions that swelled up his throat, he squeezed her fingers gently. She didn't stir at first, but then her eyes fluttered open. She blinked a few times before her gaze focused on his face.

"Jace," she barely whispered.

He forced the best smile he could muster. "How do you feel?"

Kyrin drew a heavy breath. "Awful." She offered a weak smile in return.

Jace reached with his free hand and brushed away some of the hair sticking to her damp forehead. "Kyrin, I'm leaving . . . for Valcré."

Her face scrunched, and she grew more alert. "What?"

"I'm going to get the remedy for this fever."

She processed his words for a moment, her frown deepening. "What if you get caught?"

"I won't." He squeezed her hand again. "Holden is going with me. We'll look out for each other." He glanced around him. Kyrin's family had moved away from the bed, giving them a little privacy.

Jace leaned closer, his heart thumping. "Kyrin, listen to me. I will get that remedy and you will get better because . . . I want to marry you."

Her eyes widened, and she looked as alert as he'd seen her since she'd fallen ill.

"I still have uncertainties about the future, but I do know I don't want to face it without you. I want you to be at my side, always." This was not at all the moment he wanted or had planned for so long, but this might be his only chance. He wasn't going to wait any longer and lose it. "Kyrin, will you marry me?"

Her eyes turned a misty blue as a smile spread across her lips. "Yes, Jace, I will."

Despite the fear lurking under the surface, joy spread through Jace's heart. They'd gone through so much and had much more yet to face, but it was finally official. He was betrothed to Kyrin Altair—the only woman he could ever imagine loving the way he did. She would be his wife. He couldn't let the possibility of anything else take hold.

"As soon as I get back and you've recovered, we'll get married."

She nodded, her smile a little faded with weariness but still in place.

Rising from his chair, he leaned over the bed and pressed a kiss to her forehead. Her skin burned against his lips, reminding him of how important his mission was. For a moment, he couldn't breathe at the thought of losing her.

"I'll be back as fast as I can." His voice sounded hoarse even to his own ears.

Hating to tear himself from her side, he turned and headed for the door where he met Kyrin's family. They traded brief goodbyes, and Jace left the cabin. Walking away weighed down every step he took. His heart was just as heavy as it lifted up desperate prayers for success. As much as he wanted to do whatever he could to save Kyrin and Rayad, it tore him up inside to leave them.

When he reached the dragons, Holden already had Gem saddled for him. Trask and Daniel were there to see him off. So were Leetra and Elanor. Jace locked eyes with his sister and stopped short of her.

"You shouldn't be so near to us," he said quietly.

She glanced down at the snow. "I know, but . . ." she looked up at him. "I'm going to help with the sick."

The weight inside Jace increased, but Elanor continued before he could speak.

"I know it's hard for you, but I need to help. I can't just wait and do nothing."

Slowly, Jace nodded. More would get sick. He was certain of that. They would need as many people as they could to help.

She closed the distance between them, and they hugged tightly.

"Be careful," she murmured in his ear.

"I will."

They parted, and Leetra stepped forward. She had always been a master at concealing her emotions, but this evening she let her vulnerability show.

"Make sure Timothy is all right," she said almost pleadingly. She then added hastily, "And the others."

She cleared her throat. No doubt, if her skills weren't so needed here, she would fly to Valcré along with them.

"We will," Jace promised.

That brought Daniel forward. He handed Jace a small piece of paper. "These are directions to Ben and Mira's house. If Timothy and the others aren't with them, they'll know where to find them."

"Thank you." Jace tucked the paper into a secure pocket of his coat.

Trading their final goodbyes, Jace and Holden mounted the dragons. With one last look toward the Altair cabin where Kyrin's brothers stood watching, Jace gave Gem the signal, and they launched upward into the darkening sky.

JACE STRAPPED ON his snowshoes and lifted his pack. He then turned to Gem commanding her to stay. "*Tolla.*" Elôm willing, they wouldn't have to leave them here long. They needed to get the remedy back to camp before people started dying. Jace had prayed the entire way that they would find Avery quickly and make the deal without difficulty. If it were up to him, they would be on their way back within twenty-four hours.

Leaving the two dragons deep in the forest where they wouldn't be discovered, Jace and Holden trekked westward. It was slow going in the deep snow. Some of the drifts they had to avoid were nearly as tall as Jace.

A good hour after leaving the dragons, Jace spotted towering stone through the trees—the surrounding wall of Valcré. When they reached the snow-packed road, they paused. Jace wasn't sure what to expect when they entered the city, but armed with the rumors of the violence inside, he traded a glance with Holden. Whatever they were walking into, this was the best hope of survival for their camp.

After removing their snowshoes, they trudged on toward the nearest gate and entered cautiously. Though the gate stood unguarded, a foreboding hostility permeated the air. They came across only a few people at first. Jace gripped the hilt of his sword, keeping a sharp eye out for anyone who posed a threat, and made sure his cloak concealed the money bag. The strange quietness of the usually bustling city sent a shiver down his back. Whether it was the extreme cold or the danger that kept people indoors, he could not say.

Though the crowds increased a little as they went deeper into the city, each person seemed to look on the other with suspicion. Jace and Holden received more than a few shadowed looks from people who gave them a wide berth. Many people held pieces of cloth tightly to their noses and mouths and avoided close contact with anyone.

Holden stepped closer to Jace, his voice lowered. "I wonder if Davira ever gets out to see what she's turned the city into."

Jace shook his head. From what he knew of her, he doubted it. Even more, he doubted she would care. The death of her father had unleashed a beast no one had expected.

Following Daniel's directions, Jace and Holden strode through the city. They passed by tall shops on either side of the icy, cobbled street, but many appeared closed or vacant. Their path took them steadily closer to the palace. Jace glanced at it a few times and prayed Davira would never know they were here. In a city of many thousands of people, surely he and Holden wouldn't be noticed. Yet Jace couldn't shake the feeling of having a target emblazoned on his back for every one of their enemies to see.

Finally, they arrived at a long row of merchant houses and found the one they sought. Jace scanned the area for any sign of trouble and then knocked on the door. They hadn't heard anything from their friends in Valcré in a while. He prayed that none of them had been caught in the meantime.

The door opened, and an older man matching the description Daniel had given them stood on the other side. He eyed them cautiously, and it occurred to Jace how threatening he and Holden probably appeared.

"Can I help you?" the man asked.

"Ben?"

He nodded slowly, and Jace glanced over his shoulder before murmuring, "I am Jace Ilvaran, and this is my friend, Holden. We are from the Resistance camp in Landale. We are followers of the King as well as supporters of Prince Daniel."

Ben's face relaxed and he released a long breath before a smile broke out. "Please, come in, brothers."

Jace hesitated. "We've been exposed to Miner's Fever."

Ben's smile morphed into a grim expression, but he said, "So have we."

Jace glanced at Holden, and they stepped inside. The sheltered warmth of the house was a welcome comfort after the long trek.

"Allow me to take your cloaks and coats," Ben said.

They shrugged them off and handed them over to the man.

"If I may, how is Prince Daniel?" Ben asked as he hung their cloaks near the door.

"He is well . . . at least he was when we left." Jace winced. "But the fever is spreading rapidly through our camp."

"I'm terribly sorry," Ben said, true concern wrinkling his forehead. "We had all hoped and prayed that you would be spared."

A woman entered the foyer then. She was a robust lady with an olive complexion and long, dark curls. Ben introduced her as his wife Mira. Jace greeted her with a smile. He had heard Daniel speak highly of her. This couple was to him as Kalli and Aldor had been to Jace. Mira ushered them all into the living room, where a fire burned. As they sat around the fireplace, Jace and Holden shared the recent events in camp.

"I'm so sorry for your losses," Mira said gently. "We've been praying for all of you in Landale, and we'll certainly increase those prayers."

"Thank you," Jace replied, thinking of Kyrin. She and the others needed all the prayer they could get.

"So what brings you to Valcré?" Ben asked.

"We need the remedy for the fever. We heard Alex Avery has a stash of it and hope to get some from him."

Ben nodded slowly. "I see."

"Do you think it's possible?" Jace held his breath. He couldn't bear to return to Landale empty-handed.

"Perhaps," Ben said. "Aaron is looking into the same thing. Many from our congregation are ill as well." His brows drew together as regret claimed his expression. "We've already lost a couple of people."

"I'm sorry," Jace murmured. Leetra and her request when they'd left sprang to mind. "How are Aaron and Timothy?"

A bit of a smile brightened Ben's weary face. "They're doing well, and their presence here has been a great blessing. Timothy is a gifted teacher, and everyone loves him. Our congregation has almost doubled since his arrival. Thank Elôm our meetings are yet undiscovered by the queen."

"Has Aaron had any contact with Avery about the remedy?" Jace didn't mean to change the subject so abruptly, but time was their enemy.

Ben shook his head. "Not yet. Avery is a hard man to find, with good reason. But Aaron has made connections and is confident he can set up a meeting now. The problem, however, is finances. We don't know how we'd pay Avery even if we did meet with him. The price of food and supplies is staggering, and many of our members are very poor. What money we've gathered has gone to supplies and warm clothing."

"The leaders in our camp sent along money." Jace rested his hand on the bag he'd kept at his side. "Perhaps, with whatever you have, it will be enough to get the remedy for everyone."

"You're very generous to share, and we'd be most grateful."

This would change their plan to buy supplies to bring back to camp, but Jace knew Trask would approve. Saving the lives of those who were sick was of immediate concern.

"Where are Timothy and Aaron now?"

"Helping with the sick. We converted one of my warehouses into a shelter for everyone." Ben rose from his seat. "I'll take you to them if you'd like. I'm sure you're anxious to talk to Aaron."

"Yes, thank you."

They returned to the foyer and put on their cloaks. Jace noticed Ben attach a large dagger to his belt as well. Ben gave his wife a quick kiss goodbye and then led Jace and Holden outside.

As they walked the cold streets, Holden said, "We've heard how dangerous the city has become."

Ben shook his head in dismay. "I've lived here my entire life. You never expect to see a murder in broad daylight on streets you've traveled almost every day, but I have . . . twice. I can't be sure if they were believers or not, but that's what the assailants always claim."

He sighed heavily. "People are scared, and those bent on harm are getting bolder every day. It's a wonder we haven't descended into pure chaos. I will say one thing; people are starting to see just how far our country has deteriorated." He lowered his voice. "I believe that's why our congregation has grown. The horror is opening people's eyes and causing them to seek answers. After all, it's in the name of Aertus and Vilai that so many of them are being killed—believers and non-believers alike."

"Perhaps Elôm is using Davira's ascension to the throne to draw people back to Him, same as the captivity in Samara," Holden suggested.

"I pray so," Ben replied, "and that people will pay attention."

Down near the docks of Valcré's vast harbor, they arrived at a warehouse. The worn exterior gave it the appearance of being abandoned except for smoke rising from the chimney at the far end.

"This is it." Ben opened the door and ushered them into a small entrance room.

It was dim inside, but light came from another doorway leading into the main area of the warehouse. So did the sounds of coughing and the distinct scent of herbs and tea. They stepped through the doorway and found rows of cots along the center of the warehouse. Most were full—about thirty in all—and other men and women moved among them with compresses and mugs of tea. Jace's stomach cramped at the sight. Would this soon be the sight at camp as well?

Not if he could help it.

His gaze caught on a familiar face.

Aaron smiled when he noticed them and called quietly, "Hey, Tim."

Jace spotted Timothy at the far end of the warehouse as he turned. He, too, smiled and joined his brother to meet Jace and Holden. It was good to see them. Jace had missed them in camp and the studies he used to have with Timothy and Kyrin.

They met each other near the door and clasped arms firmly in greeting.

"What are you two doing here?" Aaron asked. The excitement of seeing them faded from his face, his expression growing serious. "Has something happened in camp?"

Jace grimaced. If only he could say no. "We were attacked two weeks ago by Dagren and the General." He drew a hard breath as his chest tightened. "We lost several men . . . including Michael."

They stared at him in shock for a moment, sorrow building in their expressions. Aaron shook his head wordlessly, anger mingling with the sadness in his dark eyes.

"How are Kyrin and her family?" Timothy asked.

"It's been hard for them." He sighed, the heaviness of the situation weighing down. "One of the soldiers we captured got the fever. We tried to keep it contained, but it spread. Kyrin and Rayad are both sick, as well as several others."

Aaron just shook his head. There were no words at this point.

"How long have they been sick?" Timothy asked.

"Four days for Rayad and two days for Kyrin." Jace summoned his determination to dispel the dread and fear threatening to rise up at the thought of them lying ill back at camp. "We came to try to get the remedy from Alex Avery." He looked at Aaron. "Ben said you might have a way to contact him?"

Thank Elôm Aaron gave a confident nod. "I believe I've located his right-hand man, Tavor. If we want a meeting with Avery, it'll be through him."

"Then we must set up that meeting as soon as possible."

"It won't be cheap," Aaron warned.

"Trask sent money. Combined with whatever you can gather, hopefully it will be enough for everyone."

Daniel turned to the next page in the King's Scrolls. He figured he could sit and worry about everyone in camp, or he could study. The latter seemed a far better option. If he was going to be king one day, he should know as much as he possibly could about Elôm. That didn't exactly make it easy to focus, though. Any minute another person could fall ill, including Elanor. Of course, the only thing he could do about that was pray and trust Elôm. He wouldn't have to worry nearly as much if Jace and Holden managed to get that remedy, so he prayed for them too.

About an hour into his study, the cabin door opened. Cold air rushed in, but at least it was sunny outside. For the moment, anyway. Balen hurried inside and stomped snow from his boots before striding to his bed. Kneeling down, he pulled his bow and quiver out from underneath it.

"Where are you going?" Daniel asked.

"Hunting." Balen rose and strung the longbow. "Someone should be out checking the area for game in case the riders Trask sent out don't find anything."

Despite the freezing temperature, braving the cold seemed a whole lot more preferable to sitting around here waiting for the next bit of bad news. Not that Daniel could call himself much of a hunter. Sure, he'd been on hunts with his father. Hunts that involved dozens of men and staff herding deer toward the hunters. There wasn't much skill to it, and lives certainly hadn't depended on success.

"Mind if I join you?" Perhaps Daniel could pick up some skills from Balen. After all, he was said to be one of the best trackers and hunters in camp. It was his hunting skills that had landed him the position of king after saving Samara's previous king from a killer wildcat.

Balen looked only mildly surprised and nodded. "Sure. It's probably best not to head out alone considering how quickly the fever strikes."

Daniel agreed. He might not be much of a hunter, but at least he could help make sure they both made it safely back to camp. So much rested on the two of them surviving. Did Balen feel the weight of that as keenly as Daniel did?

He set his study material aside and rose to pull on an extra wool shirt and his warmest winter gear. The most time he'd spent outside lately was brief strolls with Elanor and traveling from cabin to cabin. Usually not more than twenty minutes at best. This hunting trip would be much different. While he had lived a much more pampered life than Balen up to this point, he was determined to hold his own beside the Samaran king. If Balen could endure the cold, then he could too.

They both grabbed their snowshoes and headed outdoors. A little twinge of uncertainty gnawed at Daniel when the icy breeze blasted him. This would not be a particularly pleasant excursion into the surrounding forest, but he'd be dead before he'd back out now. He had to prove he was up to such challenges. If he couldn't manage a bit of foul weather, how could anyone expect him to rule a country?

On the way toward the edge of camp, Balen detoured to the supply shed and collected an axe and shovel that he attached to his pack.

"What's that for?" Daniel asked.

Balen glanced at him. "I have an idea we haven't tried yet."

He didn't explain further, and they strapped on their snowshoes. Sucking in a cold breath, Daniel followed Balen away from the packed snow in camp into the deep drifts amidst the trees. They didn't say much as they made their trek. Though Daniel had questions he would have liked to ask, he didn't want to scare away any game that might be in the area. Balen appeared too focused on the surroundings for conversation anyway. Daniel scanned the snowy terrain as well for footprints or anything else that might lead to much needed food for camp. He'd heard from their other hunters how desolate the forest seemed, and now he witnessed it firsthand.

For over half an hour they trudged through the woods with not a sight of game to be found. Daniel was beginning to think this would be all their day consisted of until he picked up the sound of trickling water. Just ahead, one small hole opened up in the snow where the stream ran just fast enough to keep from freezing over. Faint indents in the snow around the hole offered hope that maybe there were still game animals around and this was where they came to drink. They continued past this small break in the monotony of the frozen forest for another several yards before Balen stopped and shrugged off his pack.

"There's a deep pool here that I saw last fall. If we can get through the ice, we might be able to bring back fish." He grabbed the shovel and set about clearing the snow. "Why don't you gather some wood for a fire?"

Daniel wasn't sure what a fire would do besides keep them warm while they attempted fishing, but he turned to search for wood buried in the snow. It was better than standing and watching Balen do all the work. Once he had a nice pile off to the side, Balen paused and rummaged through his pack. He pulled out a pouch and produced a wad of tow, birch bark, and flint and steel. Daniel watched closely, hoping his interest wouldn't betray the fact that he had never started a fire before.

With practiced ease, Balen soon had a small fire crackling amongst the wood Daniel had gathered. He stowed his fire kit and then pulled out a fry pan and a bundle of what Daniel realized was animal fat.

"We haven't had much luck with regular game," Balen said as he laid the strips of fat in the pan over the fire, "so we'll try drawing in predators instead. Maybe a wolf or two or even a fisher. If they are having as hard a time hunting as we are, they'll be hungry."

Drawing in hungry, potentially dangerous predators didn't seem to be an especially wise move, but they did need any meat they could get. Daniel figured he was probably with just about the most capable person for dealing with such a situation. Balen seemed perfectly confident in what he was doing.

"Keep watch," he told Daniel, getting up and brushing snow from his knees. "I'm going to see if I can get through this ice."

He picked up the axe and went to work hacking at the frozen stream he had uncovered. Daniel watched him for a moment before turning his gaze to the forest. Good to know Balen trusted him to watch his back, at least from hungry predators. The fat in the pan started to sizzle, the scent rising into the air for the wind to carry it deep into the trees. Surely something would be drawn to it.

Nearly twenty minutes later, after an impressive amount of work and effort, Balen broke through the ice. Tugging off his glove, he used his bare hand to scoop out the ice chunks in the way and then warmed up by the fire before gathering his fishing supplies. He baited the hooks with leftover fat and lowered a couple of lines into the dark hole.

"Now we wait."

For several minutes, the two of them sat quietly—Daniel near the fire watching their surroundings and Balen beside the hole to monitor the fishing lines. Finally, Daniel asked, "Do you think Jace will be able to get that remedy?"

Balen glanced at him. "Kyrin is sick. He won't leave Valcré without it."

Daniel nodded. Jace wouldn't leave willingly, at least. He just prayed nothing would happen to Jace and Holden in the city. He also prayed his old friend Alex would be accommodating. If only he could have gone himself. He'd wanted to offer, but he knew better. They wouldn't let him risk it. Too many people in Valcré might recognize him. He hated being one of the main pieces upon which their victory rested. It left him feeling rather useless most of the time.

"Do you ever get sick of being treated like you're something fragile and valuable that has to be protected at all cost?"

Balen cast him a wry smile. "I do, yes."

"How did you ever choose to be king? I would have refused. I was born a prince, and I still considered running away many times." Daniel couldn't imagine having a normal life and then choosing to accept the heavy mantle of king.

"I did refuse . . . at first."

For some reason this surprised Daniel. Balen was one of the most humble people he had ever met and always seemed to make the right choice when it was presented to him. But, he was only human. Daniel would do well to remember that when comparing himself to the fellow king.

"When King Alton first asked me to be his heir," Balen continued, "I told him no and immediately returned home. I hated disappointing him, but I knew I could not be king when I was nothing more than a farm boy."

A wistful smile overcame his focused expression. "When I told my uncle, he asked if I had prayed before I made the decision. I hadn't, of course. I felt so unqualified it never even occurred to me that it might be Elôm's will. My uncle then impressed upon me how important it was to seek Elôm in every decision. So I did pray about it, even though I had no intention of changing my mind. A week later, I couldn't ignore the prompting I felt to return to Amberin."

Daniel shook his head, mostly to himself. Would he have listened to Elôm's prompting? He wanted to believe he would have. He had, after all, defied his own father and put his life on the line to follow Elôm in the first place.

Before Daniel could respond, Balen's full attention shifted to the fishing lines. A moment later, he yanked one of the them, and then promptly pulled in a thrashing trout. His face lit up with a grin. This would be the first game anyone had brought back in days. A single fish might not feed the camp, but it was a start. At least it proved they could catch them.

Balen baited the hook again and lowered the line back into the water before pulling out a knife and skillfully gutting the trout. "When we leave, we'll set snares and use the guts as bait. I'll give the heads to Tyra when we get back."

Jace would appreciate that. He had to worry about his wolf with their meat supply dwindling.

Over the next hour, Balen caught another half dozen fish to add to their supply. Their fried fat didn't seem to attract anything until a little flash of movement caught Daniel's eye. He focused on a dark spot near a brush pile. It didn't appear to be more than a shadow until it finally moved again.

"Looks like your bait is working." He motioned to the lynx crouched in the snow several yards away.

Balen slowly reached for his bow and knocked an arrow. The lynx didn't make a very large target, but he took the shot anyway. The lynx leapt into the air and bolted, but didn't make it five feet before collapsing. Balen hurried to make sure it was dead, and Daniel followed. Examining the lynx, he found that Balen had made a perfect shot right in the chest. A quick kill.

"Is there anything you can't do?" He cast Balen a teasing grin, though he actually did want to know the answer.

Balen just laughed. However, his expression sobered a moment later. "Keep my people out of captivity."

All humor left Daniel. "You and me both."

Balen looked at him. Despite his somber look, hope remained in his eyes. "We will get them back. I trust that Elôm hasn't brought us this far just to fail."

JACE AND HOLDEN followed Aaron through the city. The farther south they went, the seedier it became. Trash and garbage heaps littered the streets. If it were the middle of summer, Jace could just imagine the stench that would have burned their noses. Dark figures in tattered clothing slunk away down the alleys as they approached. Others ignored them, digging through the piles of refuse. Those who did notice cast them vacant looks. Jace had seen such broken, lifeless expressions growing up in slave yards. His nerves prickled, and he kept his cloak around his money satchel. They carried enough valuables to make even an honest person consider robbing them if desperate enough.

Even so, Aaron strode confidently past the figures. The man had more guts than someone twice his size. Like Jace, he had seen his fair share of hardship growing up as a miner in the Graylin Valley. The people there were often little better than slaves themselves.

"Avery's supposed to have his loot stashed in some of the abandoned buildings around here, but he does his business in the taverns," Aaron told them. Despite his confidence, he did scan each street with an alert and watchful eye. "In this part of the city at least, there is no love lost between the people and the queen or her men. Soldiers won't even go into the taverns. Any who do don't come out alive, or so I've heard."

Jace raised his brows. These men had to be pretty bold to kill off soldiers. "Do you think Avery's men will speak to us?"

"We want to do business. That should be enough to get us a meeting."

A stiff breeze gusted toward them as they turned into an alley, and Jace shivered. Just ahead, several shady characters milled out-side one of the doors along the alley walls. They looked like hired muscle, each one bearing a variety of swords and knives. The hair along Jace's arms rose under his sleeves at their shifty glances.

However, when they spotted Aaron, they seemed to stand down. Jace glanced at the sign hanging over the narrow street. *Briar Pub.* Aaron pushed the door open, and they stepped inside, unhindered by the men. The pungent scent of alcohol, sweat, and smoke hung thick and heavy in the air, and the hum of voices filled the dim room. It was not unlike the few Jace had seen as a slave. Occasionally, Jasper had drummed up interest in him, the half-blood, by taking him into taverns while he ate. News always traveled fast that way.

Aaron paused to scan the round tables, most of which had two or more men sitting around them. "I don't see him. We'll wait a bit. He usually shows up around now."

He walked to the bar, Jace and Holden trailing him. Jace kept watch on the other patrons out of the corner of his eye. At least, according to Aaron, they weren't loyal to Davira.

Aaron nodded to the barkeeper, a burly, dark-haired man. "Three for my friends and me." He laid a silver coin down, and the man filled three mugs with ale, the froth overflowing the rims. Aaron grabbed them and handed one each to Jace and Holden.

Jace eyed the foamy amber liquid. He'd never cared for ale.

"You sit around a tavern without a drink and people will think you're looking for trouble," Aaron told them quietly as he led them to an empty table. "It's better to blend in."

Jace took a seat and a sip of the biting liquid. He much preferred Rayad's coffee, strong as that was.

"So, how do you know this Tavor will be here?" Holden asked, settling back in his chair. He looked as comfortable here as Aaron did. No doubt he'd spent his fair share of time in places like this as the emperor's informant.

"I don't, for sure," Aaron answered, "but there are two or three taverns he visits frequently. This seems to be his favorite."

Jace couldn't see why. It was dirty, crowded, and the stench weighed on his lungs. He never understood the draw of such places.

While they waited, they talked of Landale and of Timothy and Aaron's time in the city.

"It's a lot different from camp life," Aaron told them, "but not so different from living in Dunlow. I do miss camp, but Timothy is doing a lot of good here. Everyone has really taken to his teaching. Now if we can only get past this sickness."

He raised his mug to take a sip of ale but paused, his gaze shifting past Jace and Holden. Jace glanced over his shoulder. A barmaid approached their table. She was a slight girl with dark hair and eyes and a youthful look about her. She wore a low, silky red dress that barely covered her shoulders. Jace cleared his throat and steeled himself for any advances, but her attention focused on Aaron. She smiled at him when she reached the table, though it wasn't the seductive smile Jace would have expected from a woman of her occupation. Actually, it was quite lovely and sweet, a little like Kyrin's.

"Good afternoon," she told Aaron.

He smiled comfortably as well. "Afternoon."

The woman glanced at Jace and Holden. "Can I get you gentlemen anything?"

"I think we're good." Aaron leaned toward her. "Actually, we're hoping to meet with Tavor. Have you seen him?"

She stepped closer to his side and lowered her voice. "Not today, but he was in yesterday."

"Thank you."

With one more smile, she stepped back. "Just let me know if any of you need anything."

Some might have taken that as a less than pure invitation, but Jace couldn't sense anything like that behind her friendly personality. He watched her walk back to the bar before shifting his gaze back to Aaron. "A friend of yours?"

Aaron gave a brief nod, his attention lingering noticeably on the woman. "Lacy. A few weeks back, a couple of guys started getting too possessive of her. I persuaded them to leave her alone."

Jace traded a glance with Holden. Something told him that persuasion involved more than a friendly chat.

"I'm trying to get her to come to the meetings. I think she wants to, but she's afraid her boss will throw her out." Aaron's forehead wrinkled. "Her father died a few years ago and her family is deeply in debt. This is the only way she can help support her family."

Jace looked over at Lacy again as she moved around the bar. The sunny smile she'd given Aaron was gone, and he saw the desperation, pain, and hopelessness in her eyes that he knew too well. She might not be a slave, but she was trapped in her life the same as he'd once been, forced to do things that slowly destroyed a person inside. Compassion settled inside of him, and he turned back to Aaron.

"I hope she'll come sometime." She needed Elôm, desperately.

Aaron nodded slowly. "Me too."

They were silent for a moment. Aaron finally took the drink of his ale, and Jace watched him. Perhaps it was being around Kyrin so much, but Jace was getting better at reading the little clues to people's emotions.

Aaron caught him staring. He then looked at Holden and frowned. "What?"

Jace glanced over at his friend who wore a slight smile.

"She's pretty," Holden said.

Aaron huffed. "Since when did you two become match-makers? I thought that was old Mrs. Hess's job."

The old woman back at camp, who had once set her sights on Rayad, was notorious for trying to set people up. Holden chuckled and shared a smile with Jace, but Aaron didn't say anything more in protest. He just shook his head and stared at his ale. When he looked up again, his chagrined expression turned serious.

"Looks like we've got company."

Jace stiffened and whipped his head around to look toward the door. A group of men strode straight for their table. The brawny man at the head stared Aaron down. Jace let his hand slide toward his sword, though he did not draw it. He didn't want to invite trouble.

Without even a word of greeting, the man pulled out a chair and sat down just to Jace's right, directly across from Aaron. The men spread out behind him. Jace took stock of them and their weapons. Each looked ready for a fight. Heat curled through his blood. He let it simmer, ready in case he needed it.

"I hear you've been asking a lot of questions."

The man's rough voice drew Jace's attention back to the table.

Aaron eyed the man coolly. "You're Tavor?"

"Maybe."

Jace took stock of him now. His sturdy clothing pointed to more of a woodsman than a man of the city. The end of his longsword scabbard rested on the floor, and the hilt of a large dagger protruded on the other side of his belt. His worn and calloused hands said he wasn't afraid of rough work.

"We're looking for Lord Avery." Aaron gestured to Jace and Holden.

Tavor sent them each a piercing glance. The man was no ryrik, but he certainly had the ferocity of one.

"What for?"

"Business." Aaron sat up straighter, not appearing intimidated by the man before them. "He has supplies, we have money."

Tavor narrowed his eyes and stared at him for a long moment. "What do you need?"

"The remedy. We have friends sick and many more in danger of getting it."

The man contemplated the request and then pushed to his feet. Jace was afraid he would just leave, but he said, "The Red Crane tomorrow at noon. Just the three of you. If you show up with anyone else, we'll drag you off to the queen." He leaned over the table, leering at Aaron. "We know who you are and what you're worth."

He then turned and strode out of the tavern with the other men. Once the door closed behind them, Jace, Holden, and Aaron looked at each other.

"Well, I guess we have our meeting with Avery," Aaron said.

It wasn't the quick meeting Jace had hoped for, but he would take it. Tavor could have refused them . . . or worse. The thought of the man knowing they were followers of Elôm made the back of Jace's neck prickle.

Aaron pushed back his chair. "We might as well head back to Ben's and let them know. We'll need more money before tomorrow."

Leaving their half-empty mugs behind, they headed for the door. Aaron sent Lacy a smile on the way out. Matchmaker or not, Jace wouldn't be surprised if something grew between the two

150

of them—that is, if Lacy could find a way out of this life and come to know Elôm. If not, Aaron was likely in for heartache.

Back out in the cold, they trudged through the streets, away from the more lawless area of the city. Jace was glad to arrive back at Ben's large house, out of the cold and the unsavoriness of the tavern and its patrons. Mira had hot coffee waiting for them, and they gathered in the living room.

"At least you got a meeting," Ben said. "I'll have to see about gathering funds for you. I'm sure everyone will give what they can."

Mira took a sip of her coffee and focused on Aaron, "Did you see Lacy?"

So she knew of the pretty barmaid. It seemed Aaron's interest, whether romantic or not, was no secret.

"Yes."

"How is she?"

"Still working at the Briar," Aaron responded rather glumly. He shot Jace and Holden a look as if warning them to keep their thoughts and speculations to themselves. "We didn't have a chance to talk."

"That poor girl," Mira fussed. "I do pray Elôm gives her the courage to at least visit us. You did tell her she's welcome here, didn't you?"

Aaron nodded. "I did. I don't believe she thinks she's fit for your company. But I'll invite her again when I get a chance."

"You do that. We're more than willing to do what we can to get her out of that place."

Jace had to smile. He'd heard Daniel speak of Ben and Mira's kindness and compassion, but seeing it himself made him think of Kalli and Aldor. They were very much alike—inviting into their home people who most would shun.

After downing the last of his coffee, Ben rose from his chair. He looked at Aaron and Timothy. "We should start gathering that money. If this is our one chance to meet with Avery, we'd better make sure we make it worth his while."

LYDIA SAT NEXT to the bed and stared at Kyrin. The thought of losing another child left a chill deep in her bones and a gnawing panic inside her chest. She begged Elôm to heal Kyrin and to keep the boys from getting the fever too. They'd all had such precious little time together as it was.

"Here, Mother, drink this."

She startled and looked up. Kaden held a mug out to her with some of the broth they'd made. She had forgone supper the night before, her stomach too knotted with worry. It didn't feel any better now, but the way Kaden's expression drew together in concern prompted her to action. She mustered a smile and took the mug. "Thank you."

He remained standing there a moment as she took a sip, and then he walked back to the table where he and Marcus quietly prepared breakfast. Lydia glanced across Kyrin's bed. Liam sat asleep in his chair on the other side. He'd worked so hard these days, caring for so many people. It was good that he could rest for a time. She'd never imagined him as a physician's assistant, but he certainly had the compassion for it. If only she had realized and encouraged his strengths sooner.

She took another sip of the warm broth and blinked sleepily. Liam had already admonished her in his own quiet way concerning her lack of rest. But how could she sleep when her child was so sick?

Several minutes later, Kyrin mumbled. Though her eyes remained closed, her lips moved with quiet, unintelligible words. Her hands shifted fitfully under the blankets, and her breathing quickened. Lydia set her mug aside and stood, laying her hand on Kyrin's cheek. Heat radiated into her palm. She felt her daughter's other cheek and then her forehead. Even the cold compress didn't dispel the warmth. *Please no.*

"Mother?"

The worry in Kaden's voice forced her to face facts. She looked back at him and Marcus. "Her fever is getting worse. I need fresh snow."

They both dropped what they were doing. Marcus grabbed a bowl and headed for the door, while Kaden hurried to Kyrin's bed with Ronny, whose face paled with fright. The commotion woke Liam. He too felt Kyrin's face and forehead and then reached for his coat. "I'll get Josef."

When Marcus brought in the snow, Lydia made fresh compresses and draped them over Kyrin's head and neck. Her mumbling increased.

"Father," she cried softly. Her eyes fluttered open, though she clearly wasn't aware of anything.

Lydia glanced at Kaden and smoothed Kyrin's hair. "It's all right, we're here," she said softly.

Liam returned a couple of minutes later with Josef. The old physician's eyes were bloodshot with exhaustion. He set his small medical bag on the bed and examined Kyrin. His tight-lipped expression did nothing to soothe Lydia's fears. Finally, he reached for his bag again.

"We need to get more tea into her. I'll make something stronger. It will be bitter and hard to get down, but the more she can take, the better."

He sorted through his bag for the right herbs, and Lydia rushed to put a kettle of water on to boil. When she returned to the bed, Josef said, "Roll up her sleeves and bathe her arms and chest with cool water. It will help in bringing the fever down."

Lydia pushed aside the covers and rolled up the sleeves of Kyrin's nightgown, which was damp with perspiration. When she rolled up the right sleeve, it revealed the brown trillium tattoo Kyrin had gotten in memory of her father. Lydia's ribcage tightened around her lungs. If only William were here now to help them through this. She desperately missed her husband's strength. Strength she had never appreciated until now when he was gone. Hot tears seared her eyes, but she blinked them back as Marcus brought her a basin.

She dunked a cloth into the cool water and dabbed Kyrin's burning skin. Liam moved to the other side of the bed and did the same, while Kaden, Marcus, and Ronny looked on helplessly. Such heaviness rested around them that Lydia felt she might break under the weight of it. *Please Elôm, don't take any more of my children.* The silent, broken plea ached inside of her. She didn't feel her faith was strong enough for this. Not yet.

For the next hour, they continued their ministrations, and Josef helped Kyrin drink as much tea as she could get down. Every minute of waiting and praying passed in agony. At last, the fever subsided a bit, and Kyrin rested quietly. Only then did Lydia breathe more easily.

With the danger passed for the moment, Liam followed Josef to help with the others, saying he'd be back to check Kyrin in a little while. Marcus left as well to check on his militia. The cabin grew quiet, and Lydia looked over at Kaden, who had claimed the chair on the other side of Kyrin's bed.

"If you want, you can check on your men. Ronny can go with you and get some fresh air."

Kaden said nothing for a moment but then shook his head.

"I don't want to leave you in case . . ." he cleared his throat, "in case she gets worse again."

Lydia straightened, fighting to draw strength she didn't have. It wouldn't do any good to have all of them sitting around just waiting for the worst.

"I'll be fine. I'm sure Liam will check in before long."

At first, it didn't seem that Kaden would move. He just stared at Kyrin as if sheer willpower alone could cure her. Finally, he stood. "We won't be gone long." He motioned to his little brother. "Come on, Ronny."

They walked to the door and pulled on their coats as they left the cabin. Silence fell again. Lydia drew a deep breath and rubbed her hands over her skirt, battling the tears that bit her eyes with a vengeance now that she was alone.

But she didn't fight it for long. After a moment, she gave in and let the tears fall. She covered her mouth as deep sobs seized her chest and wracked her body. She couldn't do this. She couldn't sit and watch her children slowly die. What if her sons fell ill? What if she lost all of them? She would have no one left. She could barely breathe through the agony of that possibility and the desperate cries that clawed her throat.

The darkness of such a bleak future almost suffocated her until a knock came at the door. She gasped for breath and struggled to get a hold of herself. Wiping her cheeks with her sleeves, she forced herself to her feet at the third knock and answered the door. Aric stood on the other side. When he saw her tear-streaked face, his brow knotted.

"I heard about Kyrin. Is she all right?"

"Her fever is back down." Lydia's words barely choked past her swollen throat.

She stepped aside to let Aric in, out of the cold. When he closed the door, he rested his hand on her shoulder. "Are you all right?"

She bit her lip, the emotions threatening to overwhelm her again, but she just didn't have the strength. "No," she cried, the tears starting fresh. No more words would come. She buried her face in her hands.

A moment later, Aric grasped her shoulders and pulled her close, wrapping his arms around her. Lydia melted into him and abandoned her struggle for strength. She had not been held in so long. Right now it was exactly what she needed.

Liam ground the pestle against the dried herbs in the mortar, working on a new, stronger batch of tea while Josef checked on others throughout camp. All around him, men coughed and groaned as their fevers led to delirium. He glanced up to make sure Leetra didn't need help holding anyone down. Not that she typically needed help. Small as she was, the girl was strong and not at all timid about what needed to be done.

If only Liam had an ounce of her confidence and gumption. She certainly had enough to spare. She'd scared the wits out of him before he'd gotten to know her.

"How is Kyrin?"

Liam looked up, slightly startled by his grandfather's voice. He was the last person Liam wanted to deal with during this crisis. How was he supposed to respond to a man who had caused him nothing but grief his entire life?

He cleared his throat. "Her fever spiked. It's back down now, but she's not getting better."

He returned his attention to his work. He wouldn't be distracted. But now his thoughts drifted back to Kyrin. If her fever spiked again . . . He shook his head. He had to be optimistic. It was the only way he could do this job—with hope that his efforts would make a difference. This was especially true when it came to his family. He dragged in a hard breath, his vision going a bit blurry with moisture. He blinked it away and forced himself to focus.

The meeting hall door opened and closed, but he didn't look up until footsteps approached. When he raised his eyes, they rested on a slim young woman, her dark blonde hair in a long braid over her shoulder. She had arrived in camp with her brother shortly before the first snowfall. What was her name again? It started with a C . . .

He racked his brains. Her lovely brown eyes trained on him turned his thoughts to a blank, useless mush. He'd noticed how pretty she was right away but had never worked up the guts to talk to her. Especially with how sad she'd seemed her first several weeks here. He'd been too afraid of blundering through an awkward introduction.

Exactly what he was doing now.

He grimaced internally as the silence between them grew. Why couldn't he at least remember her name?

She took another step closer, a gentle smile easing the awkwardness a bit. "Is there anything I can do to help?"

Liam hesitated. Cassie! That was her name. A lot of good that would do him now. He cleared his throat and heat flushed his face. Great, he probably looked like a tomato. "I'm afraid . . . I'm not very good at . . . explaining things."

He was good at following and retaining Josef's instructions, but relaying them to someone else was a different thing entirely. His cheeks burned hotter. He'd never claimed to be particularly intelligent, but making an utter fool of himself was never his intent either. So far he was doing an outstanding job.

However, Cassie's smile only grew, and she pulled off her knitted gloves. "That's all right. I know what to do."

She laid the gloves aside and reached for Josef's extra mortar and pestle. Liam stood motionless as he watched her measure out each of the herbs for the tea with practiced ease. As she ground them together, he stood in silence for another few seconds before his brain would form a suitable response.

"Are you a physician?"

She looked up at him, her smile taking on a wistfully sad quality. "Not quite, but I was training with my father, who was a surgeon . . . before he died."

"I didn't know that," Liam said quietly. He winced. He should have said something more sympathetic. Her father had been executed in Valcré for being a believer—something he understood all too well.

Before he could think of something more to say, Cassie spoke again. "It's hard to talk about and doing this reminds me so much of him that I thought I'd give it up . . . but people need help, and my father wouldn't want me to turn my back on them."

Liam looked at her with respect. "I'm sorry . . . about your father."

"Thank you." Sympathy warmed her eyes. "I'm sorry about yours too."

They worked in silence for a time. When Josef returned, he thanked Cassie for joining them. With a fresh pot of tea, Liam went around to administer it to their patients, starting with the most serious cases. The first soldiers who had fallen ill appeared so gaunt and pale that it was a wonder they had not died yet. Liam had found it difficult at first to care for them, but that was a physician's job. It didn't matter who it was.

When he turned to get more tea, he noticed Leetra watching Josef intently. The physician looked nearly dead on his feet with exhaustion. Not a one of them had seen more than a couple of hours of sleep at a time in days. Apparently making up her mind, Leetra strode over to Josef and all but ordered him to sit down. He sank wearily down on an empty cot, a cup of tea in one hand and a basin in the other. Liam approached slowly, a knot forming in his gut. Cassie drew near as well.

With a tight-lipped expression, Leetra put her hand to Josef's forehead. Then she checked beneath the collar of his shirt, confirming what she must have suspected. "You're sick."

Liam's stomach cramped more tightly. Josef tried to rise, but Leetra held him in place.

"I can still help," he said.

The crete shook her head stubbornly. "Not a chance. You'll just collapse. Now lie down and rest."

Not even Josef seemed able to argue with her. With a heavy sigh, he handed over the cup and basin and did as instructed. Leetra traded a grave look with both Liam and Cassie. It was up to the three of them now to oversee the medical care of this camp.

Jace held the money close as he and Holden followed Aaron through Valcré again. Traveling a similar path to the one they had the evening before, they entered the rough part of the city. It wasn't too far from the old bell tower where he had hidden with Kyrin and her brothers when they'd rescued the boys and Meredith from Tarvin Hall. A deep ache engulfed the center of Jace's chest just thinking of Kyrin. How was she doing? Could she possibly be getting better? Or was she worse? He tried to shake off these questions and focus on what would heal her.

A couple of blocks from the tavern they had visited previously, Aaron brought them to a looming building with a large sign hanging out front—the Red Crane Inn. They stepped inside the establishment. Though much larger than the tavern from yesterday, it was just as dingy and distasteful. They paused as Aaron scanned the patrons.

"Do you know what Avery looks like?" Jace asked quietly. Any of the younger men sitting around the tables could be him.

Aaron shook his head. "No, but I think that's one of his men in the back."

Jace followed his line of sight to a scruffy man giving them a dour look. Aaron strode ahead, and they crossed the crowded tavern. The man rose from his table as they approached, his hand on his sword.

"You the ones wanting to see his lordship?" he asked in a low growl when they reached him.

Aaron nodded.

The man jerked his head. "This way."

He led them through a dim hall to the inn's private rooms. Prickles crawled up Jace's back. What if it was a trap? For all they knew, Davira's men could be waiting for them while Avery sat counting his reward money in a different tavern. But they had to follow the man. They wouldn't get the remedy otherwise. Besides, these men were just as likely to be arrested as they were. It wasn't much of a comfort, but it was something.

At the far end of the hall, the man knocked four times on a closed door. It swung open a moment later. Tavor stood silhouetted by the candlelight inside. He gave Jace, Holden, and Aaron a shrewd look before focusing on the other man.

"They came alone?"

He nodded.

"All right, go back and keep watch," Tavor ordered.

As the other man marched back down the hall, Tavor motioned Jace and the others into the room. Jace quickly scanned the occupants. Two more heavily armed men stood near a round table, while a third man sat casually at the head. Jace focused on him. He was about Daniel's age and black-haired. His clothing, though practical, had enough detailing to suggest wealth, especially the subtly-brocaded, deep scarlet jerkin beneath his black leather coat. Despite his comfortable posture, his dark eyes were very observant.

"I hear you gentlemen are looking to do business." He spoke smoothly and with a tone of refinement, but Avery clearly wasn't afraid to get his hands dirty if he'd managed to put together an operation like this. Not to mention taking out the emperor.

"Yes," Aaron answered.

Avery waved to the empty chairs. "Have a seat."

The three of them approached the table and sat down. As they settled in, Avery held up a dark-tinted bottle. "Wine?"

Jace glanced at Aaron. He wasn't interested in the wine but didn't want to offend Avery by refusing. Social rules were not his strong suit.

Aaron accepted, and Avery poured them each a glass. Jace took a sip. He didn't know anything about wine, but it tasted expensive, and he hadn't used such fine goblets since he'd dined with his family at Ashwood.

After taking an appreciative drink from his own glass, Alex once more focused on them. "What can I do for you?"

Jace hoped his sociable manner boded well for them.

"We need the remedy for the fever," Aaron told him.

Alex nodded as if this was a common request. "How much do you need?"

Aaron glanced at Jace and Holden before answering. Between the congregation here and the number of people back at camp, this would be no small request. "Enough for about five hundred. Whatever we don't need we can return to you."

Alex's brows lifted and then he laughed. "You're joking, right?"

None of them spoke. Jace didn't find anything amusing about the situation, and he was sure it showed on his face.

Once Alex realized they were serious, his incredulous smile faded. "Well, I hope you've brought payment. That remedy doesn't come free or cheap."

Aaron set the bag of money he and Ben had gathered on the table, and Jace set his bag next to it. Alex eyed them and then reached across the table to inspect the contents. With one brow raised, he looked at Aaron.

"That's it?" He settled back in his chair. "I think you gentlemen underestimate what this remedy is worth."

The beginning of fear wormed its way through Jace's gut. They had to get the remedy.

"That's all we have," Aaron said coolly.

Alex gave a shrug. "Sorry, but that's not going to get you what you're after."

Jace breathed harder, his lungs feeling like they'd shrunk a bit. "How much will it get us?"

Alex looked at the bags again. "Enough for about forty, maybe fifty people."

Jace's heart plummeted. There were nearly that many sick people here among the believers in Valcré alone. No doubt the number at camp would soon match and likely surpass it.

"We need more than that," Aaron said.

"Well then, you'd better find some more money."

Jace ground his teeth, the temperature of his blood rising with his desperation. "I thought you were the one people came to when they needed help."

Alex pierced Jace with a cold look. "Most people only need one or two vials for a handful of people, but you're talking a village. That's a good chunk of my supply and worth a whole lot more than what you're offering."

Jace struggled to keep his blood cool. Kyrin's life was essentially in this man's hands. Life was worth more than a thousand bags of coins.

"Now, before you go accusing me of being a greedy cad," Alex said as if reading Jace's mind, "do you have any idea how many men I have working for me in this city? Do you know the kind of funds it takes to feed and clothe them all? I'm not greedy; I'm just trying to keep this business going. A business you'll find has been quite generous to those less fortunate if you ask around."

Jace rubbed his forehead, the same helplessness he'd felt seeing Kyrin collapse outside the cabin returning in full force. What could they do now? Then he remembered what Daniel had told them before they left. He didn't fully trust Alex, but they were running out of options.

"We're from the Resistance camp in Landale." He nodded toward Holden. "The same camp that is sheltering King Balen and Prince Daniel. If we don't get the remedy, they could die. They are our best chance of righting things in Ilyon. Surely you can't have any love for Davira."

Alex snorted. "That witch? Had I known she would steal the throne, I would've poisoned her too. Don't think I haven't tried since."

Jace looked him dead in the eye. "Then help us. We need that remedy if we are to have a chance of restoring Balen and Daniel to their thrones and ending Davira's rule."

"Both Arcacia and Samara are suffering under Davira's tyranny and Daniel and Balen are fugitives. So far, you're doing a splendid job of righting things."

His sarcasm grated deeply on Jace's already frayed nerves. The man didn't take them seriously, never mind the lives they had saved over the years.

"I'll give you what you pay for," Alex continued, "which will be more than enough for Daniel and King Balen. Beyond that, you'll have to come up with a way to pay for whatever more you want."

Jace clenched his fists under the table. How would they ever choose who received the remedy and who didn't? He could see Rayad and several of his other closest friends refusing it so that others could have it. Refusing it and dying. And if they made this deal now, they would have nothing more to bargain with. No chance of getting any more of the remedy.

As a last-ditch effort, Jace said, "What about Prince Daniel? As rightful king, would you refuse him what we need?"

For a long moment, Alex stared at him, and Jace prayed desperately he would relent.

In a low voice, Alex finally spoke. "Daniel may be the rightful king, but I am a smuggler outside of the law. I am not bound by a king's commands."

This declaration felt like a blow to the gut as the last of Jace's withering hope died.

"Now," Alex said, "unless you're willing to do business on my terms, my men will show you out."

They sat in silence for a moment, the air around them growing heavy with tension. Finally, Aaron stood and picked up his bag of money. Apparently, he wasn't ready to give up their only bargaining piece just yet. Jace followed more slowly, every muscle taut. Part of him wanted to stay and fight, but that wasn't the way. This was not an instance where he could fight to save the lives of those he loved. And that was the worst part.

DANIEL STEPPED OUT of Trask's cabin and released a heavy sigh into the frigid air. The meeting that had just concluded consisted of only himself, Trask, Balen, Sam, and Captain Darq. Nearly half the camp was sick now, including Warin. Daniel could sense the underlying panic that threatened to overtake their community.

That panic weighed heavily on his mind as he set out through camp. He glanced at the sky that seemed to be in as bleak a mood as he was. "I have no idea what to do, Elôm. I want to help these people—my people—but I don't know how. Please, give Jace and Holden success in Valcré. We need that remedy."

By the time he finished his prayer, he stood at the door of the meeting hall. He opened it and stepped inside, scanning the room. It was nearly full now with the sick. The only ones not lying on cots or blankets on the floor were their remaining physicians and volunteers as well as the only two soldiers who had not fallen ill. One of them was General Veshiron. It couldn't be pleasant to be surrounded by sick people day after day, but they were the ones who had brought the fever here. Daniel couldn't summon much in the way of sympathy toward them.

All thoughts of the soldiers vanished in a blink when his gaze caught on one of the volunteers. Elanor sat beside one of the cots, dabbing a cloth over Josef's face. Daniel admired her bravery. Here she was in the thick of things when others in camp went out of their way to keep their exposure to the fever at a minimum. A woman like that would make a great queen one day . . .

However, such a future was a long way off, especially considering their current plight. Even so, she had a way of brightening his spirits. He felt rather foolish at how distracted he'd been by her just after arriving in camp last summer and hoped no one had noticed. After all, he'd been exhausted, in pain, and still half-dazed by everything. At least that's what he told himself.

Setting her cloth aside, Elanor reached up and brushed a couple of strands of dark hair out of her face. Daniel drew his brows together. Her face looked pale in the candlelight, her expression sagging with weariness. His stomach turned to rock. What if she was falling ill?

He strode across the room. "Are you all right?"

Her head snapped up in surprise. "Daniel." She then nodded. "I'm all right."

His gaze dropped to her neck. Though there was no sign of the telltale rash, his concern didn't subside. Before he could stop himself, he pressed his fingers to her forehead, and then to her cheek. It was warm, but not overly. Warm . . . and soft. His heart gave his chest a powerful thud as memories of their first kiss the other day rushed to mind. He met her gaze, and a small smile lifted her lips.

"Your fingers are cold."

He jerked his hand away. "Oh, I'm sorry." Even though they had kissed, he should be more careful about taking such liberties.

Her smile widened. "That's all right."

Daniel cleared his throat, his own face and neck a bit warm. He looked around the hall in an attempt to compose himself. He'd always been so good at flirting . . . too good. So why did he find himself so awkward and stupid with her? Maybe because it had never mattered with anyone else.

Regaining some semblance of control, he turned back to her and smiled. "Do you want to have lunch with me?"

Elanor's brows lifted, and she cast a glance at Josef, who lay unconscious on the cot next to her.

"I think he would agree that eating and taking a break now and then is a good idea to keep you healthy," Daniel said.

Elanor's smile returned. "You're right." She stood. "I'll be right back."

She crossed the room to Leetra. Apparently, the crete had taken over in Josef's unplanned absence. When Leetra nodded, Elanor retrieved her coat and turned back toward him. He met her in the middle of the hall and offered his arm. Her brows lifted again.

"What? Even if it's just a simple lunch with Trask and Anne, a lady should be properly escorted."

Elanor laughed lightly, a wonderful sound in this gloomy place. He loved that she still held so firmly to hope.

She slipped her hand around his arm and squeezed gently. "Thank you."

Daniel grinned and led her outside.

Liam hadn't been so bone-weary since the battle in Samara. There were far too many sick now and barely enough volunteers. Elôm would have to provide superhuman strength to care for everyone. Between administering tea and changing compresses, he barely had a moment to catch his breath.

As he returned to the table for fresh tea leaves, a loud metallic banging grabbed his attention. He looked to the only two soldiers who had not fallen ill yet—the General and one of Dagren's men. Dagren's soldier slammed his tin cup against the floor and sent Liam a scowl.

"When are we going to get some food?"

It was past noon now, and they'd been so busy that Liam hadn't even eaten yet. Their prisoners were the last people on everyone's mind, especially when there wasn't much food to go around.

Liam ignored the man and his incessant cup banging. There were more important things to worry about.

"Did you hear me, boy? I said when are we going to eat?" The soldier sneered. "Or are you too slow to understand? I heard that's why you were never a good soldier."

Liam gritted his teeth and fought back the reaction to the man's words. He knew better now, but such insults did still carry a bit of a sting and bring back memories.

The soldier slammed his cup down harder, threatening to give Liam a headache. He could only imagine how it would disturb those here clinging desperately to life. Before he could respond, a firm female voice cut through the racket.

"*Enough.*"

Liam looked over to see Cassie standing there, hands planted on her hips, glaring down at the soldier. His first instinct was to back her up, but she appeared to have the situation well handled.

"There are people dying here, thanks to you, and we are doing everything we can to save them, including your comrades. Instead of complaining, be thankful you are not yet one of them, and keep in mind, that the man you seem bent on insulting is one of the physicians who will be tending you if you do fall ill." Her eyes flashed and shifted to Liam's grandfather. "And you,

General, you may be a prisoner, but you are still a general. I expect you to keep your men in line."

Liam had never heard anyone speak to the General that way before. It was one of the most incredible things he'd ever seen. He just stared at her as she gave the other soldier one last warning look and then turned to Liam.

"Why don't you check on Josef? I'll put more tea on." Her voice and manner had returned to its normal, gentle tone.

All Liam could do was nod. As he turned away to check Josef, he heard the General order the other soldier in a low voice, "Not another word."

Despite everything, Liam couldn't help but smile.

Kaden trudged through the snow, his hands stuffed in his pockets. While he wanted to spend every moment near Kyrin, he loathed the inaction. He felt so helpless sitting there. He needed to *do* something. Not that there was much to do in this situation, but he could make it a habit to check on his men at least once a day. He did still have that responsibility even if his personal life had been turned upside down.

He'd just left the last cabin his dragon riders shared. Several of them had fallen ill—some doing well and others in more serious condition. He glanced at the meeting hall-turned-infirmary. Indignation stirred inside his stomach like a spoiled meal. If the soldiers had never attacked—if his grandfather had never led the attack—Michael would still be here and Kyrin and so many others would not be fighting for their lives too.

With these thoughts still brewing like a storm inside of him, he veered to his right and came to the cabin Jace shared with some of their friends. He'd made a point of checking on Rayad while Jace was away. It was the least he could do. When he stepped inside, he surveyed the occupied beds. Besides Rayad, Mick and Elian were sick now. None of the three were conscious, though Elian didn't appear as sick as some. What would happen if more people fell ill than there were healthy people to care for them? They already felt stretched thin. He shook the thought away. No use borrowing more trouble. He just prayed Jace and Holden returned soon . . . with the remedy.

Kaden quietly crossed the cabin to join Trev who sat between Rayad and Mick. Tyra lay on the floor near Trev's feet and looked up at Kaden with eyes that seemed to share his concern. Kaden reached down to rub her ears but grimaced at the sight of Rayad's gaunt, fever-dampened face. "How is he?"

Trev glanced at him. The shadows and redness of his eyes proved that he hadn't slept much in the last couple of days. Kaden doubted his own appearance was any improvement.

Trev shook his head regretfully. "Weaker. It's getting harder to keep him hydrated. He hasn't been awake at all since yesterday."

Kaden grabbed an empty chair to set near Trev and sank down with a heavy sigh. "What has Leetra said?"

"There's nothing we can do but try to keep him cool and get as much liquid into him as we can."

Kaden watched Rayad in silence, focusing on the rise and fall of his chest. It appeared difficult for him, and a wheezing came with each breath. Kaden had heard that a couple of the sick members of camp were starting to get better, but he could find no such improvement in Rayad. His stomach clenched as reality settled. Rayad wouldn't get better. Not without the remedy. If Jace and Holden didn't make it back soon . . .

Kaden cleared his swelling throat. Ever since his father had died, Rayad had been something of a father figure to him. He wasn't ready for such a loss. Especially not with Michael gone so recently.

Kaden stayed for a while longer, talking quietly with Trev and helping in any way he could, though it mostly involved sitting and waiting. Finally, when it neared suppertime, he took his leave.

Stepping back out into the freezing air, he looked around. He stared at his cabin a moment, but still felt he had things to work through before he could go back to sitting and waiting for the evening. Aric had been there when he'd left. He would come to get him if Kyrin's fever spiked.

So he started walking again. Rayad's condition weighed on him. He passed the meeting hall, and the anger toward his grandfather swelled once more. But it wasn't necessarily the anger he found so difficult to deal with—it was the bigger questions it led to.

He had prayed more in the last few days than he probably ever had before but, as more and more fell ill, it grew more difficult. *I don't get it, Elôm. I just don't understand any of this.* And that was what was so hard. How could this fit in Elôm's plans? Wouldn't things be better going forward if they were stronger, not weaker? Kaden shook his head, suddenly wishing Timothy were here. He could use his friend's spiritual wisdom right now.

Still struggling with the why of it, he paused near the edge of camp where the soldiers had first attacked. Fresh snow had erased the signs of the struggle, but it couldn't erase how it had affected all of them. What purpose could Elôm have in allowing such an attack? Or in letting it further devastate them with this fever? He breathed hard and tried to blink away the burning in his eyes.

Snow crunched behind him. He glanced over his shoulder as Marcus joined him. They nodded to each other and then just stood in silence for a moment as they both stared into the trees. Working down the lump in his throat, Kaden finally asked, "How are your men?"

"We lost two this morning." His voice was low and it sounded to Kaden like his throat was thick too.

"I'm sorry," he murmured.

Marcus nodded slightly. "What about your men?"

"Hanging on for now, but I don't know how long that will last." Kaden glanced at the sky, longing to see Jace and Holden's dragons appear.

Again, silence fell between them. Kaden didn't intend to speak his thoughts out loud, but they came anyway.

"How many of us do you think will be left once this is over?"

The question hung heavy in the cold air. When Marcus didn't answer, Kaden looked over at him. His older brother's face was set with the look of calm determination that Kaden was used to, but his eyes gave away his shared uncertainty. It took another moment before he spoke.

"I don't know." There was nothing optimistic about it, just a quiet, painful honesty. He took a deep breath as if strengthening himself and turned to Kaden. "But enough to carry out Elôm's plans, whatever they may be."

Kaden stared at his brother for a long moment. He still read the questions and uncertainties that battled within him—the same ones Kaden struggled with—but, despite them, Marcus had accepted this as Elôm's will, and there was peace in that. It bolstered the weak areas in Kaden's faith, and he nodded firmly.

ALL NIGHT LONG, Jace tossed and turned, sleep coming in rare snatches as he struggled to find a way—*any* way—to get the remedy from Avery. After the meeting, Aaron and Ben had discussed where they could get more money, but the facts were undeniable. They couldn't get more, at least not enough for what they needed. There just weren't enough people in their congregation with anything to spare.

Images of Kyrin and Rayad lying at camp, sick . . . dying, tormented him when he tried to sleep. He reached out to Elôm constantly, but it didn't alleviate the fear coursing through him like a violent, icy river. He *had* to figure something out. He could not let them die.

When dawn arrived, Jace slid out of bed in one of Ben and Mira's guest rooms and trudged downstairs. His entire body felt heavy with the lack of sleep and weight of his concerns. Voices drew him into the living room. Ben and Holden sat near the fireplace, their low tones echoing their helplessness.

"Has Aaron come by?" Jace asked as he joined them. Knowing Aaron, he hadn't slept much either, and he'd mentioned something the night before about visiting some friends to find out if they could share any funds. Jace prayed this would yield something, but doubt had a firm hold on him this morning.

Ben shook his head. "Not yet."

Silence fell. Without good news, there didn't seem to be much to talk about. After a moment or two of mulling over his thoughts, Jace asked, "How quickly does the fever kill?"

Ben and Holden both looked at him. It wasn't really a question he wanted answered, but he had to know. Ben appeared as reluctant to share the answer as Jace was to hear it.

"How soon do infected people usually die from it?"

Ben let out a heavy breath. "It is highly dependent on the person and their health to begin with. Younger, healthier people have held on for two weeks or more. For others, it's been three to six days. Quicker if they were in poor health prior."

Jace gritted his teeth. Rayad wasn't in poor health other than his wound from the attack, but he wasn't young either. Six days had already passed since he'd fallen ill. An ice-cold stone formed in Jace's stomach and worked its way up to lodge in his throat. Rayad was already on borrowed time, if he was alive at all.

He pushed to his feet. "I'm going for a walk."

Sitting here waiting would drive him mad.

Holden rose as well, but Jace held up his hand. "I think I'd like to go alone." He had things to think about and consider—things to do if all went as he hoped and prayed they would. Things it would be easier to do without Holden's influence.

Slowly, his friend returned to his seat. "Be careful out there."

"I will," Jace replied quietly as he turned for the door. He was far more afraid of what was happening back at camp than the dangers of Valcré's streets.

At the front door, he pulled on his coat and gloves and buckled on his sword before he let himself out. The cold blasted him after the warmth of being near the fire, sending a shiver down his back. He glanced up at the sky. A peek at the sun or the slightest hint of its warmth would have been a welcome and almost hopeful sign, but dark gray clouds choked out any hint of it. He pulled his collar close against his neck and set off away from the house, resting his hand on his sword hilt.

Careful to scan the streets for any danger, Jace headed in the direction of the taverns. He tried not to think too deeply about what he had in mind. If it could save Kyrin, Rayad, and the others, he had to do it. Still, an ache grew inside his chest around his heart. He forced it down. This could be Kyrin's only hope for survival. How could he not take it?

When the Red Crane came into view, he drew a hard breath to steel himself. Avery probably wouldn't even be there this time of day, but Jace prayed he would. He had no time to waste trying to find the smuggler. Turning the knob, he pushed the door open and stepped into the tavern's dim interior. So close to dawn, the main room was nearly empty, yet a few men occupied the tables, including one who looked like he'd passed out there with his overturned mug of ale the night before.

The barkeeper sent Jace a probing glance but said nothing. Ignoring him, Jace scanned the room. His heart gave an elevated thump. One of the men at the back corner table had been in the room guarding Avery yesterday. Jace set out across the room. He was halfway there when the man spotted him. His brows creased as he eyed Jace, his hand dropping to his sword. Jace stopped a couple of feet from the table and stared the man down.

"I need to speak to Avery."

The man traded a glance with his companions before fixing his keen eyes back on Jace. "Have you brought adequate payment?"

Jace took care to keep his voice even. Riling the man would not help the situation. "No, but I have something else I think he'll want. Something worth a small fortune."

The man seemed to take stock of Jace before lazily pushing away from the table. "This way."

They headed for the hall to the back rooms. Jace breathed out slowly, relief and hope mingling with the persistent ache writhing inside of him. He'd gained his audience with Avery, but now he had to go through with it. At one of the doors, they paused, and the man tapped the door with his knuckle. It opened partially a moment later, and Tavor stood on the other side. He took one glance at Jace, and then opened the door wider to let him in.

Jace stepped through and found Avery reclining at the table, a half-eaten plate of eggs and sausages set before him. His dark eyes locked on Jace, and a half-smile lifted his lips.

"Ready to do business, are we?" He tilted his head as he looked Jace up and down. "I don't see anything that could contain the payment we talked about. Where are your friends?"

Jace took a step toward the table, careful not to appear too threatening. "I have a different proposition for you."

"Have a seat."

Jace pulled out the chair across from him and sat down. His stomach knotted, but he forced the sensation away. "We can't get the money we need, but I do have something to trade for the remedy."

"And what might that be?"

Jace's mouth went dry, his tongue growing thick in his mouth at the sick feeling in the pit of his stomach. He had to do this. If only it didn't hurt so much. "I have a dragon."

Avery's brows rose. "A dragon?"

Jace drew a strangled breath and tried not to choke on his own voice. "Yes."

"Now that *is* a tempting offer. Under different circumstances, I'd take it; however, considering how hard it is just to keep people fed this winter, the cost of feeding a dragon would outweigh its worth."

A warped mix of sheer disappointment and relief swirled inside Jace. Avery would really turn down a dragon? Though the thought of giving up Gem had torn him up, the gnawing desperation to save Kyrin was even worse. Why was this man so determined to thwart their every effort?

His heart pounded loudly in his ears, his blood warming. His voice strained through his tight throat. "We *need* that remedy. People are dying."

Avery's good-natured expression dimmed. "People are dying all around us, thanks to our queen," he spat. "You're not the only ones in dire need."

Jace clenched his fists. Avery was right, of course. In reality, their camp was but a small part of the thousands who suffered because of Davira. However, that didn't mean Jace would stop fighting to save those he loved.

A flicker of knowing amusement returned to Avery's eyes. "You're not here for your resistance camp, are you?"

Jace frowned. "What do you mean?"

"You're not here for the good of your cause; you're here for someone in particular . . . someone special. It wouldn't happen to be Miss Kyrin Altair, would it?"

Jace stiffened. What did Avery know of Kyrin?

With Jace's hesitation, Avery continued. "Don't look so surprised. I know who you are. You're the half-blood. Jace, is it? Anyone with interest enough to pay attention knows there's talk of you and the Altair girl having something between you."

Jace held his gaze coldly, forcing aside the discomfort that clawed for a hold inside of him. He didn't like this man or anyone knowing so much about him or Kyrin. "Does it matter who I am trying to save?"

Avery shrugged, but his eyes held more interest. "You do know it was what she told the emperor that got my father killed?"

Tension zinged through Jace, and he leaned forward a little. "That was never her intent. The emperor had her trapped. What was she supposed to do?"

Avery shrugged again. "Regardless, my father was murdered after Miss Altair gave a report that called his loyalties into question."

"You don't think Daican was suspicious already? There's a reason he had Kyrin watch your father." Jace bit back the rest of his retort. The heat rising in his chest wouldn't help the situation, nor would arguing. He'd come here for the remedy. His plan to trade Gem had failed, but he still had a second option. He'd prayed it wouldn't come to this, but he was willing, for Kyrin's sake.

"If you won't trade for a dragon, then I have another offer."

"I'm listening."

"Since you know who I am, you know there's a price on my head." Jace paused, letting grim determination harden inside of him so that he wouldn't think of the pain this would cause Kyrin. His goal was to save her life. "Hand me over to Davira and consider the reward as payment for the remedy."

If Holden only knew what he'd just done. Jace could imagine him immediately offering to take his place had he been here. But Jace had to do this, not just for Kyrin, but for Rayad and the others at camp. The men and women who had taught him there were people who cared and brought light to the world despite its evils.

Deafening silence hovered in the room before Avery snorted out a laugh. "You really are desperate to save her."

Jace speared him with a hard look. "Will you do it, or not?"

"As much as I have to admire your willingness to sacrifice yourself, I'm afraid I can't accept."

Jace's breath gusted out in frustration. Was there *anything* Avery would accept? "Why not? The reward would more than cover the cost of the remedy."

"But how do you suppose your friends would feel about that? I'm not interested in making more enemies than I have already."

"I'd make sure they knew it was my idea."

"Still, it's not a deal I feel comfortable accepting."

Jace wanted to shout at him. Did the man realize that every time he declined the offers, Jace could see Kyrin and Rayad dying? He worked to smother the emotion feeding the flames in his blood, but his voice tremored as he forced it past his tongue. "There must be something I can do to get that remedy."

"I told you what I want . . . unless . . ." Avery paused, calculating thoughts playing out on his face.

Jace straightened, his desperation gripping him full force. "I'll do anything. I just need the remedy."

A grin rose slowly on Avery's face. "Anything?"

Jace's stomach twisted as dread tingled down his spine, but he said nothing. Kyrin's life was at stake.

"Well then, how about this—I'll accept your current payment for the remedy *if* you also do a favor for me."

Jace stared grimly at him. "What kind of favor?"

"I need you to kill someone."

JACE'S BREATH DIED in his lungs. "What?"

"My uncle, Baron Reynold, is here in the city, enjoying the queen's *hospitality*. He is the one who stole the position of baron from me. I want him dead."

Jace let out a half-choked breath. "And you want me to kill him?"

Avery nodded. "Since his schedule hasn't changed in the last week, finding and ambushing him will be simple."

Jace narrowed his eyes. "If it's so simple and you want him dead so badly, why not do it yourself, or have one of your men do it?"

"Oh, as much as I would love to, I'd be spotted before ever getting close enough, and why risk my men when I have you?"

Jace shook his head, pushing back his chair. "No." He would not be Avery's assassin.

Avery waved toward the door. "Your choice. It just depends on how badly you want to save your ladylove. I can guarantee you won't be getting the remedy from the queen."

Jace ground his teeth together, halfway to his feet. He could *not* do this. He would not murder a man again.

"He has killed dozens of Elôm followers in Keaton."

Jace paused.

"He makes a sport of it. If you kill him, it could save a lot of lives he might take once he returns home."

A drowning sensation overwhelmed Jace as indecision flooded him. A man like Avery's uncle, a man who murdered people for their belief in Elôm, should be stopped, and if that was the key to saving Kyrin and the others . . .

He shook his head. No. This was not the way. He forced himself to his feet, though lingering desperation stiffened his joints. He headed toward the door without another word to Avery, disgusted that he would try to force Jace to make such a choice. Avery's voice halted him at the door.

"If you change your mind, you can get word to me here."

Jace didn't turn around or respond. He walked out and didn't stop until he stepped out of the tavern. He expected relief to wash through him at rejecting Avery's offer, but nausea gripped his stomach, threatening to upturn it. Kyrin and Rayad still lay at camp, dying, and the closest he'd come to being able to save them involved taking a life. They would die and Avery's uncle would live to continue terrorizing the followers of Elôm. How could that be?

He looked up at the sky, his soul crying out for an answer that would show him what to do. But Elôm seemed silent lately . . . almost like the days when Jace had struggled with not knowing whether or not he had a soul. He could almost feel the darkness of that time creeping in now. He'd seen Elôm save and protect them from danger before. He'd been face to face with Elon . . . why couldn't he see or hear anything now when the need was so dire?

Like a gaping hole, the silence inside him rapidly filled with all his fears as he made his way back to Ben and Mira's. He fought to banish them when he reached the front door, but they lingered, digging in, using devastating what ifs to hold on. He let himself inside and slipped off his coat. As he hung it up, he recognized Aaron and Timothy's coats already on the pegs near the door.

Following the murmur of voices, he found them all gathered around the dining table, breakfast half-eaten. Mira rose when he entered and motioned to one of the empty chairs next to Holden. "Jace, have a seat. I kept breakfast warm for you. I'll get it."

Jace stopped her before she turned to the kitchen. "That's all right. I'm not very hungry this morning."

Mira gave him a look of motherly concern but didn't press him to eat. Holden also cast him a questioning glance as he took a seat.

"At least have some coffee to warm up." Mira set a steaming mug near his elbow.

"Thank you," he murmured, reaching for the handle.

Silence surrounded him as he took a sip. It seemed the others were waiting to see if he'd say anything, but he remained silent. He didn't feel like speaking of his failed meeting with Avery, especially not of the man's last deal, though a small voice inside him said he should let them know. When he did not say anything, Holden spoke up.

"We've been discussing alternate options to pay for the remedy." He paused, and Jace noted a slight grimace cross his face. "I'm going to trade Thron for it."

Holden's dragon, the one who had replaced Brayle after the fight in Dorland last summer.

Jace slowly let the air seep from his lungs and shook his head. "It won't work. I already tried."

Holden's gaze zeroed in on him. "You spoke to Avery?"

Jace nodded. "This morning. I offered him Gem, but he declined."

"Why would he refuse a dragon?"

"He said it wouldn't be worth trying to feed it this winter."

Holden released a defeated sigh, and Aaron looked equally disappointed. Like Jace, they must have thought it would be the perfect solution, albeit difficult to go through with.

As the quietness settled again, Jace thought of his second offer to Avery. It was still an option . . . if he could get his friends to agree. At least they understood the situation and had a personal investment in it. He cleared his throat.

"I know another way we can get the money we need."

They all stared at him.

He hesitated. They weren't going to like this. "Turn me in to Davira and use the reward money to pay Avery."

For one heartbeat, everyone reacted with only stunned horror and head shaking.

"No," Holden said.

Jace clenched his fists. "This is the only way. If we don't do something *now*, a lot of people will be dead."

"And if we turn you over to Davira, you'll be dead."

"I am one person. We're talking about hundreds who could die if we don't do this."

Holden shook his head as if he wouldn't hear another word about it and then met Jace's eyes. "Fine, if that's the case, then turn me in, and *you* take the remedy back to camp."

Jace stared at him, his tongue frozen in his mouth. It was one thing to sacrifice himself but entirely another to sacrifice a friend. He shook his head. "I can't do that."

"Neither can I," Holden responded.

Jace's shoulders sagged, and he rested his head in his hands. Was there no way to get that remedy and save their friends?

"I know our options are limited," Holden said, "but turning each other in is not one of them. We'll find another way."

Jace bit down hard, threatening to crack his teeth.

They didn't have time.

Kaden pushed himself up and sat on the edge of his bed, craning his neck first to the right and then to the left. He winced. Sitting at Kyrin's bedside for hours on end killed his back. He looked over at her. She laid disturbingly still, her face ashen. No improvement.

Kaden ran his hand through his hair and sighed. He wasn't sure he had the energy to stand. He'd tried to rest after his turn sitting up and trying without success to get their mother to go to bed. However, sleep came only in brief, unfulfilling snatches. Not enough to renew the energy that worrying depleted.

Through sheer willpower, he shoved to his feet. Marcus crouched at the fireplace, stirring a pot of porridge. Kaden glanced at it as he passed on his way to the washstand. There wasn't much in it. Under normal circumstances, he could probably have eaten it all himself.

His stomach pinched. With so many sick, who was out trying to bring in more provisions? How much did they have left in the supply shack? He already noticed some of his own clothing getting a little loose. What would happen if they had to cut rations again?

With the weight of these questions dragging on him, he bent over the washstand and splashed the cold water on his face. It did little to revive him from the fatigue. When he dried his face and turned, Marcus was carrying the pot to the table. They traded a look, and Kaden read all the same questions in his brother's eyes. And neither of them had a clue what could be done to answer them.

He looked across the cabin to the chair his mother had occupied all night, steadfastly remaining at Kyrin's side. Kaden's throat tightened painfully. She looked terrible—her pale skin sagging and shadowed around her eyes.

He turned back to Marcus. "I'm going to get Mother to eat. Give her my portion with hers."

His lips set in a grim line, Marcus met his gaze and nodded. Right now, their mother needed the nourishment more than either of them. She was the one who spent so much time tending Kyrin.

Kaden crossed the cabin to his mother. She didn't even seem to notice him until he laid his hand on her shoulder. Jerking, she looked up from Kyrin and blinked.

"Marcus has breakfast ready. Go eat. I'll watch her until you're done."

She didn't respond immediately, a hollow look in her eyes. Finally, she nodded. She stood up, a bit unsteady, and Kaden grabbed her hand.

"Are you all right?"

She gave a slight, dismissive wave. "I'm fine."

Kaden watched her walk toward the table, apprehension prickling down his back. She didn't seem fine.

A moment later, she swayed.

"Mother!"

He wasn't close enough to grab her but Marcus was. He scooped her up as she collapsed. Kaden rushed to them. That's when he saw what he had missed before—the mottled red rash on their mother's neck.

The grueling treks Liam's grandfather used to force him to complete didn't compare to the exhaustion he faced now. Even so, he kept going. Thank Elôm for Cassie. Without her, he wasn't sure he and Leetra would have been able to keep up.

He sought her across the meeting hall, checking on Josef. She was the exact opposite of Leetra. While the crete certainly had a passion for her work, she went about it with stoic determination. Cassie, on the other hand, seemed to heal with her kindness and compassion as much as her medical knowledge. This aspect of her was even more beautiful than her appearance.

She looked up and caught him staring. He looked away, heat rushing to his face. A moment later she joined him at their work table. He cleared his throat, struggling to make eye contact.

"How is Josef?"

Her gentle smile eased his embarrassment. "No better, but no worse either."

"Good." He nodded but struggled for more to say. Why did it have to be so hard to talk to girls?

Liam welcomed the distraction of the door opening until Marcus walked in. His grim expression left Liam cold. Was Kyrin worse? What if they couldn't bring the fever back down the way Josef had? What if—

"Mother is sick," Marcus said when he reached them.

Liam's mind went blank for a moment before his heart thumped with a reminder to breathe. He shouldn't be shocked when more and more fell ill every day, but this was his family.

Something warm and gentle closed around his arm. He looked down to find Cassie's hand and then looked into her eyes.

"Go. Leetra and I have things handled for now."

Trask stood next to Balen as they both watched Cassie apply fresh compresses to Josef's forehead. He'd hoped to find the physician faring better than most, but he was just as sick. Sicker, perhaps. His constant care of everyone else had left him without strength to fight off the fever.

With a sigh, Trask looked around the meeting hall. Though they had volunteers, only Liam, Leetra, and Cassie had actual medical training. There was Lenae, and she helped where she could, but now she had Warin to take care of and little Meredith, who was scared to death she'd lose her new father. If Lenae got sick . . . He didn't want to consider Meredith becoming an orphan twice at such a young age.

Trask closed his eyes and rubbed them. It was all so much to think about, and there was very little hope to be found. And what was happening with Jace and Holden in Valcré? He had a bad feeling about their delay. What if they were, at this very moment, locked away in Auréa Palace's dungeon? Help certainly wouldn't be able to come for them from here.

Trask looked around again and rested his hand on Balen's shoulder. Josef was the only person who had come with him from Samara. The only person he had from home.

"Anne and I are praying for his quick recovery."

Balen nodded his thanks, and Trask turned. He needed to sit down for a bit and try to find some energy that just wasn't there. Sleep was a luxury none of them were able to afford lately. He left the meeting hall, pulling his coat close as the breeze instantly robbed the heat from his body, and trudged toward his cabin. He nodded at Darq near the dragons at the edge of camp with a couple of the other cretes. So far none of them had fallen ill. They seemed more resistant to the fever. Thankfully, Darq had kept his men searching for food while so many were ill. With the little they had been able to bring back and Balen and Daniel's efforts, the food shortage wasn't dire just yet. Thank Elôm for that.

When he entered the cabin, he was happy to find Anne there. With the two of them doing all they could to help, they didn't have much time together these days. He pulled off his coat, his worn out body aching.

"How is Josef?" Anne asked, hanging a kettle over the fire.

"Pretty much like everyone else." Trask sighed again, his body so heavy with the weight of it all. He walked to the fire and sank down in his chair. It felt so good to be off his feet. He closed his eyes. He could fall asleep right here.

"Trask."

He blinked at Anne's serious tone and looked up at her. Her brows were drawn together, and she rested her hand on his head.

"You're warm." She reached toward his collar.

He shook his head. "I'm just . . ."

Her momentary crestfallen expression and then the sight of her steeling herself said it all. She didn't even have to tell him the news. Their eyes locked, hers a little watery.

"Let's get you in bed," she said, her voice wavering slightly.

Trask shook his head again. He couldn't be sick. He had a camp to take care of, people who depended on him. But he couldn't find the strength to argue.

Anne helped him up and slipped her arm around him as she guided him toward their bed. Every step sapped more and more energy. How could it hit so fast? His legs almost gave out by the time they reached the bed. He sat down on the edge, and Anne helped him take off his jerkin and boots and get under the covers. As she arranged the blankets, he reached out for her hand. She looked down at him, a bit of her fear breaking through her mask of strength.

"I'll be all right," he told her. He had to be all right.

LARGE, HEAVY SNOWFLAKES floated past the windows in the meeting hall as Daniel did whatever he could to help with the sick. He and Balen had planned to go back out to their fishing hole today, but the heavy snowfall could easily turn into a blinding blizzard. At this point, they were of more use here. People came and went regularly, so Daniel didn't pay much attention to the door opening until he heard Sam's voice. When he looked up from helping one of the feverish soldiers drink a few sips of tea, both the talcrin and Captain Darq were on their way across the hall. Daniel's gut turned with dread. This couldn't be good.

He rose and joined Balen, Leetra, Liam, and Cassie to meet Sam and Darq.

"I just received word," Darq told them grimly, "three have come down with the fever in our northern camp."

Daniel released a long sigh. First, he'd heard that Trask was down and now this. Here they'd thought their other camps were safe, but the fever had somehow spread there too.

"The people there are starting to panic," Darq continued. "Between the fever and the rationing, Tane is afraid things will get out of hand."

Daniel couldn't blame the people for their fear, but the last thing any of them needed was a panic. It wouldn't heal or aid anyone.

"I'm heading over there to see what I can do to help," Sam said. His gaze shifted to Leetra. "I know you're already short-handed, but I'm sure the people will feel better having a trained physician there."

Leetra's lips thinned. There were so many ill here.

"I'll go," Cassie spoke up. She looked at Liam. "You and Leetra keep things going here. I'll take care of the other camp."

Liam's chin dipped in a short nod. He didn't seem particularly happy to see her go, but they all had their jobs to do.

Cassie quickly gathered the medical supplies she would need and then joined Sam and Darq. They turned to go, but Daniel stopped them. If things were getting out of hand in one of their camps, then someone with true authority should take care of it. With Trask and Warin down, the responsibility fell squarely on Daniel's shoulders. A responsibility he would not shirk.

"I'm going with you." He turned to Balen. "Watch over things here and let me know if there is any trouble."

Balen nodded, and Daniel followed Sam and Darq toward the door where he and Cassie retrieved their coats. Elanor met him there.

"Be careful," she said, her eyes earnest.

He looked down at her with a small smile he hoped would encourage her. "I will. And don't overwork yourself."

As if any of them could avoid that.

She just smiled and nodded.

Before he could make himself leave, Daniel leaned forward and planted a soft kiss on her forehead. In his heart, he silently prayed for her protection. He then followed Darq's lead out of the meeting hall and into the falling snow. He squinted up at the sky through the snowflakes. It was gray, but not overly dark. Elôm willing, it wouldn't turn into a blizzard, at least not before they reached the other camp.

At the dragons, Glynn and one of their other riders were ready to go. Daniel rode with Darq and closed his eyes as they launched upward, the icy snowflakes stinging his face. It was difficult to see much of anything as they leveled out above the treetops. Thankfully, the weather didn't seem to bother the cretes or the dragons.

On the short flight to their second camp, Daniel prayed for wisdom to handle whatever situation awaited them once they landed again. They didn't need a panicked riot on top of everything. It was far too easy in times like this for people to lose sound judgment and let fear overshadow their faith.

When they landed at the edge of camp, all seemed quiet. However, as they approached the grouping of small cabins and mounded shelters, upraised voices drifted through the hush the falling snow created. Daniel exchanged a look with Sam and picked up the pace. Just on the other side of camp, they came upon a crowd gathered around the supply shed. Angry shouts and arguments rose from the midst of it. Daniel caught sight of Tane standing at the front and facing the crowd as if guarding the door to the shed.

"No one can simply come and take what they want." Tane's raised voice held authority, yet Daniel detected a whisper of desperation. Big as the talcrin was, he couldn't take on a whole crowd. "Trask has a rationing system in place that we all must follow."

"My children are starving," someone shouted.

"How are we supposed to fend off the fever if we don't have enough to eat?" another man demanded.

Daniel shook his head. How quickly even the best people could lose all common sense. Sure, they'd had to cut down on their food intake a bit, but no one was starving yet. He tried to gain their attention. A few glanced back at him, but in the heat of the moment, it was as if no one recognized him. Their anger only seemed to escalate. Soon he was afraid the men would barge right past Tane to reach what food was left in the shed. Daniel tried to keep his own head cool. Fear turned people into something they weren't under normal circumstances, but he'd had just about enough of all this.

He thought of his father in that moment. The man had been able to command an entire throne room full of people with barely a word. As cruel and wrong as he may have been, he had known how to lead. Maybe it was about time to find ways in which Daniel could emulate his father.

Uncertainty being replaced by a fair amount of righteous anger, Daniel forced his way through the crowd toward Tane. When he reached the talcrin, he noticed an empty crate lying on its side near the shed. He grabbed it, set it upright, and then stepped up onto it. This put him at least a head taller than anyone in the crowd.

"Enough!" he shouted.

Almost instantly, all arguing ceased. The snowy hush reigned for a moment as all eyes turned to him. He wasn't sure if he had mastered his father's piercing gaze, but he let it touch on a few people who promptly lowered their eyes. Satisfied he had their complete attention, he spoke with just enough of an edge to his voice to show them his displeasure.

"I know things are difficult and uncertain right now. However, that does not give anyone the right to form a mob and march over here to take whatever you please. *No one* is starving. Anyone who has taken anything from this shed without permission is stealing and in direct disobedience to Trask's orders. Do you suppose that is pleasing to Elôm?"

More than one person fidgeted and shifted, their heads bowed. Daniel didn't like having to shame them, but they had to see what they were doing and the error in it.

"I know that everyone is afraid. So am I. But where is your faith? It is times like this where we must cling to it. Elôm has not abandoned us, and I will not see us abandon Him." Daniel drew a deep breath. What these men needed was a bit of hope and direction. It was too easy to feel helpless and that led to desperation.

"Jace and Holden are in Valcré right now trying to get the remedy for the fever. Pray that they will succeed. In the meantime, turning on each other and acting in selfishness will not help anyone. Every one of us will continue to follow a rationing system, myself included. Now, if you do not have anyone who is ill yet or are not helping with those who are, then I want you trying to contribute to our food stores. Take some of the fat from what meat we have. Go out into the forest, start a fire, and fry the fat. Elôm willing, it will draw in predators that are just as hungry as we are. Anything you can bring back will help. And if you know of any deep streams or pools nearby, clear the snow and break through the ice to fish. Do whatever you can to help contribute, but do not go out alone. Always have someone with you to help monitor your surroundings for danger as well as your health."

He let his words sink in and scanned the men's faces. They seemed to accept his words.

"We are all in this together, and I believe that Elôm *will* bring us through this. Now is when we need to trust Him the most. Don't let fear make you forget that. Be the men of honor and courage I know you are. The enemy would like nothing more than to prove otherwise and see us destroy ourselves. I will not let that happen. Will you?"

The men shook their heads, murmurs of "no" echoing around them.

"Good. Now go and do as I've commanded."

With bowed heads toward Daniel, the men turned and dispersed. Daniel released another long breath. He then caught eyes with Sam as the crowd parted around him. His friend bore a slight smile and gave Daniel a nod of approval.

Kaden squeezed out the cloth in the basin of cool water and laid it on Kyrin's forehead, pressing it against her skin. It seemed warmer than it had earlier, and he prayed her temperature wouldn't spike dangerously again. He looked over to where his mother lay unconscious. Aric sat beside her, changing the compresses on her head and neck. He'd shown up just after she'd collapsed this morning and hadn't left since. Kaden was thankful to have him there to help while Liam went back and forth between the cabin and the meeting hall.

Even from here, Kaden saw the beads of sweat on his mother's face. The fever seemed to have hit her hard. And no wonder. How much had she slept lately? Did she even have a fighting chance? He shook his head to himself before catching sight of Ronny, who sat next to Aric. His little brother looked stricken now that their mother had fallen ill. When Ronny glanced up, Kaden tried to give him an encouraging smile, but Ronny was old enough to understand how dire the situation was. Kaden wouldn't lie and tell him everything would be fine. There was just no guarantee of that.

A couple of minutes later, the door opened and Liam walked in, snow swirling in with him. It sounded like the wind was picking up. Nightfall would probably see them in the midst of another blizzard.

Liam shrugged off his coat and hung it up before turning to face his brothers and Aric. His face was grim amidst the shadow of stubble overtaking his jaw. It made him look much older than he always seemed to Kaden.

"We lost five more men," he told them, his voice low. He looked at Marcus. "Three from the militia."

Kaden didn't even know how to react to this. He was almost getting numb to the blows they kept taking.

"I just wanted to come check on Mother and Kyrin for a bit before I go back to help Leetra."

Kaden turned his attention back to Kyrin. He hadn't seen her open her eyes in what felt like days. How much longer did she have? How much longer did any of them have?

Pushing to his feet, Kaden joined Marcus and Liam near the table.

"Maybe I should go to Valcré and find out what is going on. Jace and Holden should've been back by now."

Marcus's weary gaze shifted to him. "The payment must not have been enough. If Jace had that remedy, he'd be here."

"Do you think Trask has anything more we can send?"

Marcus shook his head. "I think he sent along most of it."

"Well, maybe I can help them in some way." Kaden couldn't stand sitting here anymore, watching people slowly die.

Marcus raised his hand and rested it on Kaden's shoulder. "If it's the payment that's the problem, there's nothing you can do. Jace won't stop until he finds a way. Right now, we need everyone here."

Letting his shoulders sag, Kaden rubbed his eyes and nodded. He couldn't abandon his brothers here now that their mother was sick too.

Returning to his chair, he sank down and rested his head back against the wall. Liam sat down next to him. Kaden shifted to look at his brother. Liam's face was pale, like their mother's had been, and he slumped in his chair.

Kaden straightened, fear taking hold. "Are you all right?"

Liam looked over at him. "I'm just tired."

"Are you sure?" Their mother had said she was fine too.

He nodded. At least Kaden couldn't spot any redness around his throat. Even so, he'd keep a close watch on him.

They were all about stretched to their breaking point.

HE WAS GOING to lose everyone.

Jace rubbed his fingers against his eyes that burned with both exhaustion and emotion and then stared up at the darkened ceiling in his room. Another day had passed without getting them any closer to the remedy. It seemed they had run out of options.

All but one.

His stomach churned nauseously as Avery's offer ghosted through his mind. He tried to shove it away. He couldn't do such a thing. But Kyrin's face always followed. Not her beautiful, smiling face he loved so much—her pale, almost lifeless face, her eyes feverish. Every time it came to mind, his chest ached fiercely. He wanted to do *anything* to save her, but could he?

He looked toward the window, into the snowy darkness outside. They'd tried all day to find a solution but failed. Jace still hadn't told anyone about Avery's offer. He knew he should, but he also knew Holden would stop him if he even considered it. He didn't want to, but . . . if it was the only way to save Kyrin . . .

Groaning, Jace rolled over and closed his eyes, fighting to grasp sleep. The night hours always dragged on miserably long and heightened his sense of helplessness. His mind continued to spin but, eventually, his body won out in its need for rest.

Jace jolted awake with a gasp, cold sweat clinging to his skin like ice. His heart hammered his breastbone as images from the dreams that had overtaken him showed him his worst fears—burying Kyrin. It had been so real. He'd felt it. Felt her lifeless body in his arms as he'd lowered her into an open grave, just like he had Kalli years ago.

He shook, his eyes flooding as his throat caved in on itself. Drawing a difficult breath, he shoved back the blankets and sat on the edge of the bed with his head in his hands. He knew Elôm could save Kyrin and the others without the cure, but what if He didn't? What if the dream would be his reality? Hot moisture rolled down his face, and he scrubbed it away. He forced another deep breath, but the trembling wouldn't subside. Then, another wave of cold washed through him. Something wasn't right.

He pushed to his feet, disturbed by the twinge of weakness in his legs, and crossed the room to the washstand. He held his breath and looked in the mirror. Even in the twilight-like darkness, he could see the redness around his throat.

He braced himself against the washstand. He couldn't be sick. He needed to get the cure. He needed to save Kyrin. How long until he couldn't even stand?

He hadn't had trouble with his lungs since Elon had healed him. Jace always believed he'd been healed completely of the condition that affected him because of his ryrik blood, but what if that were not so? He would die of suffocation long before the fever took him. He placed his hand against his chest, as memories of choking on his own blood took hold. But that wasn't the worst. If he fell ill and died now, who would save Kyrin?

Unbidden, Avery's offer dropped in amidst the fear. He could save Kyrin . . . if he was willing to accept the offer. He shook his head. No, he couldn't. But didn't Avery say his uncle made a sport of killing believers? If Jace did kill him, how many others would be saved? Not only Kyrin and all those who were sick but other believers in Keaton as well. One man to save many others. Was that really so terrible?

The question unsettled him, but once again, he saw Kyrin's pale and lifeless face from the dream. He had to save her, and now he had even less time than he had thought. He turned to the window. The hazy, gray light told him it was almost dawn.

Bracing himself, Jace grabbed his clothes and dressed quickly. His discomfort sounded a warning, but fear for Kyrin drowned it out. He loved her too much to let her die, and if he didn't act now, he soon wouldn't be able to.

Once he was dressed, he opened his door and paused to listen. The house was silent and brought him a sad relief. If Holden knew what he was doing, he had no doubt his friend would stop him. He had to leave now, while they were still asleep. It was just something he had to do.

Downstairs in the dim foyer, he pulled on his coat. Just this bit of effort made him too warm and a little shaky. He had to hurry. With a glance over his shoulder that stirred the unease in his stomach, he let himself outside.

The icy breeze momentarily refreshed him, but as he walked down the street, it bit through his clothes and chilled him to the bone. He hunched his shoulders and hurried his steps. He had to finish this before the fever overwhelmed him. He thanked his ryrik blood that he wasn't already bedridden, yet he wouldn't assume it would halt the fever's effects completely.

Jace had to fight down his roiling stomach when the sign for the Red Crane appeared just ahead. His steps grew heavy, as if he had to drag them to keep himself moving forward. Gripping the cold knob, he pushed the door open and stepped inside. Would Avery or his men even be here at this early hour?

Spotting Tavor, he let out a long breath, but the nausea only grew. The man noticed him a moment later. His look said he'd been expecting Jace to show up. Something about that didn't sit well. Jace was supposed to be a better man than that. But he did this for Kyrin. She didn't deserve to die if he could do something to save her.

Pulling his shoulders back, he crossed the room, fighting to hide a wince at how much energy the walk from Ben and Mira's had consumed. Tavor looked almost amused when Jace reached the table. He leaned back in his chair and waited frustratingly. Surely, he knew exactly why Jace was here without him having to say it.

Jace gritted his teeth. He didn't have time for games. "I need to speak with Avery. I . . . I want to accept his offer."

Tavor nodded slowly and set aside the deck of cards he'd been playing with. Standing, he grabbed his coat. "Come with me."

He strode toward the door, and Jace followed, struggling to hide his disappointment that Avery wasn't here in this tavern. More walking would only deplete his energy. He willed strength into his body. In response, a bit of warmth seeped through his veins, steadying him. He would have to rely on this aspect of his ryrik blood until his task was completed.

His task . . .

His stomach threatened to turn, and he swallowed it back into place. He couldn't think about it. Like when he'd fought in the arenas, he had to shut his mind to the horrors . . . except he'd never set out to kill anyone then, only in self-defense.

But this was different. At least, that's what he told himself. He did this to save people. And Avery's uncle was not an innocent man.

This thought settled fitfully in his mind as they veered off the main street and into a narrower alleyway. Another tavern sign hung over one of the doors—the Dragon's Head. Tavor opened the door and beckoned him inside. The tavern interior was smaller than the Red Crane, though it appeared better kept—more a place for gentlemen patrons than the usual riffraff who frequented such places. The room was empty save for the barkeeper who gave them a calculating look, but said not a word as the two of them passed.

Tavor led Jace up a dark stairwell. In the hall, he spotted a man standing guard at the end near the farthest door. He eyed Jace and then traded a silent nod with Tavor as they neared. At the door, Tavor knocked. A minute later, it swung open halfway. Avery peered out. His clothing was a bit rumpled as if he'd only just gotten out of bed and tugged them on. The moment he saw Jace, the irksome hint of a grin grew on his face.

"Here to discuss our deal?"

Jace nodded curtly, and Avery opened the door wider, gesturing him inside. Tavor stepped in as well, taking up a guard position and watching Jace as though he didn't quite trust him.

Jace swept the room with his gaze. It wasn't simply a meeting room. While not overly spacious, it contained an unmade bed, a table, and a couple of cabinets. This must be where Avery lived, or at least one of the places he'd made home since he'd assassinated Emperor Daican.

"Sit," Avery said, gesturing to the table. He reached for a coffee pot with steam curling around the spout. "Coffee?"

"No." Jace's voice was clipped, but he didn't soften it, nor did he take a seat despite his body's need for rest. "How do I find your uncle?"

Avery lowered the pot and looked Jace up and down. Jace resisted the urge to throttle him. He didn't have time to waste. Avery met his gaze with a knowing look.

"You have the fever."

Jace swallowed hard, acutely aware of the swollen ache taking over his throat. He did not answer. The truth was plain enough to see.

Instead, he ground out, "Where do I find your uncle?"

Avery straightened, his expression growing more serious. At least he wasn't making light of the situation. "Every morning he attends the 'games' at the arena. Executions of Elôm believers and others who have offended Her Royal Highness." He scowled at the mention of Davira. "No doubt that's where you'll find him. If you go now, you can intercept him on the way to the arena."

Clenching his jaw, Jace nodded, making himself picture the man sitting and watching believers being killed as if it were a sport. He didn't deserve to live if it meant other good people would die.

"What does he look like?"

Avery gave Jace a detailed description of his uncle, including the manner in which he usually arrived at the arena. The entire time, Jace's heart pounded like a drum deep in his chest, the blood throbbing in his veins.

Once he was certain he could find Avery's uncle, he nodded again. After a brief pause, he looked the man in the eyes. "There's one more thing."

Avery silently waited for him to speak.

"I'm risking everything for this. My friends should get something if I fail and am captured or killed."

Avery mulled this over a moment. "Very well. If you fail and don't return, I'll give them enough of the remedy for Daniel and King Balen, free of—"

"Three people," Jace cut in. "Prince Daniel, King Balen, and Kyrin."

He felt wretched making such a deal, as if he was personally condemning Rayad and everyone else, but he had to try to save Kyrin.

"All right, three doses."

"And you will stick by that?"

"I may be a smuggler, but I'm a man of my word," Avery responded with all seriousness, and Jace believed him.

In the following silence, the discomfort tugging at him spiked again—an inner warning to turn back while he still could—but he fought to silence it. Who could blame him for doing whatever he could to save Kyrin? Hadn't he given her father such a promise?

"I'll be back for the remedy."

Turning, he headed out of the room before his inner voice could raise any further protests. He didn't slow on his way through the tavern or out onto the streets. Now that the sun was up, more people traveled the alleys, but he paid them no heed. He had to travel a couple of blocks before the Draicon Arena came into view. The moment he spotted it, his innards lurched and twisted. He'd never fought there, but it brought memories flooding back of the arenas he *had* seen.

Despite the cold, he could almost feel the hot grit of sand and hear the cheers. Why did that life he'd fought so hard to put behind him seem so suddenly near? The dark hopelessness of that time seemed to surround him, as if he were tottering right on the edge of slipping back into it. He shook his head. He had to focus. Perhaps it was the fever, warping his senses and bringing new life to those past horrors. He drew the cold air into his lungs to clear his head. Instead, a cough rose up, burning his chest. He half expected the salty warmth of blood in his mouth, yet none came.

By the time he had crossed the city and neared the arena, his clothing clung damply to his skin, and his head pounded. His elevated heartbeat worked twice as hard as normal. He paused, looking around at the people filtering into the arena. His gaze then traveled upward, climbing each of the six stories of the monstrous structure. Ice encased him, and his mouth went dry. How many people could such an arena hold? He could almost hear their screaming and chanting for death. How many had been killed here already?

Shaking off questions he couldn't answer or do anything about, he focused on what he *could* do—save Kyrin. He scanned the base of the arena until he found the entrance Avery had described as being used by nobility. He would have to get closer. Thankfully, no soldiers guarded the entrance, at least not from the outside.

Gripping his sword scabbard, he strode toward the entrance. A nearby statue provided a good vantage point and a way to conceal himself. He stepped behind it and leaned back against the cold stone, letting out a long breath. He closed his eyes and focused on his heartbeat, willing it to slow to a more normal rhythm.

Several minutes later, the sound of approaching hooves jerked his attention to the street. From the direction of the palace rolled a carriage towed by four white horses. Jace's heart lurched into his throat as it passed on its way to the arena and stopped several yards away. This was it. It had to be Avery's uncle.

He stood frozen as three men exited the coach, and a fourth jumped down from next to the driver. They weren't clad in official gold and black, but everything about them said they were guardsmen. A moment later, a fifth man joined them—tall and thin with graying hair pulled back in a tail that fell well past his shoulders. Jace's pulse kicked up yet another notch. It was him—Baron Reynold.

As the man fussed with his cloak, Jace stepped away from the statue and slipped his hand to his belt where he'd stuck his hunting knife. Move quickly, take the man out, and then run. It was all he had to do. Kyrin, Rayad, and the rest of their camp would be saved. He slipped the dagger out of its sheath, concealing it within the folds of his coat. The man's back was to him and his security didn't appear to notice. He was so close. If he lunged, he'd reach him. He squeezed the dagger as the man's defenseless back filled his sight. Heat curled through his blood. Drive the blade in, just right of the man's left shoulder and it would be done.

Jace froze.

What was he doing? Was he truly going to kill—to *murder*—this man? His grip on the dagger trembled as the voice inside him rose up, echoing Elon's voice. Elon, his Savior, the one who had died, not only in his place, but for all those in Ilyon, including Avery's uncle. Elon had paid for their lives with His own blood. Who was Jace to take another's life like this, regardless of the circumstance?

The horror of what he'd been about to do nearly sent him to his knees. "Elôm, forgive me."

He took a wobbly step back and met with a solid blow to the back of the head. Light flashed and then darkness as he crumpled.

ROUGH TUGGING AT his arms roused Jace. Muffled voices surrounded him. Then hands grabbed his arms, yanking him upward. He stifled a groan as his shoulders protested. His feet dragged along the ground, but he didn't have the strength to lift his head, much less get up. He blinked, the cobblestones a blur. None of his senses worked at first and returned slowly. Pain flooded in, and he drew a sharp breath. The back of his skull felt like it had been split open. He wasn't so sure it hadn't.

Wincing at the pain pounding behind his eyes, he raised his head and got his feet underneath him, though he stumbled a few steps before his legs regained their strength. He looked to his right and left at his captors—the same guardsmen he had seen with Baron Reynold. They led him around the side of the arena.

He hung his head again, the pain of regret swelling in his chest to rival the pain in his head. This was his fault. He'd brought this on himself with his lack of faith. He'd been so afraid for Kyrin that he'd let his fear overwhelm him. His poor decisions had been based on the desperate and misguided belief that he could save her under his own power. What a fool he was. She always had been and always would be in Elôm's hands. Whether she lived or died would be His will. What folly for

Jace to believe he could save her by taking the life of another—by forsaking all he knew of Elôm. His fear had led him to one of the biggest mistakes of his life, and now he'd pay for it.

I am so sorry, Elôm. I've done terrible wrong. I'm done taking things into my own hands. Whatever happens to Kyrin . . . whatever happens to me, I accept Your will.

Tears stung his eyes, but even now, facing his own uncertain future, a peace settled inside him that he hadn't experienced in what felt like ages. *Thank You.*

The men jerked him to the right, cutting off the rest of his thoughts. He stumbled, his legs wobbling again. He'd barely regained his balance before the men slammed him up against the side of the arena. He ground his teeth and squeezed his eyes shut at the fresh stab of pain that shot from the back of his head. When he opened them again, Avery's uncle stood in front of him, his sharp, clean-shaven chin tipped imperiously as he peered down his long nose at Jace.

"So my nephew finally hired an assassin?"

Jace said nothing, and the man snorted.

"Did he not think I would be prepared for such a thing? You poor fool. You walked right into it."

Jace let his gaze drop. He was a fool, and he was prepared to accept the consequences.

"You have the fever."

Jace looked up again into Reynold's smiling face.

"My nephew offered you the cure in exchange for killing me, didn't he?" He shook his head as if Jace were nothing more than a pathetic beggar. "Pity. You look like you would have provided good sport in the arena."

Jace swallowed hard, an involuntary reaction to the thought of finding himself in an arena again. Before he or Reynold could speak another word, a man rushed up to them. Jace didn't recognize him as being with Reynold when he'd first arrived. He stepped to the man's side and spoke in his ear. Though he barely more than whispered, Jace's sharp hearing caught the words.

"We've finally found him, my lord. He's been staying at the Dragon's Head. He's there right now."

Jace stiffened in his captors' grips. The man was talking about Avery.

Reynold's expression lifted. "Is that so?"

The other man nodded.

"Then let's not waste any time." Avery's uncle motioned to one of his guardsman, and then peered contemptuously at Jace. "Dispose of him and then meet us at the Dragon's Head."

Jace's heart pounded, each beat sluggish and heavy. Not only would he surely die, but no doubt Reynold would capture Avery and drag him to face Davira's wrath. Any small chance of ever getting the remedy from him would then be gone.

Without a second glance at Jace, Avery's uncle turned and joined several of his men, striding back the way they had come. Jace's two captors plus one other man pulled him away from the wall and led him in the opposite direction. Jace tugged against them, but even the heat working through his veins couldn't compensate for the draining effect the fever had on his strength.

Elôm, he cried out with total dependence as he should have done days ago, *I can't stop this. Only You can.*

The men dragged him into a shadowed alley up the street from the arena. Snow drifts, broken glass, and other refuse cluttered it. Several yards away, a large lump lay half buried by the snow. Jace had to swallow down his stomach. It was just large enough to be a person. Had these men killed someone here before? Would his body lay here to freeze where his friends would never know what happened to him? He released a heavy sigh. Had coming here to Valcré even been the right decision, or had he again taken matters into his own hands instead of trusting Elôm?

The men shoved him against the wall of the building. The third man reached into his coat and pulled out a long dagger. Jace fought to pull away again, but they held him in place. Resignation settled. He couldn't escape death this time and would accept it with whatever dignity he had left.

Jace closed his eyes and waited for the blade to pierce his chest or cut his throat. He focused his mind on Elôm but couldn't shake the regret that gripped him. This was not how he wanted to meet his King—not as a result of his own folly. He would rather have died for his beliefs, but these men probably didn't even know he was a follower of Elôm. To them, he was just a failed assassin. Instead of dying openly for his faith, he would die alone in an alleyway because of his lack of faith. *I am so sorry, Elôm. I failed You.*

He sensed the nearness of his killer and bit down, swallowing against the choking lump in his throat. *I don't want to die like this.*

Something hissed in the air and one of the men grunted and launched into a string of curses. Jace opened his eyes. His killer was hunched over with an arrow through his arm.

"Unhand him."

Jace could have sunk to his knees in relief at the sound of Aaron's voice. He looked to the entrance of the alley. Aaron stood, bow drawn with another waiting arrow aimed at one of Jace's captors. Holden and Timothy flanked him, swords in hand.

No one moved for a moment.

"I said, let him go," Aaron commanded, "unless you want to end up like your friend." He nodded slightly at the other man who clutched his arm and glared at Aaron. "I'm not likely to miss at this range."

Slowly, the men's holds loosened on Jace's arms.

"Good, now step away."

They obeyed, and Aaron followed their movements with his bow.

Jace sagged against the wall as the truth washed over him. He wasn't going to die. *Thank You!* Taking a long breath, he pushed away from the cold stone and walked toward his friends. His steps wobbled, and Holden grabbed his arm as he drew near.

"Are you all right?"

Jace didn't answer, a bit out of breath just from the few steps he had taken.

Realization dawned in Holden's stormy expression. "You're sick."

Jace nodded slowly and winced at the pain it caused. He raised his hand to the back of his head. His hair was matted, and when he pulled his hand away, blood coated his fingers.

"Let me see." Holden moved around behind him, and Jace bent his head as he inspected the wound.

"You've got a nasty gash." He took hold of Jace's arm again. "We need to get you back."

He guided Jace out of the alley, Aaron and Timothy guarding their backs and making sure the men didn't follow. As they rounded the corner, thoughts of Avery and his uncle crashed in. Jace froze. His brain must really be muddled since he hadn't thought of them sooner. By now, Baron Reynold could be dragging his nephew to Davira and certain death.

"What is it?" Holden asked.

"We need to get to Avery now." Jace stepped forward, but Holden stopped him.

"You're in no condition to go anywhere."

Jace turned to him and the others. "Avery's uncle knows where he is. They're on their way to get him right now. If we don't stop them, he'll be killed or taken to Davira." He shuddered to think of what horrors she would inflict on Avery for killing her father. What Jace had faced in Auréa's dungeon would be nothing compared. He looked Holden in the eyes. "We have no time. We have to stop them."

Though his face was fraught with uncertainty, Holden nodded, and they moved on swiftly, checking over their shoulders to make sure they weren't followed. After only a few yards, Jace's legs threatened to give out. *Please, Elôm, give me strength. Just enough to save Avery.* Though not overwhelming, the heat still working through his blood seemed to grow hotter as his fighting instincts kicked in, dulling the pain and weakness. He pressed forward. He only had to last long enough to foil Reynold's plans.

They traveled through the city with all haste, though the distance seemed to have multiplied since Jace had traveled it earlier. If only they had their dragons to aid them.

At last, they reached the Dragon's Head. The door stood open suspiciously. Jace glanced at Holden as they approached and drew his sword. When they neared the door, they peered inside. Overturned tables and a handful of bodies dotted the floor, but no sign of Avery or his uncle.

They stepped inside. A loud groan drew their attention to the back corner where Tavor stumbled to his feet, holding his bloodstained side. Jace rushed over to him.

"Where's Avery?"

"They took him," Tavor growled, spitting out an uncomplimentary name for the men.

Jace breathed out slowly. At least Avery was still alive. "To the palace?"

Tavor nodded, grimacing as he pulled his hand away from the slice in his coat. Blood glistened across his palm, but he reached for his sword. "I'm going after them."

Jace had never been sure if Avery's men followed him out of loyalty or for the money, but Tavor proved it was the former if he intended to face Baron Reynold and his men alone.

"How many were there?"

"Eight."

Jace glanced at his friends. Their looks offered him answers without him even having to ask his question. He looked at Tavor again. "We'll help you."

Tavor seemed to look on Jace with new eyes, and then nodded curtly. He pushed away from the table at his side and headed determinedly for the door. Jace followed with Holden, Aaron, and Timothy. It would be the five of them against eight. Two of them were hardly fit for fighting, but they had no choice.

JACE PEERED AROUND a corner, down the street. Baron Reynold and his men should appear any minute. They'd spotted them on their way to a suitable ambush site. A couple of royal guards had joined them, bringing their total to twelve men. Not great odds. They were depending on Aaron to thin their numbers before it came to any hand-to-hand combat.

Jace leaned his shoulder against the building and closed his eyes momentarily, praying for success. Twinges of weakness darted through his legs. He feared standing here idle would douse the surge of strength that had brought him this far. If he didn't get moving again soon, he might not be able to fight at all. *Lord, give me Your strength. If you want Avery to live, help us in this rescue.* He didn't know exactly why he was so determined to save Avery, but leaving him to Davira would not have given him any peace. And though he'd been no help to Jace and the others, he did seem to care about those in need. The people here needed someone like him.

A glimpse of gold caught Jace's full attention. They were coming. Jace glanced back and nodded to the others. His gaze caught on Tavor. The man could have used medical care, but at least it didn't appear he'd lost too much more blood. The wound must not be overly deep. Regardless of it, he looked ready to fight.

Too bad more of Avery's men weren't alive or nearby to help them. If only they could have gathered a larger force but, by then, Avery would have been doomed. Already, they were too close to the palace for Jace's comfort. He sent up another prayer that there weren't soldiers nearby who would be attracted to the sounds of fighting.

As they drew near, Jace looked for Avery and spotted him at the center of the heavily armed escort. His hands were bound behind his back, and blood oozed down the side of his face. His expression was hard-set and defiant. If he feared what was to come, as any man in his right mind would, he didn't give away any hint of it.

In another few seconds, they came within several yards of the ambush site. From the other side of the street, Aaron drew back his bow. The arrow sailed away a second later. One of the soldiers dropped to the ground, the arrow's fletching protruding from his thigh. Before the men could figure out what had happened, another soldier went down. This snapped the group from their shock, and they rushed toward cover near the buildings along the street, dragging Avery with them. Aaron took down one more of them before they had a chance to take shelter behind empty merchant stalls and doorways.

Now it was time to fight. Lifting his sword, Jace dashed away from the corner and charged in with the others. Well-trained, Reynold's men reacted quickly, drawing their swords. Jace raised his blade to meet that of the first man. His arms felt heavy, but he focused on the fighting blood rising in temperature inside him and the energy it provided. The blades crashed together, echoing through the street.

Another guard converged on him, but he held them off until he maneuvered around and took one down. Focused again on a single opponent, he pressed forward in attack. The guard soon fell, injured, though not mortally. With proper care, he'd survive . . . Jace hoped. He looked around for another foe and spotted Baron Reynold. The man stalked after Avery, who did his best, hands bound, to dodge his uncle's attacks. Jace rushed toward them.

The moment Reynold heard him coming, he spun around. Jace slowed cautiously. Though Reynold let others do most of his fighting, Jace would not underestimate his skill. The man lifted his blade and came at Jace, undaunted. He certainly was confident, probably because he knew Jace was sick. But did he realize Jace was half ryrik? Likely not.

The man's first strike rang against Jace's blade with surprising force. Clearly, the man had training. Jace batted the sword away and launched an attack of his own. Reynold blocked it but had to take a step back. Fresh heat surged through Jace, though weaker than usual. He'd have to be quick if he wanted to outlast the rescue attempt.

Reynold certainly wouldn't go down without a tough fight. His answering attack forced Jace back a step now. Gathering the energy he had left, Jace raised his sword and slashed downward with all his strength. The impact against Reynold's blade jolted up his arms. Surprise flashed in the man's face, and he stumbled. Using this vulnerability, Jace swung again and again. Reynold backpedaled. Not watching where he was going, he staggered against the wall of a building, and with a hammer-like blow, Jace battered his sword out of his hand. The man leaned against the building as Jace pressed his sword against his heaving chest.

Winded, Reynold gasped out, "Do you have any idea what you're doing? You're saving the man who killed the emperor. The queen will have you hunted down and killed."

Jace almost laughed. As if Davira didn't want them all dead already. He just shook his head and stared at Reynold. He had him in the perfect position to kill him and complete the deal with Avery. All it would take is a quick thrust of his sword, and he could be on his way back to camp, to Kyrin, with the remedy. He looked over his shoulder. All fighting had ceased, their opponents either dead or maimed. His friends watched him while Tavor stood with Avery. Jace nodded to the rope in Tavor's hands.

"Bring that here and tie him up." Reynold could still run to the palace for help, but tying him up would hopefully give them just enough extra time to escape the area before any more enemies arrived.

Tavor growled. "I have a better idea." He yanked out a dagger and took a step forward.

"No." Jace leveled him with a firm look.

Tavor stopped and glared at him. "He and his men killed some of my friends."

Jace spoke quietly, but firmly. "Killing him won't bring them back."

"Yeah, but it'll avenge them."

Jace gritted his teeth. His arm was beginning to tremble from the weight of his sword. Fighting to keep the weakness from overcoming the rest of his body, he looked over at Holden.

"Tie him up, please."

Holden strode over to Tavor and took the rope from him. A moment later, Tavor stepped forward like he intended to shove Holden out of the way and take Reynold out regardless. However, in an act that deeply surprised Jace, Avery held him back. Tavor gaped at Avery, who appeared just as surprised over his own actions, but he did not relent and only watched in silence.

Holden swiftly tied Reynold's hands, and Jace turned to Avery again.

"Holding him as captive may serve you better than outright killing him."

Alex nodded slowly and then ordered Tavor, "Bring him with us."

Tavor's displeasure morphed into a dark grin. Reynold glared at them and then over at Avery.

"You will pay for your crimes."

Avery stared coldly at him. "Maybe . . . once you've paid for yours."

He glanced at one of the fallen swords nearby, the desire for revenge glinting in his eyes, but he finally turned away from his uncle. Jace released a long breath and slid his own sword wearily into the scabbard. They all started down the street. After a few steps, the last of the heat in Jace's body went cold. Chilled sludge filled his veins instead. He willed his body to keep moving, but after just one more step, his knees gave out and hit the frozen cobblestone.

"Jace!" Holden was at his side in an instant, followed quickly by Aaron and Timothy. His expression sobered as he looked into Jace's face. The effects of the fever must be getting disturbingly evident. He put one of Jace's arms around his shoulders, and Aaron did the same with the other.

"We need to get you back to the house," Holden said as they helped him to his feet.

Jace tried to steady himself under his own power, but didn't have the strength, and had to rely completely on Holden and Aaron to keep him upright.

"Come with us." They looked over at Avery, who motioned to them. "He needs the remedy."

Holden and Aaron immediately followed him, but all Jace could think about was getting that remedy to Kyrin. His ryrik blood gave him a much higher chance of survival than she had. She was the one who needed the remedy.

By the time they trudged back across the city and reached one of the taverns Avery apparently frequented, Jace was drenched in sweat, yet an icy coldness gripped his bones. They stepped into the tavern, which seemed unusually full for this time of morning. Their entrance caused quite a stir, and the men immediately gathered around.

"Avery!" one of them exclaimed. "We heard what happened at the Dragon's Head. We were just about to go looking for you. We were afraid you'd be dead or in the queen's custody by now."

"I would be, if not for some help." Avery motioned to Jace and the others. Tavor then shoved Reynold into their midst. "We also managed to bring back our own captive."

The men murmured and sneered in recognition of Reynold before offering congratulatory remarks to Avery.

"Keep watch over him until I can figure out somewhere secure to keep him," he ordered them.

They seemed only too happy to comply. He then gripped one man's shoulder. "We need medical supplies. Also a dose of the remedy."

The man hurried off, and Avery addressed some of the others. "Keep watch. The queen's men will probably come looking for us. We'll need plenty of warning to get out if that happens."

In a flurry, the men grabbed their coats and weapons, heading out the door and leaving the tavern nearly empty except for those who guarded Reynold. Avery gestured to Holden and Aaron who still supported Jace. "Bring him to a chair back here."

They crossed the room and helped Jace sit near a crackling fireplace. He braced himself against the table. He might never be able to get up again now that his body had ceased moving.

The man Avery had sent for supplies returned a moment later with a plump, middle-aged woman. By the way she glanced at the burly barkeeper nearby, Jace guessed she was the man's wife. Her face took on a fussy, motherly appearance as she hurried to Avery.

"What has that scoundrel uncle of yours done to you?"

"Not too much. You should look after Tavor first."

The woman nodded, and she and the other man set trays of supplies on the table. Picking up a small tin cup, she said, "Which one of you has the fever?" Her brown eyes rested on Jace. "Ah, that would be you, wouldn't it?" She offered the cup to him. "Drink this up and you'll be feeling better in no time. I mixed it with some tea to help it go down."

Jace held up his hand, though it took a terrible amount of effort. "No." He looked over at Avery. "Kyrin needs it more than I do."

Avery waved dismissively. "Just drink it and we'll discuss that once none of us are bleeding out or about to fall out of our chairs."

Holden took the cup from the woman and held it in front of Jace. Jace stared at the murky liquid swirling inside. This small cup could save Kyrin's life. It went against everything inside him to drink it himself. But Holden didn't yield, and Jace finally took the cup. Begging Elôm to save Kyrin and the others, he gulped down the bitter mixture, and then set the cup on the table, his strength spent.

For the next half an hour, the barkeeper's wife tended each of them, cleaning and binding up their wounds. The gash across Tavor's ribs had bled a lot, but the tough man would recover. Avery had a gash to the side of his head, though it didn't require any stitches, and Jace barely felt the cut along the back of his head. His skull did still pound, though, with the effects of a concussion.

Once they were each looked after, the woman bustled off, murmuring humorously dark threats against Baron Reynold and Davira. By this time, Jace almost felt as though his fever were starting to go down, though he still wasn't sure he'd be able to stand if he had to. The remedy probably wouldn't miraculously return his strength in under an hour.

Quietness settled as they all sat around the table. Finally, Avery looked at Jace. "You had the perfect chance to complete our bargain, but you didn't take it."

Jace straightened, resting his arms on the table. "I murdered a man once." He swallowed hard at the guilt that still liked to creep in. "I won't do it again. Not even to save Kyrin."

Avery's dark eyes probed him. "Why did you stop Tavor?"

"I couldn't just watch a murder either. It wouldn't have been right."

Avery shook his head. "You Elôm followers are a strange lot." He fiddled with the empty tin cup. "I suppose now you're looking for payment for saving my life."

"No," Jace said, bringing the man's gaze back up in surprise. "That is not why I, at least, came after you. As I felt with your uncle, I didn't believe it would be right to let you die, especially at Davira's hand. I had no thoughts of payment."

Avery's expression slowly changed, becoming less cool and more open. "If any other man said that, I'd think him a liar . . . but I believe you." He sat for a moment in contemplative silence, and then turned to Tavor. "Are you fit for walking?"

Tavor straightened, only the slightest wince crossing his face. "I'm fit for fighting again if need be."

Avery gave a half smile. "Good. Have the men gather enough of the remedy for their people and bring it here."

Jace's heart leapt in his chest. Avery turned his gaze to him as Tavor left the table.

"You may not have expected payment for rescuing me, but I want to give it. Whatever you need for those in your camp and the sick here in the city, you can have."

Jace gasped out a breath, hardly daring to believe it.

Avery offered another half-smile. "I don't understand them, but I admire your convictions. If all Elôm believers are like you, then it would be a shame to lose them. After all, you may be the only ones who can restore Daniel to his throne. I dismissed your ability to do that at first, but I'm beginning to rethink it."

Jace shook his head. "I don't know how to thank you." *Or You, Lord.*

New energy coursed through him, combatting the effects of the fever. In just moments, they would have possession of the remedy! The very thing that could save Kyrin and Rayad. He turned to Holden.

"We need to leave as soon as we have the remedy." He wouldn't waste another precious second.

"It won't be an easy trek back to the dragons for you."

"I'll manage." Jace turned his attention back to Avery. "We'll see that you receive our payment for the remedy. I know it doesn't cover it, but at least it's something, and we do appreciate that you are helping people."

Avery shrugged. "Whatever you have will help. And you did save my life. I think we got off on the wrong foot. It is important to me to help the people in this city, but they are not the only ones in need of aid. At present, you are the strongest force in Arcacia standing against Davira. I may have trivialized that at first, but I wouldn't want it to change."

He offered Jace his hand, and Jace reached out to grip his forearm.

"Again, thank you."

Avery smiled and nodded. "If you're ever in Valcré again and need help, I'll be here . . . that is, if Davira doesn't succeed in killing me first." He looked at Aaron. "Same goes for you and your people."

A few minutes later, a couple of Avery's men walked in with four leather satchels they laid on the table. Avery opened the flap of one and pulled out a small vial of dark liquid. Jace's heart reacted in an elevated thump. There it was—the remedy that could save Kyrin.

"Two teaspoons is a dose," Avery told them. "For especially severe cases, you can give three. It's best to mix it with tea or something to help it go down."

Jace nodded, ready to snatch up the satchels and race back to Gem to be on their way.

"Try your best to keep them from freezing," Avery said. "Perhaps you can rig something to keep them under your coats."

"We'll have to go back to get our gear," Holden replied, looking in one of the satchels, which was filled with carefully packed vials. "We'll figure something out there."

They all stood. Aaron took one of the satchels, while Jace and Holden took the three others.

"Good luck with your trip back," Avery told them. "I hope you haven't lost too many people."

Jace's lungs seized with the thought of the losses they might face once they returned home. But he thanked Avery even though he knew the success of this trip had nothing to do with luck. Once more they clasped arms, and Avery said, "Say hello to Daniel for me." A wince crossed his face. "We didn't exactly part under the best circumstances."

"I will," Jace told him.

Itching to be on their way, Jace led them toward the door. His legs still shook a little, but he didn't think even a group of soldiers could stop him from getting the remedy back to Kyrin.

They paused at the street corner where Aaron said, "Tim and I will deliver the remedy to the warehouse. We'll meet you back at Ben and Mira's."

Jace nodded, and they parted. At first, he and Holden strode down the street in silence, but as the excitement of the last hour settled, Jace thought about what had led to all of this. No doubt Holden knew what he'd intended to do to Baron Reynold. Unease churned inside him. What did his friend think? Had

Elôm not brought him to his senses, he might have murdered a man. The very thought made him sick to his stomach.

He glanced at Holden. "How did you know where I was?"

"When I got up and realized you'd left, I went out to find you. I thought maybe you would offer Avery the deal of turning you in."

Jace would have to tell Holden that he had indeed offered, but his friend was still speaking.

"I met Timothy and Aaron on the way, and Avery told us where you were."

He stopped there and didn't mention anything about Jace's intended actions, for which he was thankful. He knew what a terrible thing he had almost done and was more than ashamed of it. He appreciated that Holden chose not to speak of it.

When they arrived, Ben and Mira waited anxiously. Apparently, they had been worried about Jace as well. He would miss their parental-like concern.

As Ben closed the door behind them, Jace lifted one of the satchels. "We have the remedy."

Mira put her clasped hands to her chest. "Praise the King!"

"Timothy and Aaron are taking some to the warehouse," Holden told them. "Jace and I need to leave immediately for Landale, but first we have to figure out how to transport the remedy without it freezing."

Mira thought for a moment and then bustled off. "I have an idea. Bring it into the dining room and I'll show you."

Jace and Holden brought the satchels into the dining room and set them on the table. Jace then turned to his friend. "I need to change into a fresh shirt and get my things."

He hurried upstairs to the guest bedroom and grabbed his pack from the floor. He pulled off his coat and sweat-soaked shirt. Once he'd put on a clean shirt and his jerkin, he stuffed everything else into the pack and carried it down to the dining room. Holden came in just behind him, carrying his own pack.

By then, Mira stood at the table and sheared a long strip from what looked to be an old bed sheet. "We'll wrap the vials up in this and you can tie them around your waist, under your coats. The closer to your skin, the better. That should keep them from freezing."

She emptied the satchels, lining the vials up in the middle of the cloth strip and wrapping it over them a couple of times so they would not slide out. Lifting it carefully, she turned to Jace. He pulled off his jerkin so that only his shirt separated the vials from the warmth of his skin, and he held them in place while Mira wrapped the length of fabric securely around him. Once she'd tied it off, she stepped back.

"How does that feel?"

"Good." Jace was happy to have the precious vials so close so he could make sure they were well protected. It was as if each one contained the lives of those he held most dear.

Satisfied, Mira turned to help Holden. Jace put on an extra wool shirt before slipping on his jerkin and buckling it snugly against the bundle around his waist. He then pulled on his coat.

Looking them both over, Mira asked, "I know you're in a hurry, but do you need anything to eat before you go?"

Holden shook his head. "We can eat once we're on our way."

Jace wasn't sure if Holden was just as anxious to return to camp or if he said that because he knew Jace would never wait. Either way, he appreciated his friend's understanding of the situation.

While they finished their final preparations to leave, Aaron and Timothy showed up, each with a full pack in tow.

"We're going back to Landale with you for a visit," Aaron told them, "in case you need any extra hands."

A bit of a smile reached Jace's face for the first time in what felt like weeks. "Everyone will be very happy to see you again."

Now the only thing left was to say goodbye. They all gathered near the door.

"We'll probably be back in a few weeks," Aaron told Ben and Mira. "Keep the payment safe, and I'll take it to Avery when we get back."

Ben nodded, and then their attention turned to Jace and Holden.

"Thank you for your hospitality while we were here," Jace told them. "With everything going on, I'm not sure we were the most pleasant guests."

"Nonsense," Mira said, shaking her head. "We were happy to have you and even more thankful that your trip was a success, thanks be to Elôm."

Not prolonging the inevitable, Ben clasped hands with each of them. "Tell Daniel he is in our prayers daily, as is the rest of your group."

Jace thanked him, and they traded reluctant farewells. Once out the door, however, Jace's mind turned toward Kyrin and Landale. If only Elôm could just place him there right this instant. The flight home would surely feel like an eternity.

Following the same path they'd traveled days earlier, they headed for the gate. They kept a close watch for soldiers who might be searching for them after the attack against Reynold. By the time they reached the gate and passed through, Jace was winded and had begun to sweat again.

"How are you doing?" Holden asked.

Jace drew in a deep breath, though the cold air stung his lungs. "I'm fine."

He wasn't going to let anything keep him from reaching Gem. As soon as he reached her, he could let his body be as weak as it needed. He just had to make it the final couple of miles into the forest where they'd left the dragons. He prayed no one had found them there. But who would venture that deep into the forest with all this snow and freezing temperatures? He comforted himself with this as he, Holden, Aaron, and Timothy detached their snowshoes from their packs and strapped them on.

Straightening, Jace lifted his pack a little higher on his shoulders and took another deep breath, blocking out the pain and weakness in his body and focusing on the path ahead. Leaving the wall of Valcré behind, they set off determinedly into the forest.

THE FAMILIAR LANDSCAPE of Landale set Jace's pulse to thumping against his ribs. How could only five days make him feel as though he'd been away for years? He glanced over his shoulder. Timothy's expression displayed his own anticipation to reach camp. After all, he hadn't seen Leetra in months. Jace didn't know how either of them did it.

He set his eyes back on the horizon, toward his home of the last two years. Everything felt as though it could turn out right . . . but would it? What would they find when they reached camp? Jace tried not to ask himself that question and focus only on what he prayed—no, *pleaded*—would be true: that they weren't too late to save the sick. That they weren't too late to save Kyrin.

Still, as they drew near, his heart changed from a rhythm of anticipation to a heavy thudding of dread. One part of him longed to urge Gem on with all speed while the other half shrank with the terror to land in camp and see what had transpired in their absence.

At last, barely perceivable wisps of smoke appeared above the trees. In another moment, the treetops thinned to reveal the snow-covered rooftops of the cabins. Gem glided downward with barely a prompting from Jace. When they set down just outside of camp, Jace looked around, hardly daring to breathe. Holden landed behind him. All was quiet and still. Aside from the smoke rising from the chimneys, there wasn't much for signs of life. Jace's throat constricted, and he had to stop himself from imagining the worst. He quickly dismounted, careful not to jostle the vials still tied around his waist. He wanted to run straight toward the Altairs' cabin, but he held himself back and looked over at Holden. His struggle must have been painted all over his face.

"Go," Holden told him. "I'll send someone for the vials and take mine to the meeting hall to distribute."

Jace nodded in thanks and was about to go but stopped himself once more. It was difficult to get words past his throat. "Will you . . . check on Rayad for me?"

Holden clapped him on the shoulder. "Of course."

Jace looked toward the cabin he and Rayad had shared. Was he still alive? Jace's heart already experienced the pain of the possibility that he was not. He'd been sick for so long . . .

Jace shook his head. Unfortunately, he could only check on one person at a time, and Rayad would understand his need to reach Kyrin's side. She was the love of his life—his soon-to-be wife if Elôm fulfilled his desperate pleas.

Half walking, half jogging, he strode toward the Altair cabin. His mouth felt as though he hadn't had a drop to drink in days. What would he find when he stepped through the door that now stood only a few feet away? Crossing the remaining distance in three strides, he reached for the knob, pausing for only the briefest moment to gasp out a prayer before pushing the door open.

He blinked as his eyes adjusted to the dim interior.

"Jace!"

It was Kaden's voice, but Jace's gaze locked on the occupied beds. Kyrin's mother lay in one and Kyrin in the other. Jace looked at Kyrin's face. Deep in his heart he'd hoped to find her awake and recovering, but she didn't stir at his entrance. She lay perfectly still, her eyes closed, her face a deathly, ashen hue just like in the horrible nightmare he'd had in Valcré. For one paralyzing moment, he feared she truly was dead until he caught the slightest rise and fall of her chest and let out his own breath that had been trapped.

"How is she?" he asked hoarsely, dragging his eyes to Kaden.

"She's not doing well. Did you get the remedy?"

Snapping fully to his senses, Jace nodded and dropped his pack, quickly tugging off his coat. "Yes." He let it drop too and unbuckled his jerkin, casting it aside. "The vials are here. Help me so they don't fall and break."

Jace lifted his wool shirt, and Kaden assisted him in unwrapping the strip of cloth.

"Get cups of tea," Jace instructed Marcus and Aric.

They jumped to do so.

Setting the bundle carefully on the table, Jace pulled out one of the vials and uncorked it. In a moment, Marcus set two cups of tea near him. Jace measured two teaspoons of the remedy into each. He handed one of the cups back to Marcus and took the other himself, crossing the room to Kyrin's bedside.

The sight of her pale, sunken face up close jolted him again. Gently, he slid his fingers through her matted hair and under her head, tipping it up. The back of her head heated his palm. He placed the cup to her lips and let a little of the tea and remedy mixture dribble in. She did nothing at first, the liquid just pooling in her mouth.

"Come on, Kyrin, swallow." *Please*. He tipped her head back a little more.

Finally, her throat moved. She coughed a little, but the tea went down. Little by little he let the rest trickle in until the cup emptied. He set it aside and rested her head back against her sweat-dampened pillow. Marcus seemed to have had success with his mother as well. Jace lightly brushed a few strands of hair away from Kyrin's face. How desperately he desired to see her gorgeous blue eyes open and looking up at him. *Please, Elôm, I love her so much.* His breath trembled as he drew it in and let it out again.

Still a bit weak from the fever and the lack of sleep, Jace sank into the chair next to Kyrin's bed and took her limp hand in his.

"I'm back," he murmured. He lifted her hand and kissed the soft skin near her knuckles. "I'm back and I'm not going anywhere until you're better and we're married."

The last few words came out in a hoarse whisper. He wanted so much for it to be true. He stared at her face. How long until they knew the remedy was working? It hadn't taken long for him, but he'd only been sick for a couple of hours, not days.

After another minute, he pried his gaze away from her to look up at the others. Kaden stood nearby. Jace had never seen him, or any of them, look so ragged and in need of a month's worth of sleep. It was a wonder they could even stand.

Jace swallowed hard. He needed to ask—needed to know—but dread lingered. Once he knew, there would be no more reason to hope. But with the hope, fear would continue to gnaw at him. He met Kaden's gaze, forcing his voice out for one, painful word. "Rayad?"

Jace's heart nearly broke apart with the force of its impact against his ribcage in the split second of unknown, waiting for Kaden's answer.

"He's still hanging in there . . . barely."

Jace's breath rushed out, and he felt a bit dizzy. Rayad could still die, but at least he hadn't yet. Hope remained. He fought back the sudden flood of moisture to his eyes. "Elanor?"

"She's fine so far. She's been helping out in the meeting hall. Josef got sick three days ago."

Jace's eyes widened at the news. It couldn't have been easy for anyone without their primary physician. He would have to go see Elanor and Rayad. For now, however, he couldn't make himself let go of Kyrin.

Timothy followed Aaron and Holden toward the meeting hall, more than a little afraid of what he'd find. He'd witnessed the ravaging effects of the fever on those in Valcré, but this camp was like home to him—the people here like family. *Lord, You see what is happening here. You've been here all along, and everyone who has fallen ill rests in Your hands. Give healing to those who are fighting this fever and peace to those who have lost loved ones. Let us all feel Your love in the midst of this hardship and tragedy.* He took a deep breath and added a personal prayer for one person in particular.

When they reached the door, Timothy braced himself. No doubt the meeting hall would resemble the warehouse in Valcré. Holden opened the door, and they stepped inside. Warm air engulfed them, but it was heavy with the smell of sweat and sickness. Row after row of cots and makeshift beds lined the floor. Timothy's gaze followed them all the way toward the back of the hall where his gaze snagged on one person.

His breath caught as everyone else momentarily disappeared except for Leetra. She stood near a table full of vials and bowls and all manner of other medicinal supplies, petite and beautiful, her long hair swaying as she reached for something. A heart-stopping mix of feminine beauty and the fierceness and pride of the cretes. The deep ache he'd held for her and kept at bay with the work he did in Valcré came free now that he could be near her for even a brief time.

She turned then, and their eyes met. Her beautiful lavender eyes. They grew wide, and she didn't even look back as she let a bowl slip from her hand with a quiet thud on the table. Skirting around the cots, she hurried toward him, running the last few feet into his arms. He wrapped her up tightly as she buried her face in his chest. Even through his coat, her warmth seeped into him, and he pressed his lips to her hair.

"I missed you so much," he whispered.

He felt each hard breath she took, no doubt a struggle to hold in tears. Finally, she stepped back, moisture around her weary, red-rimmed eyes. Knowing her, she hadn't slept in days. Timothy cupped her cheek in his hand. "Don't worry, we're here to help. We have the remedy."

Her eyes flashed wide again, and he gestured to Holden, who was already unwrapping his bundle of vials with Aaron's help.

In the space of a second, Leetra composed herself. "We must get it to everyone immediately. Some are barely hanging on."

Timothy couldn't help a small smile, in spite of the situation, as she hurried to take the vials from Holden. Leetra came across so cold and hard to others. Even he had thought so when they'd first met, but she cared more than almost anyone he knew. The coldness was merely her armor to protect how deep her feelings and care truly ran. And, Elôm willing, he wanted to spend the rest of his life encouraging that soft side of her to show.

TWENTY-FOUR HOURS. JACE rubbed his eyes and stared at Kyrin's still face. She hadn't moved at all since his return yesterday morning. Only her shallow breathing provided any sign of life. He glanced at Lydia in the other bed. She slept peacefully, having woken for the first time only an hour ago. Just long enough for Aric to give her a little of the broth Lenae had brought over. She'd stopped by early with the pot of it along with the happy news that Warin had been conscious for a short time during the night. Jace had to remind himself that Lydia and Warin hadn't been sick for as long as Kyrin had. It would take longer for the remedy to work and her body to regain the strength it needed for her to wake.

He laid his hand on her forehead. Still too warm. Shouldn't the fever have subsided at least? When Leetra had checked on them at dawn, she'd agreed that they should give Kyrin the extra half dose of the remedy. He'd been so sure that would bring her fever down.

Sighing, he leaned back and rubbed his sore neck, careful not to disturb the healing cut on the back of his head. He still kept getting headaches on and off from the concussion. Leetra was not subtle in her insistence that he should rest. But he just couldn't bear to leave Kyrin's side for more than a brief time.

Not until he saw some improvement. *Please take this fever from her and let her wake up.* He'd barely ceased praying since yesterday. He'd run out of words beyond simple pleas for her recovery.

The cabin door opened, and he looked over his shoulder. Liam stepped in, slipping his boots and coat off by the door. Fresh snowflakes fell around him. It must be snowing again. Jace hadn't even noticed.

Marcus and Kaden met him near the table, and they talked quietly, Liam reporting all those who were recovering. Jace tried not to let his anxiety grow that Kyrin wasn't one of them. When they finished, Liam joined him.

"I checked Rayad on the way here. He seems to be doing much better this morning. I can watch Kyrin if you'd like to go see him."

Jace hesitated. He wished they were all in the same place so he wouldn't have to leave her, but he did want to see for himself that Rayad was improving. It would help the knot of dread winding up his stomach.

He pushed to his feet and stretched his fatigued back. "I won't be long."

Tyra followed him outside. She'd been glued to him since Marcus had brought her to the cabin yesterday. According to Trev, she'd barely left Rayad's side while he was gone.

A light snow fell, but at least it wasn't a howling snowstorm. That would have made it difficult to get back and forth between cabins, and Leetra and Liam still made rounds regularly to check on everyone. Jace admired how they and Cassie had held everyone together after Josef had fallen ill.

When he entered the men's cabin, he found Elian sitting near the fireplace. Though still pale, he had certainly fared better than most, and the remedy had worked quickly on him. Mick was awake as well, propped up in his bed while Holden and Trev prepared lunch for them at the table. They each greeted him, and Jace made his way over to Rayad's bed.

When he'd first visited him yesterday afternoon, Rayad's gaunt appearance had disturbed him as much as Kyrin's had. He'd looked so near death, and while there wasn't a vast improvement today, a little color had returned to his face. When Jace touched his forehead, he found it a normal temperature. He breathed out a sigh. While not out of danger yet, at least Rayad had a good chance of recovering. One more day without the remedy and he might not have survived.

Jace eased down in an empty chair and reached over to straighten Rayad's blankets. As he tugged them into place, Rayad drew a deep breath and stirred. Jace stilled and looked at his face. A moment later, Rayad's eyes parted slowly. He blinked a couple of times before any clarity came to them, but then they focused.

"Jace," he breathed out, his voice rough but a wonderful sound.

Jace couldn't help the grin that split his face. "Yes, I'm here."

Rayad's eyes slid closed, his breathing deep and even. Jace thought he might be sleeping again, but his eyes opened once more, heavy but not lacking coherence.

"Kyrin?"

"She's still asleep." Jace swallowed hard. "But she'll wake up." She had to.

Rayad gave the barest hint of a nod and slipped back into unconsciousness. Jace sat still for a long moment. His heart rejoiced to have spoken with him, however briefly, when he'd been so close to death. At the same time, he ached like never before to hear Kyrin's voice again.

Fighting to hold onto the hope that Rayad's improvement offered him, Jace stayed at the cabin for close to a half an hour before his need to be with Kyrin grew too strong. As he pulled on his coat, Holden approached him.

"Leetra told me something this morning that I thought you should know. Dagren passed while we were gone. I guess the fever hit him hard."

Jace paused. The man responsible for Kalli and Aldor's murders and Baron Grey's execution was dead. He wasn't sure how to feel other than that Elôm's justice had been done. Perhaps he'd feel more strongly about it once Kyrin was out of danger.

Daniel dismounted Captain Darq's dragon and looked around. It was good to be back in the main camp. He'd felt isolated while he was gone, even if it was for only a couple of days. He had wanted to return the moment one of the riders had brought news of Jace and Holden's success and enough of the remedy to treat those who had fallen ill in the northern camp. However, he had felt he should stay a bit longer to make sure everything would go smoothly. Now that the sick were improving and no one was threatening to raid the supply shed, he and Cassie could return home while Sam remained behind to help Tane just in case things got out of hand again.

Daniel turned to Glynn's dragon to help Cassie down, and the two of them headed toward the meeting hall. When they entered, they found it still full of cots and beds, though the atmosphere had changed dramatically. Those who had been so ill when Daniel had left now rested comfortably or sat up eating and talking quietly to one another, praise Elôm.

Across the room, Elanor passed between the cots offering what smelled like a savory broth from a kettle to those who were awake. The bright smile on her face combatted any lingering signs of fatigue. It drew a wide smile to Daniel's lips. He was convinced that she could brighten anyone's spirits.

When she spotted him, her smile only deepened. She quickly returned the kettle to the fireplace and hurried to meet him.

"You're back." Her joy to see him erased the chill from the flight. "How are things in the other camp?"

"There was a bit of a ruckus when I arrived, but I took care of it."

"Of course you did."

The way her eyes beamed with pride made Daniel feel downright good about himself. A man could accomplish just about anything with a woman like her supporting him. He quite liked making her proud.

"How is everyone here?" he asked before the urge to kiss her could overtake him.

"Improving, thank Elôm. I don't know what we would have done if Jace and Holden hadn't made it back with the remedy."

Daniel was anxious to find out how things were in Valcré but wasn't quite ready to give up Elanor's company. The news could wait a bit longer.

"Is there anything I can help with?"

Something in her expression told him that she knew exactly what he was doing. With a satisfied little smile, she said, "You can help distribute broth. We're working to get everyone's strength up."

"Whatever you command, my lady." He gave her short bow, causing light laughter to bubble out of her.

Daniel thanked Elôm that he no longer had to worry that she would catch the fever and die. It had come to the point where he couldn't quite imagine his life without her in it.

Another day dawned. Jace sat in the same chair he had occupied for most of those hours, staring at Kyrin's face, willing her eyes to open. Why hadn't she wakened yet? Why wasn't she recovering? Why wasn't the remedy working? The questions ate away at his sanity. He hung his head, his heavy eyelids sliding closed. He hadn't slept at all in two . . . three days?

"Jace."

He looked up at Kaden. Kyrin's twin glanced at her, worry lines deeper than they should be for someone only nineteen. But determination settled in his expression as his attention returned to Jace. "You should rest or at least get some air. I'll watch her, and one of us will get you at the slightest change. You've barely left the cabin."

Jace rested his gaze on Kyrin again. It was hard to tear himself away from her. He wanted to be here the moment she opened her eyes, or . . . if the worst should happen . . .

Moisture blurred his vision, and he swallowed nearly overcome. Kaden was right. He needed a moment to compose himself and gather strength for whatever today would bring.

Without a word, he rose and collected his coat. Tyra followed, as always, her quiet presence comforting, though she was more subdued than usual. He knew she could sense his mood. She might even know things weren't right with Kyrin. He looked toward the other cabins as he stepped outside. Rayad had woken up again yesterday, even taking some broth, which would surely help his recovery. Jace should visit him, but something tugged him toward the forest instead. A soul-deep need.

Turning, he crossed camp, passing the cabin he'd put so many hopes and dreams into before everything had collapsed. It seemed like a different lifetime. He didn't go far outside of camp in case someone came looking for him but far enough to feel the solitude of the forest. Here, beside a towering maple, he sank to his knees and bowed his head.

For a long moment, he knelt in silence as emotions, fears, and heartache roared inside him. At last, he forced his mind to quiet as much as possible and reached out for the presence he knew was always there.

"Elôm." The name hung before him with his frozen breath. "I can't lose Kyrin. I can't . . ." Tears left scalding streams down his face. "But . . . I know she's in Your hands. You can save her . . . or You can take her. I don't know how I'd survive the loss . . ."

He hunched over, the pain already almost too much to bear. In the midst of it, a question seemed to whisper through his soul, gently but firmly, asking him who was more important to him—Kyrin or Elôm? He choked down a sob that lodged in his throat with the rising flood of pain. How could he answer that question? He shook his head, but after the initial wave of grief, quietness followed, and he straightened up again, swiping away the tears with his gloves. More threatened, but he looked up at the sky.

"I tried to save Kyrin myself and almost went against everything I believe. I doubted You, Lord, and forgot my faith. I never want to do that again." A couple more tears made their escape. "Kyrin is Yours. I love her more than anything in this world, but You love her even more. If You want to take her . . . I know, even if I don't understand, that it's best. I couldn't survive it on my own, but if that's what You want of me, then I know You'll give me the strength I don't have."

The grief descended again, and Jace let it course through him, spilling out in his tears and heaving breaths as he surrendered entirely to Elôm's will.

After a time, he mastered his emotions, feeling beyond spent, yet possessing a quiet peace he'd needed so desperately.

Tyra padded up to him, nosed his face, and then started licking away the remnants of his tears. Jace scrubbed his fingers through the fur around her neck.

"Let's go back," he said hoarsely.

Bracing his hand against the tree, he rose stiffly to his feet, and they trudged back into camp. Jace steeled himself as they entered the Altair cabin. Kaden sat at Kyrin's bed. Clearly, she had not moved since he'd left. Jace hung up his coat and reclaimed his seat at her side.

The morning stretched out into afternoon. His elbows propped on the bed and forehead resting against his hands, Jace prayed. He'd let go and accepted the possibility of Kyrin's death, but it didn't stop him from pleading for her recovery as well as for the strength he just did not have. He prayed until he thought his heart might break apart with the intensity of his pleas and the emotions within him.

"Jace."

Everything stilled. He sat frozen for the barest second, afraid to hope, and then raised his head. Dusty blue eyes met his. He gasped out a breath and shoved to his feet. "Kyrin!"

He put his hand to her face as she stared up at him, the barest hint of a smile lifting her lips. He stroked her cheek and then touched her forehead as Kyrin's brothers crowded around him. The heat of the fever had nearly vanished. She closed her eyes as if savoring his touch, but his heart dropped, wanting to see them open again. They opened a moment later, though she obviously struggled to stay awake. Jace looked over his shoulder at Kaden. "Get some broth."

They needed to get food into her while she was still conscious. Kaden rushed to the fireplace where they kept the kettle of broth warm and hurried back with a cup of it. Jace took it from him and lifted Kyrin's head, putting the cup to her lips.

"Kyrin, drink as much of this as you can. It will help you feel better."

She murmured a quiet syllable, her eyes closed, but she took several swallows of broth before she lost consciousness again.

Jace gently let her head rest back. She'd awakened. Though still too early to know for sure if she would recover, hope surged through him. He pressed his fingers hard against his eyes lest the tears break free and whispered, "Thank You, Elôm."

Trask blinked, struggling to dispel the grogginess from his mind, and let out a small groan. He never wanted to be sick again. He rubbed his face, though his arms felt like they had grain sacks tied to them. The swish of fabric drew his attention, and he dropped his hands from his eyes to reveal the lovely sight of his wife.

"Hello, beautiful."

She laughed lightly, a grin lighting up her previously taut face. "Well, you must be feeling much better."

Trask raised his brows. "Define better."

She sat down near him on the edge of the bed. "At least you're in the mood to flirt instead of lying there half dead and scaring me to death."

He could see in her face how true that was. Reaching for her hand, he drew her a little closer. "I'm sorry." He meant it with all his heart. Still, he couldn't stop a grin from forming. "As soon as I've recovered my strength, I'll make it up to you."

Anne shook her head, trying to hide a smile and the bit of a blush that added color to her pale cheeks. "You're lucky we're the only ones here."

"Really?" He lifted his head to look around the cabin, but even that took extreme effort, and he let it fall back again with a heavy sigh.

Anne lifted her brow in amusement. "There will be no mischief from you until you've had proper time to recover."

She knew him too well. "Killjoy."

She laughed again, a most delightful sound, and then leaned over to kiss him. He wrapped his arm around her, pulling her close. He'd come far too close to losing such precious moments when they'd barely been married for half a year.

After a minute or two, Anne pulled away a little and gazed into his eyes. "I can't tell you how thankful I am that you're feeling better. We came so close to losing so many."

Trask smiled gently at her. Oh, if only he could give her a more stable and quiet life. Someday, he prayed. He brushed his fingers through her hair. "I know you were worried, but I'll be fine now. You don't have to worry anymore."

Her lips twitched in a quick smile, but something else flashed in her eyes.

"What is it?"

She shook her head. "It's nothing."

"Come on, if something is upsetting you, I'd like to know."

"It's hardly worth thinking about compared to what we've dealt with for the last couple of weeks."

Trask tipped his head a little, questioning her with his eyes. He truly wanted to know.

She let out a light sigh. "For the last few days, I thought . . . maybe . . . I was pregnant. But I guess I'm not."

Trask's heart thumped. Though it took almost all the strength he had, he pushed himself up to his elbow so he could face her better. "You thought you were pregnant?"

Her chin dipped in a quick nod.

"Are you sure you're not?" The thought of having a child was . . .

"Unfortunately, I'm sure." She gave him a sad little smile.

They both fell silent for a moment. Trask hadn't even had a chance to think she might be pregnant before learning she wasn't, yet a keen disappointment took hold.

"I suppose it's for the best," she said. "With all the stress, or if I still get sick, I might have miscarried. It's not the best time for a baby anyway."

Trask reached out for her hand again. "Any time is good for a baby."

A smile finally bloomed on her face once more. "You think so?"

"Absolutely." He drew her closer. "And just because you aren't pregnant now doesn't mean you won't be in the near future."

They shared a grin and another kiss.

All day Jace waited and watched for Kyrin to wake up again while helping her brothers get more fluids into her. She didn't wake up, but at least her fever had broken.

The waiting remained difficult, though. Jace found himself caught between the desire to let Elôm work the way He willed and his concern. It took nearly constant prayer to hold onto that peace he'd felt earlier in the woods. But he'd meant what he had told Elôm. Whatever Elôm willed for Kyrin, Jace would accept it.

Sometime after a quiet supper, Kaden approached Jace. "Why don't you get some rest?"

Jace hesitated. It was just so hard to leave Kyrin.

"You're going to end up killing yourself with lack of sleep. Then what would we tell Kyrin?"

Jace had to smile at Kaden's firm tone. It was the same one Kyrin used when he was being foolishly stubborn. No doubt he'd hear it plenty of times as Kyrin's husband.

He looked up at Kaden and nodded. "All right."

Kaden looked both surprised and relieved. "Why don't you sleep in the loft? Marcus, Liam, and I will take turns watching Kyrin. We'll wake you if there's any change."

Jace nodded again, staring at Kyrin's face. He wanted a turn watching her too, but that wouldn't speed her recovery, and he needed a full night's rest more than he wanted to admit. Every ache and weakness in his body proved this as he pushed himself up from his chair. He brushed his fingers gently against Kyrin's cheek and then turned toward the loft. Murmuring goodnight to Kyrin's brothers, he climbed the ladder.

In the loft, he paused and scanned the small area. This was where Kyrin and her mother usually slept. Jace's gaze touched each of her things, imagining them in their own cabin. If they'd been married already, he could have fallen asleep at her side. Soon, he told himself. Elôm willing, that would come soon.

JACE BLINKED HIS eyes open, the warm comfort of sleep fading slowly. He didn't remember the last time he'd slept so soundly. Morning light shone through the windows downstairs. As comfortable as he was, his thoughts turned immediately to Kyrin, and he pushed back the covers.

Below him, dishes clinked quietly and male voices murmured. A female voice joined in, and Jace's pulse quickened. Yet, listening closer, he recognized Lydia's voice, not Kyrin's. He tamped down disappointment. Just because it wasn't her didn't mean she wouldn't be improved this morning.

He got up, straightened out his sleep-wrinkled clothing, and buckled on his jerkin before descending the ladder. His gaze went straight to Kyrin's bed. Her eyes were closed, and Marcus sat beside her. Jace walked over to them.

"How is she?"

"Better, it seems." Marcus smiled.

Jace studied Kyrin's face. She did look better, like she slept peacefully and not on the verge of death. He prayed a night of rest without fighting the fever would make all the difference in her recovery.

Relieved, Jace looked around the cabin. Lydia sat propped up in bed, her expression weary but alert. Ronny occupied the chair next to her while Kaden and Liam worked on breakfast.

"You can sit here." Marcus rose from his chair.

"Thank you." Jace switched places with him and scooted the chair a little closer to the bed. Careful not to wake her, he slipped his hand under hers and cradled it, gently rubbing his thumb over her fingers. She was so beautiful. He'd never wanted anything the way he wanted to love and cherish her for the rest of their lives.

The morning passed quietly, the oppressiveness of fear and worry not nearly so heavy. Kyrin's brothers took turns getting much needed rest, and Jace eventually visited with Rayad. Though still weak, Rayad seemed much more like himself.

When Jace returned to the Altair cabin shortly before noon, he noticed Kyrin stirring as he hung up his coat. He hurried to her side just as her eyes fluttered open. They rested on him, clear, vivid, and alert. Her soft lips turned up as she smiled at him.

"How do you feel?" he asked.

She drew a deep breath and shifted under the covers. "Weak . . . but better."

A full grin came easily to Jace. "Good."

Her eyes shifted past him, her smile returning. "Hey."

Jace looked over to see all her brothers gathered around the bed.

"You're always fussing and worrying over us," Kaden said in a teasingly scolding tone, "but here you're the one who worried us all sick."

Kyrin breathed a tiny laugh. "I'm sorry." She seemed to take in their faces, and the humor faded, her forehead wrinkling. "Where's Mother?"

"I'm here."

Kyrin turned her head to her mother's voice. Lydia had propped herself up to look over at Kyrin. Her brown eyes filled with moisture, but she smiled widely.

"You were sick?" Kyrin asked.

Lydia nodded. "Yes, but thanks to Jace, we're all recovering."

Kyrin slowly tipped her head back to look up at him. "You got the remedy?"

Still holding her hand, Jace squeezed it gently. "Yes."

She smiled softly again. "I knew you would."

Jace's own smile faltered at what had almost happened in Valcré. He would have to tell her. But for now, he would just revel in her recovery.

"Kyrin, do you want some broth?" Marcus asked.

"Yes, please. I am a bit hungry."

"We should hope so," Kaden said, sitting down at the foot of the bed. "You've been sick for ten days. I would've died of starvation by now."

Kyrin raised her brows at him. "Ten days?"

They all nodded.

As Jace helped Liam prop an extra pillow behind Kyrin, she looked up at him, her face strained with concern.

"How is Rayad?"

Jace rested his hand on her shoulder. "He is recovering well. I just visited with him this morning."

Kyrin let out a long breath. "Thank Elôm."

"You're the one we've all worried about," Jace told her quietly. "The fever hit you hard. For a while, the remedy didn't seem to be working."

She gazed at him soberly and, with effort, reached up to place her hand over his. "I'm sorry I worried you so."

No doubt she could see the toll these days had taken on him.

Jace shook his head. "It's all right. I learned a great deal about faith and trusting Elôm while waiting for you to recover."

Kyrin slept for most of the next two days, but each day she grew a little stronger. Now that the danger had passed, Jace moved back into his cabin, though he still spent most of his time with the Altairs.

On the third morning, he visited with Rayad, who was now sitting up in bed and getting a bit restless, before heading over to see Kyrin. She was awake when he walked in and had a smile for him that immediately set his heart to praising Elôm for her recovery. Jace nodded in greeting to Lydia, who stood at the table kneading dough. Though she still took it easy at her sons' insistence, she was clearly happy to work around the cabin again. Jace looked for Kaden and the others, but it appeared they had all gone out. Perfect. It would give him a chance to talk to Kyrin in relative privacy.

He took his seat and smiled at her, resisting the urge to give her a good kiss. There would be time enough for that soon, he hoped.

"You look much better today." She looked adorable, actually, with her mussed up hair and healthy color returning to her cheeks, but such observations just tempted him more and he reined them in.

The playful sparkle in her eyes suggested she read his thoughts. "At least I can lift my head and arms now without feeling like they're tied down. How are the others?"

"Everyone is doing very well. Josef is back on his feet, though Leetra keeps a close eye on him and orders him to lie down if she thinks he's overdoing it."

Kyrin laughed merrily at this.

Jace chuckled too. "Timothy has to keep reminding her that Josef's not a child."

Kyrin shook her head, still giggling. "How are they getting along?"

"Well, you know Leetra. No one but you could probably tell how much she's missed him, but Timothy can't stop smiling and is spending as much time with her as he can. She's not discouraging him, so I wouldn't say anything has changed since he left."

"Good." Kyrin readjusted her blankets with a satisfied look. "I do hope he and Aaron can stay for a bit." She cast him a cute little grin. "At least long enough for our wedding."

They hadn't spoken of their betrothal since she'd woken up, but Jace welcomed the topic. "When do you want to have it?"

"As soon as I can walk ten paces without falling over."

Jace had to laugh. He'd see to it she was a little more recovered than that. "A couple of weeks then?"

Kyrin nodded.

This suited Jace just fine. The sooner the better in his mind. "I guess we should start planning then. I'll talk to Trask about it now that he's up and about."

"I just want it small," Kyrin said. "I know we don't have enough food for a celebration feast, and that's all right. I just want to get married."

Jace smiled, gazing at her. How was it possible to love someone even more with every moment you spent with them?

"That sounds perfect." He leaned over and placed a kiss on her forehead. How wonderful to feel the natural warmth of her skin and not the burning heat of fever.

As he pulled away, she looked into his eyes and asked, "What was it like in Valcré?"

Jace settled in his chair with a wince. He hated to speak of it, especially just after discussing their wedding, but it was time to tell her. He took her hand in his. By now, concern had furrowed her brow, her expression gently seeking answers.

He fortified himself with a quick prayer. "I almost did something terrible, and I am ashamed at how close I came to doing it."

Quietly, he told her everything that had taken place in Valcré. Just as he'd come to expect from her, she looked on him with nothing but compassion and love in her eyes, even as he confessed how weak his faith had been. When he finished, a bit of a burden lifted, though lingering guilt still clung stubbornly.

Kyrin squeezed his hand. "You didn't do it, Jace. You thought about it, but you knew it was wrong and you didn't go through with it."

She was right, of course, though he still hated how close he had come to doing it at all. "I just lost faith in that moment. I didn't know if Elôm would save you, and I felt I had to do it myself. I was just so afraid to lose you."

She smiled lovingly at him. "I know. But just look at how Elôm took your weakness and used it for good anyway. If you hadn't been caught by Reynold's men, you wouldn't have overheard that they were going after Avery. He would have been taken to Davira and killed, and many more would have died here without the remedy."

Jace shook his head as he pondered it. What an incredible thing. Mortals could mess things up so terribly, yet Elôm could still use their mistakes to bring about good.

Kyrin rested against her pillow, basking in the warm emotions of her visit with Jace. It pained her deeply to think of what he'd gone through in Valcré and having to watch her on the verge of death. Yet, the pain didn't quite stifle the giddy fluttering in her chest at the thought of their wedding. A couple of weeks! In only days, she would be Kyrin Ilvaran, Jace's wife! She'd wanted it for so long. If only she were well enough to marry him now, but she would strive to practice patience in the next two weeks.

Smiling to herself, lost in daydreams, she almost didn't notice her mother rustling around up in the loft. When she came down the ladder, she had a long bundle draped over her arm. Kyrin peered at it curiously as she walked toward her.

Her mother laid the bundle across the end of the bed and loosened the ribbons that held it together. "I couldn't help overhearing your wedding plans."

She shared a smile of delight with Kyrin.

"I thought now would be the perfect time to show you this." Her mother reached into the bundle and lifted up a simple yet beautifully elegant, long-sleeved white gown. Kyrin's heart skipped a beat. She'd seen that dress once before when she was just a little girl.

"It's your wedding dress," she said, breathlessly.

Her mother nodded, her eyes misty. "Yes. I brought it back when we visited Mernin. I thought . . . maybe you would like to wear it."

Kyrin pushed herself up higher in bed to see the dress better, but it blurred in a rush of moisture. To wed Jace in the same dress her mother had worn to marry her father . . .

She nodded, sniffling as tears tracked down her face. "I would love to."

Her mother smiled, tears running down her cheeks as well. "You'll look lovely in it." She laid the dress down gently. "I told your brothers to bring us a tub. I think both of us could use a warm bath."

Kyrin wiped at her wet cheeks, nodding eagerly. She might not be able to walk farther than the fireplace, but she'd been in this bed for far too long.

"Perhaps after, if you're up to it, you can try the dress on and we'll see if any alterations need to be made."

Kyrin could hardly wait.

A short while later, Kyrin's brothers returned, tromping in with a metal tub between them, full of snow to melt near the fire. They set it down next to the hearth and eagerly took part in the lunch their mother had waiting for them. Once the snow melted, their mother added kettles of boiling water to it and shooed the boys out once more. Drawing the curtains for privacy, she turned to Kyrin.

"You can go first."

Kyrin sat up and slipped her legs over the side of the bed. Her mother put a supporting arm around her waist, helping her toward the fireplace. Kyrin's leg muscles shook like they hadn't been used in ages, but she made it across the cabin and braced herself as her mother helped her undress. Stepping into the tub and sinking down into the water, she sighed. Yes, this was every bit as heavenly as she imagined it would be.

With her mother's help, she scrubbed her skin and hair, and then rinsed it well. Nodding in satisfaction, her mother said, "You can just soak for a bit, and I'll change the sheets on your bed."

"Are you sure?" Kyrin didn't want her mother overexerting herself.

"This won't take long. I'll be fine."

Kyrin didn't have much energy to argue, so she just rested back against the tub and closed her eyes, drifting on the edge of consciousness until her mother finished. She helped Kyrin out of the tub, drying her off and wrapping her in a blanket to sit by the fire where her hair would dry faster. Adding a couple more kettles of hot water, she took her turn in the bath.

For a long while, silence settled as Kyrin stared at the logs in the fireplace and thought back over the days she was sick. The fever had brought vivid dreams, many of her father. She pulled her blanket more tightly around herself, longing for his hugs and loving voice.

Before she could let herself get overwhelmed with emotion, she focused on the bits and pieces she remembered that weren't dreams. She glanced at her mother. "Aric was here while I was sick."

"Yes, he was a big help to me and then to the boys."

Kyrin frowned at the fire, a hazy image floating in her mind. How odd to have a memory that wasn't clear. Still, she remembered it. It wasn't the same as the dream images. "I saw him holding you."

The bath water swished, and Kyrin looked over at her mother. Her expression was tense.

"It's all right," Kyrin said quickly. "I'm glad he was here . . . and I'm glad he cares." She paused for a moment. She wasn't often wrong about such things. "Maybe I'm reading too much into this, but . . . don't feel bad if you are interested in Aric."

Her mother looked down at the water, her voice quiet. "He's been very kind and . . ." She seemed to struggle for words.

"I know it's hard because of Father." Kyrin's chest squeezed with memories. "I think we all want to hold onto him as much as we can, but I do think he would want someone here to take care of you if you found the right person. Aric was one of his best friends. I think that would make him happy."

Tears rolled down her mother's face, rippling the water as they dripped off her chin. Kyrin had to wipe her own cheeks.

Her mother nodded shakily before finally looking at her. "I don't know if that is really what's happening, but thank you. I wouldn't want to do anything that would upset you or your brothers."

Kyrin sent her an encouraging smile. "I think we all understand how important it is to have people in our lives who love us and are there for us with all that's going on. I don't think that would upset them."

A trembling smile graced her mother's lips and she nodded. Reaching up, she wiped her face and drew a breath. She then grabbed a towel and got out of the tub. Once she was clothed, she offered Kyrin a much stronger smile. "Do you want to try on the dress?"

KYRIN PRESSED HER hand to her stomach where the butterflies fluttered like crazy. Could this day really be here? After a week of bedrest and another week of taking it easy, her strength had yet to recover completely, but it didn't matter. Today she would marry Jace, and that gave her all the strength and energy she needed.

"How are you feeling?" her mother asked as she brushed her fingers through Kyrin's hair and twisted pieces up in a long, elegant style.

"Like I can barely sit still."

Her mother laughed lightly. Only the two of them occupied the cabin. Kyrin was glad of this quiet time before the ceremony, though she was as jittery as her first day at the palace. Still, the emotions and anticipation were significantly more pleasant.

"I just can't believe today is finally here." She felt like she'd known Jace for half a lifetime already. They'd gone through so much together and, within an hour, she would be his wife. All she wanted was to run to him and marry him right this second, but she forced herself to remain still. She'd waited this long, she could wait a bit longer.

"There," her mother announced a minute later. She stepped around the chair to face Kyrin with a bright smile. "Now the dress."

The butterflies all fluttered anew. Kyrin stood up and her mother helped her slip on the dress. The fine, soft linen fell comfortably against her skin. Her mother laced up the back and, with the slight alterations she'd made, it fit Kyrin perfectly—the bodice snug, but comfortable, flaring gradually at the waist to a full skirt. Small gold trimming lined the collar, following the lines of the bodice and then around the waist.

Kyrin's mother reached around her and fastened a dark cord around her neck. Kyrin lifted her hand and clasped the familiar blue stone hanging from it—the necklace she had given her father. She squeezed it, breathing deeply to keep the tears from falling, and let the stone rest in front of her dress. Now she would have something of both her mother's and her father's when she married Jace.

"Come see." Her mother guided her toward the long mirror they had borrowed.

Kyrin smiled widely at her reflection. The dress was beautiful, and her mother had done a wonderful job with her hair, pinning up the sides and accenting the style with small gold combs. Another level of reality settled. She was a bride! In all her years at Tarvin Hall, she never could have imagined this day. Tears filled her eyes, especially when she spotted those just about to splash down her mother's cheeks.

"It's so beautiful," Kyrin said, choking a little on her words.

Her mother stepped in front of her, clasping her arms in her hands. "You're so beautiful."

At a gentle knock on the door, her mother turned to answer it.

"May I come in?" Kaden's voice drifted from the other side. "Yes."

Their mother opened the door wider, and he stepped inside. He stopped when he saw Kyrin and looked her up and down. She turned to face him fully. The cutest smile lit his face, and she could swear there were tears in his eyes, though he'd probably deny it.

"You look beautiful," he said.

"Thank you." It was certainly a better reaction than when he'd first seen her all made up at Auréa Palace. That seemed like an eternity ago. They'd both grown up so much.

"Could I talk to Kyrin for a minute before Marcus gets here?" Kaden asked.

Their mother smiled at him and nodded. Taking her cloak from one of the chairs, she slipped it around her shoulders.

"I will see you soon."

Kyrin grinned, her heart almost leaping from her throat to think of Jace waiting for her not far away. What would he think of her dress? She was sure he'd appreciate the simplicity of it.

Once their mother left the cabin, Kyrin looked up at her twin. For most of her life, Kaden had been her protector—the one she turned to in both the good and bad. Even here, it was natural for her to look on him like that. But things would change today. That role would now fall squarely on Jace as her husband. In a way, it was sad, but Kaden didn't look too heart-broken over it. She could see in his eyes how happy he was for her.

"So," he said.

She grinned. "So."

"I always knew you and Jace would get married someday."

"Did you?"

Kaden shrugged. "Well, maybe not always, but you two have been pretty much inseparable since you met. I think most people probably figured it would come to this."

Kyrin laughed a little. "That's true." She looked him in the eyes. "You are happy about it, aren't you?"

"Of course." Kaden shook his head. "I could never see you with anyone else. And I trust Jace. When it comes to you, I don't give that trust out easily. Besides, he's a lot better than Collin."

Kyrin laughed again at the memory of the flirtatious young man at Tarvin Hall who Kaden had disliked so much. "That is true. Thank you for taking such good care of me. I'm glad you feel Jace is worthy of your trust."

Kaden's expression grew more serious. "Father liked him too."

The breath hitched in Kyrin's lungs. One of her biggest regrets was that her father hadn't had more time to get to know Jace. "Did he?"

"Yes. The day he, uh . . ." Kaden cleared his throat. "The day he left for Valcré, I overheard him talking to Jace. He told him that he saw in him a man of strong character and not to believe any lies to the contrary. I think he'd be happy to have Jace as a son-in-law."

Kyrin put her hand to her chest, which suddenly ached fiercely. She'd done well with her tears all morning, but now they spilled over. "I wish . . . he was here." She hiccupped, trying not to fall apart completely. "Both him and Michael."

Kaden's eyes were definitely full of tears now. "Me too." He reached for her, and she hugged him tightly.

After a moment, she stepped back and reached for the handkerchief her mother had left on the table. Dabbing her eyes, she worked to control her emotions. Today was a day for happy tears, not sorrowful ones. Both her father and younger brother would agree. She smiled, still a bit tearful, at Kaden. "Thank you for telling me. It means everything to me to know Father would have approved of Jace as my husband."

Kaden smiled in return. "I know he would." He cleared his throat again, appearing to gather his own composure. "Why don't I go get Marcus?"

Kaden let himself out, and Kyrin waited. For a long time she'd imagined Kaden walking her down the aisle, but when they'd discussed it, he'd insisted it should be Marcus, as the oldest and now head of their family. Kyrin thought it was one of the sweetest things he'd ever done, giving up such an important role to their brother. Kyrin had seen the surprise and gratitude on Marcus's face when Kaden told him. She loved her brothers so much. They'd come so far.

A moment later, the door opened, and Marcus stepped inside. He looked very handsome in his militia uniform—very much like their father, and it warmed Kyrin to see that in him. She squeezed the stone necklace again and smiled. Like Kaden, he took in her appearance with a bit of awe.

"You like it?" she asked.

He grinned. "It's beautiful. I think Jace will be speechless."

Kyrin laughed, something that came as easily as tears today. "Hopefully not so much that he can't say his vows."

Marcus chuckled in agreement. "Are you ready?"

Kyrin glanced around the cabin to make sure she wasn't forgetting anything and then nodded. "Yes, I think so."

She reached for the white cloak Anne had somehow found for her, and Marcus draped it around her shoulders. He then offered his arm to her.

"Let's get you to your anxiously waiting husband-to-be."

Jace took a deep breath in and let it out slowly. He'd imagined this day countless times in the past. Almost always, he'd imagined himself nearly sick with nerves, similar to what he'd experienced during Warin and Lenae's wedding. But he wasn't. Oh, the nerves were there, making him fidget and shift around so much it was a miracle both Rayad and Holden hadn't grabbed him to hold him still. Yet, it wasn't fearful nerves. It was the sort of anxious anticipation that tempted him to dash over to the Altair cabin, grab Kyrin up, sweep her over here, and get their vows said so they wouldn't have to be apart for another minute longer.

He nearly laughed at himself. What had happened to him? A year ago, those feelings would have been replaced with the urge to run out into the forest and hide for a while. Now he wanted this so badly he had to wrestle with impatience. Of all the men in the world, he would have considered himself the very last to ever find a woman he loved with the intensity he loved Kyrin. What a special and incredible person Elôm had created and brought into his life. He sure didn't deserve it, even now. Thank Elôm for His grace and infinitely patient love. Jace prayed he could shower Kyrin with even a fraction of that great love for the rest of their lives.

Rocking from his toes to his heels and back, Jace looked over at Rayad, who barely hid a grin. Jace attempted to settle himself, but it was starting to feel as though he'd been standing here all day. He looked around the meeting hall. The General and the three other soldiers who had survived the fever had been relocated, thank Elôm. Jace didn't want the sight of Kyrin's grandfather to ruin the day for her. The men had set up benches and chairs to accommodate all of their closest friends. Almost everyone was here now. Everyone but Kyrin and Marcus. Surely they'd be here any minute.

Distracting himself from the torturously slow passing of time, Jace glanced over at Timothy. Leetra sat tucked in close to Timothy's side, their hands clasped together. Would today set their minds toward marriage? Their relationship seemed to be moving in that—

The door opened, and Jace straightened, all thoughts vanishing. He locked his gaze on that open door. With a swish of white, Kyrin entered the hall with Marcus. They paused where Kaden waited and took the white cloak from Kyrin's shoulders to reveal the full splendor of her dress. Jace couldn't breathe. When their eyes met as she and Marcus started down the aisle, Jace's heart didn't even beat. She was here, and she was gorgeous, and in moments, she would be his. Elôm's grace and love were magnificent indeed.

Shortly, she stood in front of him, the picture of perfection in his eyes. She gave her older brother a smile and a quick hug before he handed her over to Jace. Jace took her hands in his, gazing down at her. Only when Daniel spoke did Jace shift his attention away from her, but only momentarily.

Daniel shared a bit of their story, and Kyrin's eyes glittered, her smiling lips twitching mirthfully in memory of their early days. He still didn't know how she had stuck with him and endured his misery. She'd been right there with him on some of the darkest paths he'd ever traveled.

At last came the vows—words Jace meant with his whole heart and couldn't wait to give in pledge to Kyrin.

"I, Jace Ilvaran, take you, Kyrin, to be my wife, to share in Elôm's plans for our lives together, for better or for worse, in sickness and in health, in joys and sorrows, until death do us part. I give you all that I have of myself and my love, with Elôm's help, to be your supportive and strong husband. All these things I pledge before our eternal King Elôm and those gathered here as witness."

Tears gathered in Kyrin's eyes as she smiled the biggest smile Jace had ever seen. She gazed up at him with a love he would happily drown in, her earnest voice touching his heart.

"I, Kyrin Altair, take you, Jace, to be my husband, to share in Elôm's plans for our lives together, for better or for worse, in sickness and in health, in joys and sorrows, until death do us part. I give you all that I have of myself and my love, with Elôm's help, to be your supportive helper and wife. All these things I pledge before our eternal King Elôm and those gathered here as witness."

Aside from Elon, Jace had never heard sweeter words.

With joy in his voice, Daniel said, "By the power vested in me by Elôm and as the crown prince of Arcacia, I pronounce you husband and wife . . ."

Jace held his breath, waiting for the last part, and caught Daniel grinning out of the corner of his eye. Had he not been so intent on Kyrin, he would have cuffed him on the shoulder for delaying, prince or not.

"You may now kiss your bride."

Jace barely waited for him to finish. He scooped Kyrin into his arms and kissed her deeply as he'd wanted to so many times before. Her arms wrapped around his neck, and she returned the kiss with just as much enthusiasm. All around them, their friends erupted in cheers, whoops, and applause, but Jace's sole focus was his bride. They may have a month together, a year, ten years, or a hundred. However long Elôm gave them, this moment would live in his memory as one of the happiest times of his entire life.

As they swayed gently to the lovely melody Talas and some of their other crete friends played on their flutes, Kyrin rested her head against Jace's chest, savoring the warmth of his arm wrapped around her. Today had been everything she'd dreamed of and more. Perfect in every way except for those who could not be here with them. She let a long contented sigh escape. Jace's lips pressed against the top of her head, and she looked up into his smile that sent warmth cascading all the way down to her toes. He bent his head farther and kissed her lips, sending tingles after the warmth.

"Are you enjoying yourself?" he asked in a low murmur.

"Very much."

He glanced around before his attention focused again on her. "Would you be very disappointed if we left?"

Kyrin's heart fluttered. Though she'd enjoyed their wedding celebration, she was growing a bit weary and was more than ready for some time alone with her new husband.

"Not at all."

Jace grinned and captured her hand to lead her toward the door. He pulled on his coat and then retrieved her cloak, wrapping it around her shoulders and planting a soft kiss at the base of her neck in the process. She grinned to herself. She already loved being a wife.

With a most handsome smile, he offered her his arm and led her outside, holding her close as the icy breeze swept past them.

"So, where are we going?" Kyrin asked as they walked through camp.

She'd wondered where the two of them would stay as newlyweds, but her mother had told her that Trask and the others would figure something out. She hadn't thought about it much again, too focused on the wedding.

Jace didn't look at her, but she could still see his smile, even in the dark.

"You'll see."

She hugged his arm, trusting him completely.

After another little ways, they came around the corner of one of the cabins. A pathway of flickering lanterns greeted them, leading to one of the farthest cabins whose windows glowed invitingly. They stopped, and Jace looked down at her.

"This is our cabin."

"*Our* cabin?"

He nodded, his blue eyes shining with excitement. "Trask gave it to us. I started cleaning it up just before . . . everything happened, and I finished it in the last two weeks. It's all ours, at least for the time being."

Kyrin sucked in her breath and gazed once more at the cabin. Their cabin. Their *home*. Tears burned her eyes.

Jace slipped his hand into hers. "Let me show you."

He led her along the lantern-lit path and up to the cabin. Casting a dazzling grin back at her, he opened the door and tugged her inside. Kyrin stared around, overwhelmed. A gorgeous blue quilt covered the bed in the corner and blue curtains were drawn across the windows. A table sat near the fireplace, along with cabinets, chairs, and even some dishes.

"Your mother, Lenae, and Anne helped me gather things for it."

"Oh, Jace," Kyrin breathed. "It's so beautiful."

She turned to him, so full of love she thought she would melt into a puddle. He almost seemed to know this, because his arms were around her in a moment, and she gazed up into his eyes.

"I love you so much."

"And I love you even more."

He pressed his lips against hers, and Kyrin blissfully lost herself in their shared love.

CHARACTERS
AND
INFORMATION

Returning Characters

Aaron—A half-crete and former miner from Dunlow. Timothy's older brother.

Alex Avery—An old friend of Daniel's who assassinated Emporer Daican.

Altair (AL - tayr)—Kyrin's family name.

Anne—Trask's wife.

Aric (AHR - ick)—Emperor Daican's former head of security.

Ben—Wealthy merchant and leader of the believers in Valcré.

Carl—The Altair's groundskeeper. Ethel's husband.

Dagren (DAY - gren)—Arcacian captain with a vendetta against Rayad and Warin.

Daniel—Rightful king of Arcacia.

Davira (Duh - VEER - uh)—Queen of Arcacia.

Elanor—Jace's sister.

Elian (EL - ee - an)—Elanor's bodyguard.

Elôm (EE - lohm)—The one true God of Ilyon.

Ethel—The Altair's housekeeper. Carl's wife.

Glynn (GLIN)—A crete from Dorland. Captain Darq's lieutenant.

Holden (HOHL - den)—A former informant for Daican but now part of the Resistance.

Jace—A half-ryrik former slave and gladiator.

Josef—A physician from Samara and close friend of Balen.

Kaden (KAY - den)—Kyrin's twin brother.

King Balen (BAY - len)—Exiled king of Samara.

Kyrin (KYE - rin)—A young Arcacian woman with the ability to remember everything.

Leetra Almere (LEE - truh AL - meer)—A female crete from Dorland. Talas's cousin.

Lenae (LEH - nay)—Warin's wife and adoptive mother of Meredith.

Liam—Kyrin's older brother and training physician.

Lydia—Kyrin's mother.

Marcus Altair—Kyrin's eldest brother and captain of the Landale militia.

Marcus Veshiron (Veh - SHEER - on)—Kyrin's grandfather and an Arcacian general.

Meredith—Lenae's adoptive daughter.

Mick—A Resistance member from a wealthy mining family.

Michael—Kyrin's younger brother.

Mira (MEER - uh)—Ben's wife.

Rayad (RAY - ad)—One of Jace's close friends and mentor.

Ronan "Ronny"—Kyrin's youngest brother.

Sam "Endathlorsam"—A talcrin man and formerly Tarvin Hall's wisest scholar.

Talas Folkan (TAL - as FAHL - kan)—A friendly crete from Dorland. Leetra's cousin.

Tane "Imhonriltane"—Sam's nephew.

Timothy—A half-crete young man from Dunlow, and the Resistance's spiritual leader. Aaron's younger brother.

Trask—Resistance leader and son of Baron Grey.

Trev—A former member of Daican's security force. Now part of the Resistance.

Tyra—Jace's black wolf.

Verus Darq (VAYR - uhs DARK)—A crete captain from Dorland.

Warin (WOHR - in)—One of Trask's right hand men and husband of Lenae. Lifelong friend of Rayad.

NEW CHARACTERS

Baron Reynold (RAY – nahld)—Alex Avery's uncle.

Cassie—A training physician and new member of the Resistance camp.

Lacy—A barmaid at the Briar Pub in Valcré.

Tavor (TA – vohr)—Alex Avery's right hand man.

DRAGONS

Exsis (EX - sis)—Kaden's dragon.
Gem—Jace's dragon.
Ivoris "Ivy" (EYE - vohr - is)—Kyrin's dragon.
Storm—Talas's dragon.
Thron—Holden's dragon.

LOCATIONS

Arcacia (Ahr - CAY - shee - uh)—The largest country of the Ilyon mainland.

Ilyon (IL - yahn)—The known world.

Landale—A prosperous province in Arcacia formerly ruled over by Baron Grey.

Valcré (VAL - cray)—Arcacia's capital city.

RACE PROFILES

Ryriks

Homeland: Wildmor

Physical Appearance: Ryriks tend to be large-bodied, muscular, and very athletic. They average between six, to six and a half feet tall. They have thick black hair that is usually worn long. All have aqua-blue colored eyes that appear almost luminescent, especially during intense or emotional situations. Their ears are pointed, which makes them very distinct from the other races. They have strong, striking features, though they can pass as humans by letting their hair hide their ears and avoiding eye contact. Ryriks typically dress in rough, sturdy clothing—whatever they find by stealing.

Physical Characteristics: Ryriks are a very hardy race and incredibly resistant to physical abuse and sickness; however, they have one great weakness. Their lungs are highly sensitive to harsh air conditions, pollutants, and respiratory illness. Under these conditions, their lungs bleed. Short exposure causes great discomfort, but is not life-threatening. More severe, prolonged exposure, however, could cause their lungs to fill with blood and suffocate them. It is said to be a curse from choosing to follow the path of evil. Ryriks' eyes are very sensitive, able to pick out the slightest movement, and they can see well in the dark. Both their sense of hearing and smell are very keen—much higher than that of humans. In times of great distress or anger, ryriks can react with devastating bursts of speed and strength.

Race Characteristics: Ryriks are the center of fireside tales all across Ilyon. They are seen as a savage people, very fierce and cunning. To other races, they seem to have almost animal-like instincts; therefore, it is commonly believed they don't have souls. They are a hot-blooded people and quick to action, especially when roused. They have quick tempers and are easily driven to blind rage. They prefer decisive action over conversation. Most have a barbaric thirst for bloodshed and inflicting pain. They view fear and pain as weaknesses and like to see them in others. They are typically forest dwellers and feel most comfortable in cover they can use to their advantage.

SKILLS: Ryriks are highly skilled in the woods and living off the land. They are excellent hunters and especially proficient in setting ambushes. They're experts in taming and raising almost any type of animal. They make the fiercest of any warriors. A ryrik's favorite weapons are a heavy broadsword and a large dagger. Ryriks aren't masters of any type of craft or art. Most of their possessions come from stealing. What they can't gain by thieving, they make for themselves, but not anything of quality. They think art, music, or any such thing to be frivolous. Most ryriks can't read or write and have no desire to.

SOCIAL: Ryriks are not a very social race. Settlements are scattered and usually small. They have no major cities. Families often live on small farms in the forest and consist of no more than four to six people. Children are typically on their own by the time they are sixteen or seventeen—even younger for some males. Ryriks have a poor view of women. They see them as a necessity and more of a possession than a partner. Once claimed, a ryrik woman almost never leaves her home. She is required to care for the farm while the men are away. Most ryrik men group together in raiding parties, pillaging and destroying unprotected villages and preying on unsuspecting travelers. Ryriks have an intense hatred of other races, particularly humans.

GOVERNMENT: Ryriks have no acting government. Raiding parties and settlements are dictated by the strongest or fiercest ryrik, so the position can be challenged by anyone and changes often.

PREFERRED OCCUPATIONS: The vast majority of ryriks are thieves. A few hold positions as blacksmiths and other necessary professions.

FAITH: Ryriks disdain religion of any kind. They were the first to rebel against King Elôm and led others to do so as well.

Talcrins

Homeland: Arda

Physical Appearance: Talcrins are a tall, powerful people. Talcrin men are seldom less than six feet tall. They have rich, dark skin and black hair of various lengths and styles. Their most unique feature besides their dark skin is their metallic-looking eyes. They have a very regal, graceful appearance. Men often dress in long, expertly crafted jerkins, while women wear simple but elegant flowing gowns of rich colors, particularly deep purple.

Race Characteristics: Talcrins are considered the wisest of all Ilyon's peoples. Some of their greatest pleasures are learning and teaching. Reading is one of their favorite pastimes. They have excellent memories and intellects. Talcrins are a calm people, adept at hiding and controlling strong emotion. They are peace-loving and prefer to solve problems with diplomacy, but if all else fails, they can fight fiercely. They have a deep sense of morality, justice, loyalty, and above all, honesty. They are an astute people and don't miss much, particularly when it comes to others. Besides learning, they are also fond of art and music. Most talcrins are city dwellers, preferring large cities where libraries and universities can be found. Of all the races, they live the longest and reach ages of one hundred fifty, though many live even longer. Because of this, they age slower than the other races. Talcrin names are known to be very long, though they use shortened versions outside of Arda.

Skills: Talcrins excel in everything pertaining to books, languages, legal matters, and history, and are excellent at passing on their wisdom. They are often sought as advisors for their ability to easily think through situations and assess different outcomes. They are master storytellers and delight in entertaining people in this way. Though they strive for peace, most talcrin men train as warriors when they are young. They make incredible fighters who are highly skilled with long swords, high-power longbows, and spears. When not reading, many talcrin women enjoy painting and weaving. Their tapestries are among the most sought after. Both men and women enjoy music and dancing. They are expert harpists. Beautiful two-person dances are very popular in talcrin culture and are considered an art form. Metal-working is another skill in which talcrins are considered experts. Their gold and silver jewelry and armor are some of the finest in Ilyon.

SOCIAL: Talcrins are a family-oriented people and fiercely loyal to both family and friends alike. Families are average in size, with between three to seven children. Men are very protective of their families and believe their well-being is of utmost importance. Their island country of Arda is almost exclusively populated with talcrins. Scholars from the Ilyon mainland often come to visit their famous libraries, but other races rarely settle there. Many talcrins inhabit the mainland as well, but are widely scattered. The highest population is found in Valcré, the capital of Arcacia. They get along well with all races, except for ryriks. Though generally kindhearted, they can hold themselves at a distance and consider others ignorant.

GOVERNMENT: The governing lord in Arda is voted into authority by the talcrin people and serves for a period of two years at a time, but may be elected an unlimited number of times. His word is seen as final, but he is surrounded by a large number of advisors, who are also chosen by the people, and is expected to include them in all decisions. Those living on the mainland are under the authority of the king or lord of whichever country they inhabit.

PREFERRED OCCUPATIONS: Scholars, lawyers, and positions in government are the talcrins' choice occupations, as well as positions in artistry.

FAITH: Talcrins are the most faithful of all races in following King Elôm. The majority of those living in Arda are firm believers, but this has become less so among those living on the mainland.

CRETES

HOMELAND: Arcacia and Dorland

PHYSICAL APPEARANCE: Cretes are a slim people, yet very agile and strong. They are the shortest of Ilyon's races, and stand between five foot and five foot ten inches tall. It is rare for one to reach six feet. They are brown-skinned and have straight, dark hair. Black is most common. It is never lighter than dark brown unless they are of mixed blood. Both men and women let it grow long. They like to decorate their hair with braids, beads, leather, and feathers. Crete men do not grow facial hair. A crete's eyes are a bit larger than a human's, and very bright and colorful. A full-blood crete will never have brown eyes. They dress in earthy colors and lots of leather. All cretes have intricate brown tattoos depicting family symbols and genealogy.

PHYSICAL CHARACTERISTICS: The crete's body is far more resilient to the elements and sickness than other races. They are very tolerant of the cold and other harsh conditions. Their larger eyes give them excellent vision and enable them to see well in the dark. They don't need as much sleep as other races and sleep only for a couple of hours before dawn. Their bodies heal and recuperate quickly.

RACE CHARACTERISTICS: Cretes are tree dwellers and never build on the ground except when absolutely necessary. They love heights and flying and have a superb sense of balance. They are very daring and enjoy a thrilling adventure. They mature a bit more quickly than other races. A crete is considered nearly an adult by fifteen or sixteen and a mature adult by eighteen. They are a high-energy race and prone to taking quick action. Cretes are straightforward and blunt, coming across as rather abrupt at times. They are not the most patient, nor understanding, and they have high expectations for themselves and others. They are a stubborn, proud, and independent people, and don't like to conform to the laws and standards of other races.

SKILLS: Cretes are excellent climbers, even from a very young age, able to race up trees effortlessly and scale the most impassible cliffs and obstacles. Because of this fearlessness and love for heights, they are renowned dragon trainers. They are masters at blending in with their surroundings and moving silently, which makes them excellent hunters. All crete males, as well as many females, are trained as skilled warriors. Their choice weapons are bows and throwing knives, though they can be equally skilled with lightweight swords. Cretes are also a musical race, their favorite instruments being small flutes and hand drums.

SOCIAL: Cretes live in close communities and often have very large families, maintaining close connections with extended family. They are very proud of their family line and make sure each generation is well-educated in their particular traditions and histories. They consider it a tragedy when a family line is broken. Still, all children are cherished, both sons and daughters. Every crete is part of one of twelve clans named after various animals. Men are always part of whichever clan they are born into. When a woman marries, she becomes part of her husband's clan. Though cretes are proud of their clans, they show no discrimination, and their cities always have a mixed-clan population. Cretes are hospitable to their own people and well-known acquaintances, but suspicious and aloof when it comes to strangers. It takes time to earn one's trust, and even longer to earn their respect.

GOVERNMENT: The highest governing official is the crete lord. He is essentially a king, but directly below him are twelve men who serve as representatives of each of the twelve clans. The lord is unable to make any drastic decisions without the cooperation of the majority of the twelve clan leaders. Each crete city has a governing official who answers to the twelve representatives. Directly below him is a council of men consisting of the elders of each major family in the city. In the past, the cretes ultimately fell under the authority of the king of Arcacia, but with the deterioration of the Arcacian government, they've pulled away from its rule.

PREFERRED OCCUPATIONS: Hunters, dragon trainers, and warriors are the favored occupations of the cretes. But leather-working is another desirable occupation. This is typically done by the women of a household.

FAITH: Most cretes have remained faithful to King Elôm, or at least are aware of Him.

GIANTS
(Also known as **Dorlanders**)

HOMELAND: Dorland

PHYSICAL APPEARANCE: Giants are the largest race in Ilyon. Standing between seven to nine feet tall, they tower above most other peoples. They are heavily built and powerful, but can be surprisingly quick and agile when the occasion calls for it. They are fair-skinned, and their hair and eye color varies greatly like humans. They dress simply and practically in sturdy, homespun clothing.

RACE CHARACTERISTICS: Despite their great size and power, giants are a very quiet and gentle people. They dislike confrontation and will avoid it at all cost. They are naturally good-natured and honest, and enjoy simple lives and hard work. To those who don't take the time to get to know them, they can seem slow and ignorant, but they are very methodical thinkers, thinking things over carefully and thoroughly. While not quick-witted, they are very knowledgeable in their fields of interest. They are generally a humble race and easy to get along with. They tend to see the best in everyone. Their biggest failing is that, in their methodical manner, it often takes too long for them to decide to take action when it is needed.

SKILLS: Giants are very skilled in anything to do with the land. Much of the gold, silver, and jewels in Ilyon come from the giants' mines in the mountains of northern Dorland. They are also excellent builders. While lacking in style or decoration, the architecture of their structures is strong and durable, built to last for centuries. They have often been hired to build fortifications and strongholds. Unlike other races, it is not common for giants to train as warriors. Only the king's men are required to be able to fight. While not a musical or artistic race, giants do love a good story, and they've been said to have, beautiful, powerful singing voices.

SOCIAL: Giants typically live in tight farming or mining communities. Family and friends are important. Families usually consist of two to three children who remain in the household for as long as they wish. Many children remain on their parents' farm after they are married, and the farm expands. Giants are known throughout Ilyon for their hospitality. They'll invite almost anyone into their homes. Some people even find them too hospitable and generous. They are very averse to cruelty, dishonesty, and seeing their own hurt. Despite moving slowly in most other areas, justice is swift and decisive.

GOVERNMENT: Giants are ruled over by a king who comes to power through succession. However, most communities more or less govern themselves. The only time the king's rule is evident is when large numbers of giants are required to gather for a certain purpose.

PREFERRED OCCUPATIONS: The majority of giants are farmers, miners, or builders.

FAITH: Almost all giants agree King Elôm is real, but in their simplistic and practical mindset, fewer giants have actually come to a true trusting faith.

Want to find out what happens with Aaron and Lacy? Check out the Jaye L. Knight companion novella!

DAICAN'S HEIR

ILYON CHRONICLES – BOOK SIX

For three years, the Resistance has suffered under oppression, first from Emperor Daican, and then from his daughter. Now it is time to fight back.

COMING SOON

For more "behind the scenes" information on Ilyon Chronicles, visit: **www.ilyonchronicles.com**

To see Jaye's inspiration boards and character "casting" visit: **www.pinterest.com/jayelknight**

ABOUT THE AUTHOR

JAYE L. KNIGHT is an award-winning author, homeschool graduate, and shameless tea addict with a passion for Christian fantasy. Armed with an active imagination and love for adventure, Jaye weaves stories of truth, faith, and courage with the message that even in the deepest darkness, God's love shines as a light to offer hope. She has been penning stories since the age of eight and resides in the Northwoods of Wisconsin.

To learn more about Jaye and her work, visit:
www.jayelknight.com

www.ingramcontent.com/pod-product-compliance
Lightning Source LLC
Chambersburg PA
CBHW050015120726
47903CB00006B/1779